# Archer's Arrow

# Archer's Arrow

ALEXA WHITEWOLF

**Archer's Arrow**
An *Immortal Rogues* **novel**

by Alexa Whitewolf
Copyright ©2022 Alexa Whitewolf

Cover design by Y. Nikolova at **Ammonia Book Covers**
Editing and formatting by Luna Imprints Author Services
Kindle First Edition

This is a work of fiction.

# AUTHOR'S NOTE & ACKNOWLEDGEMENTS

Wow, what a year 2022 has been. I thought my vampire series gave me a headache last year, but it's nothing compared to this one! So by the time you hit the ending, if you feel like your head is spinning and there are *so many* gods and goddesses mentioned… Rest assured, we get to see way more of them in later books! Yep, this might end up being my longest series to date.

Anyway, I mentioned in Hades' acknowledgements how one of my favorite books (and first!) that I read growing up was Legends of Olympus, by a Romanian author. As the title implies, it had compilations of stories on every Greek god and this really brought them to life for me. But, in *Archer's Arrow*, I wanted to show a bit more of tugs and scuffles between pantheons. The differences, as they were. Fenrir and Artemis are, in my eyes, a bit of a Romeo & Juliet couple, minus the tragic ending. Delving deep into what makes them tick was…eye-opening, to say the least. I hope you enjoy them!

A few readers have asked me if the books in this series are standalones. I'll be honest, after this one…probably not. The romances, as always, are a one-book thing, but the overall arching plot grows and expands (believe me, it kills me keeping track of everything!), which means for a better reading experience, you'll want to stack up and read all of the *Immortal Rogues* in order. Does this mean you need to read the rest of the Rogues Universe? Nah. But if you have, you'll notice some cameo appearances tee hee. :)

*A* note, as always, that the book contains swearing and sex scenes, and if those might offend you… You might want to skip this. Sorry! The gods are raw, and edgy, and very human. Very, very human.

Now, for the thanks:

Huge thanks to my family for sticking by me. To my doggos, for their ever-growing patience…and reminders that I need to move, and eat, and breathe fresh air.

Siobhan, a million thanks for your beta feedback and helping me whip this one into shape!

To all the bloggers and readers supporting this universe, you guys rock!

Huuuuge thanks to Y. Nikolova at Ammonia Book Covers for the amazing work you do each and every single time!!!!

Thank you to Tracey, my lovely PA, who keeps me on track and takes on all the tasks I hate, so I can have more time writing!

And as always, on the cover and all the extra

work you do! And the team at LIAS for formatting and edits (special thanks to Milica for such a short turn-around!! I promise I'll be better!) :)

Happy readings,

Alexa :)

# Rogues Extended Universe – Reading Order

Moonlight Rogues
Flaming Rogues
Immortal Rogues
Lost Royals of Transylvania
Vârcolac Legacy (coming 2022)

# Quick Glossary

Not as much Romanian in here as you've come to expect with the Rogues, but! Since Ileana and Făt-Frumos show up, I thought it only fair to mention there are *some* words.

*Da/nu – Yes/no*

*Scuze – sorry*

*Zmei – Carpathian dragon shifters (plural; sing. zmeu)*

*And the names…*

*Ileana – pronounced E-lya-nah*

*Făt-Frumos – pronounced Fuh-th Fruh-mohs*

**\*These last two are heroes of lore in Romanian folklore** :)

For Evelyne
This one's for you. Parce que chaque jour tu me
rappelles qu'il y a du bon dans le monde.

# PROLOGUE

Clotho stared at the spinning thread, biting her thumbnail. Her silky white toga had seen better days, and her long, raven locks were looking a tad mussed.

"Clotho?"

She turned to her sister. Atropos seemed equally tired, and haggard, almost. Her lavender toga had a rip at the bottom. "How bad is it?"

Clotho shrugged. "Well…"

"Are you two worrying over the state of the threads once more?" Their third sister, Lachesis, entered the room. She held a goblet of ambrosia in one hand, and she was the only one to seem some-how put together. Her hair was in a neat dark braid—for once—and she wore a clean brown toga.

"Yes!" Clotho whimpered. "Lach, maybe this wasn't such a good idea. Screwing with the gods' threads…"

Lachesis waved her hand in irritation. "You worry too much. Everything is *fine.*"

"But it's not fine, Lachesis!" Atropos' sharp voice drew all their attention. Her sharp, bird-like features seemed more prominent than before, with her large nose and thin lips almost taking full center of her features. "This is bad. Real bad."

They each turned their gazes to the imposing spinning wheels. Threads that had previously seemed clear, each following the gods' journey, now seemed intertwined. And some…had darker colors rising within them. Colors that didn't belong.

"I've tried to remove that darkness," Clotho whined, "and nothing works. It keeps coming back, time and time again."

Lachesis downed the rest of her drink, then moved closer, inspecting the thread in question. "Whose is it?"

"Fenrir, the wolf god of the Norse pantheon."

Lachesis made a face. "Ah, him."

"Yes, *him*," Atropos shot back. "If we hadn't messed with Hades' thread, perhaps his wouldn't have gotten so out of…sync." She gulped, tears brimming in her eyes. "We need to do something.

We need to fix this."

Lachesis rolled her eyes. "We don't *need to* do anything. But, fine, if you insist." She handed her empty cup to Atropos, then headed to the threads. Looked at all of them...then picked one of the lighter ones, with a brilliance that seemed to seep into the others. She intertwined it with Fenrir's thread, and stepped back, smiling. "There!"

Clotho gasped, dropping the goblet. "What did you do, Lach?"

"I fixed him. Or, tried to. Adding a little light to his darkness should do the trick."

Atropos looked at her. "Unless the darkness infiltrates the light, too..."

Lachesis shrugged, then picked up the goblet. "Too late now. We will have to wait and see how it plays out."

# CHAPTER 1

**Artemis**

Faint brown eyes meet mine. Widen in fear. And then she's gone, limber legs jumping through the tall grass, taking off on a gallop.

I curse under my breath, re-notching my arrow and turning in the doe's direction. I'd had her in my sights, but something scared her too early. And I never miss.

"Artemis."

I blink, then drop my arm to my side. The wooden bow in my hand fades, its golden string shimmering. It's there one moment, gone the next— returning to the ether, along with the gold-tipped arrow that's my signature. The leather quiver by my feet joins them. Being in this realm has meant learning how to dissipate my weapons faster, until they're needed again.

Not that the newcomer who'd scared my doe would be surprised at said weapons. My eyes land on him—a man—a few feet away. Dark salt-and-pepper hair, eyes that have seen too much.

"Hades."

He casts an amused glance over my shoulder at the disappearing doe. "You know mortals in these times have stores where you can buy the meat you seek?"

I roll my eyes. "Yes, it has come to my attention. Not to my taste, though."

He nods, as though he'd predicted I would say so. "Is the earthly realm all you expected, then?"

I can't contain my moue of disagreement. *All I'd expected? Hardly.* Despite centuries of existence, the mortals still care only for their materialistic needs and inner growth is not even on their radar. The men can be disgusting pigs, as I've learned, and the women… I miss the days of my temples and priestesses, of teaching the chosen ones about true strength of character.

"I take it that's a 'no' then."

"Hades…" I shake my head. "Did you know it's gotten this bad?"

He shrugs. "I keep an eye on things, occasionally. We all do. But I cannot say I was blessed enough to interact with many mortals recently." The corners of his eyes crinkle when he smiles. "Unlike you, by the looks of it."

"Yes, and it's why I much prefer staying *away* from their polluted cities and noisy crowds. Easier to go about my business this way."

If nothing else, living in the wilderness the last six months has only confirmed my first impressions of mortals. I can't wait to get my task done and return home, to Olympus and my regular existence. To ambrosia and sweets and food that isn't contaminated by things that should never be in it.

His amused expression disappears, giving way to something much more serious. "And how goes your other hunt?"

A sigh leaves my lips. Not of defeat, not entirely. "It goes…"

"It has been twenty years, and you're Olympus' best tracker. But even I must admit when it seems we were wrong. Perhaps it's time to call it in, and return home."

Thoughts of golden marble floors, nymphs with aromatic beverages and various luxuries I've forgone fill my mind. As quickly as they've come, I push them aside, into their little compartment. I haven't crossed multiple realms and wasted years in each of them, only to retreat now.

"You tasked me with a mission, Hades. I intend to see it through to the end."

"I know that." He hesitates, as though trying to find a way to speak without offending me. Surprising, given it's not a trait that runs in our family and it's definitely not something my father, Zeus, practices. "But tell me, in just many realms have you pursued him?"

"Many. You know that." I toss my head back and look at the sky, wishing the crushing shame of this quest wasn't quite so heavy.

"And that's precisely it, Artemis. How many more will you go into? Don't forget, I received your reports at the end of every failed attempt." He raises his hand and starts counting off his fingers. "First with Asgard—and what a mess that was! Did you really need to face off against Heimdall himself?"

I lower my head, hair covering my flaming cheeks as I stare at the ground this time. "He asked for it," I mutter. "All I wanted to know was if Fenrir had been seen in their pantheon. Given he's the protector to the Norse gods and to that rainbow bridge leading to the many realms, Heimdall should have known better than to test me."

"And yet, I had to douse out the flames before he went crying to Odin, who in turn would've sought out your father. We both know how that would've ended."

I raise my gaze to his. "I'm sorry, Uncle. Truly.

And thank you for that."

He shakes his head, and goes back to counting. "Next you burst into the Duat, and we all know how the Egyptians took *that*."

I wince at the recollection. Bastet, their goddess of protection, pleasure and good health, told me she'd heard rumors of Fenrir hiding with one of their gods. And like an idiot, I listened. I'd been desperate for a new lead after the encounter with Heimdall, and had figured that despite her obvious dislike for Olympians, we had something in common. As it turns out, I couldn't have been more wrong.

"OK, granted, Osiris was a bit ticked off. And Anubis will likely take a few centuries to forgive me for the broken nose. But I smoothed out those waters myself, Uncle."

Hades closes his eyes, as though restraining himself. When he opens them again, he drops his hand by his side. "Artemis, this isn't about where you failed. I'm not trying to make you feel like shit, but to point out how futile this quest seems to have become." He spreads his arms wide open, encompassing the surrounding area. "What even brought you here, on Earth? Out of all the realms?"

My voice is quiet when I answer him. "Morrigan did."

That stops him in his tracks. This bit, I'd left out of my last report—delivered to him by my brother.

To say Apollo had been surprised to find me in the Mayan heavens, holding a message from a Celtic goddess' immortal guardian, would be an understatement. As was my reason for being there, but that's a story for another time.

"Morrigan?" Hades asks.

"Rather, her immortal. I'm assuming he was sent by her, though." I meet his gaze again. "He told me Morrigan believed Fenrir might be on Earth. In these last few months, I found his trail—faint as it is—and it led me here. To Ireland, and Dingle." I shrug. "I figure an seaside town is the ideal place for a Norse god to want to hide in. All I need to do now is find him."

"Artemis… You always were stubborn." Hades sighs, then watches me for a long moment. Finally, he inclines his head. "Very well, continue as you were. But you should know your brother misses you."

I know he does. Apollo was never able to handle us being apart for more than a few days, and this time around it's been years. Before he'd seen me in the Mayan heavens, we hadn't spoken for nearly a decade. The distance was compounded by the fact I was never in the same spot for too long, and that time in Olympus and other realms moves differently—given gods generally lose track of it.

Seeing him was bad enough, reminding me there was a time when I hadn't been so alone. I'd cried like a newborn babe after he'd left to deliver Hades my report. Landing on Earth right after, and going about my quest here for the past six months, only enhanced that sense of loneliness.

"As do I," I whisper. "Is he staying out of trouble, at least?"

Hades chuckles. "Can Apollo truly keep himself out of trouble? If he could stop going after other gods' women, perhaps. As it is, he's embroiled in a rather amusing feud with Hermes."

A shiver runs up my spine. The messenger god is way too fickle. "Tell him to be careful. Hermes isn't to be trifled with."

Once more, Hades' amusement fades. "No, he is not. And I will pass on the message." He turns as though to leave, then casts me another glance over his shoulder. "Are you quite certain you wish to stay?"

"Yes, Uncle. I will find Fenrir, even if it takes me the next twenty years."

He sighs, turns, and opens a portal. I watch the air ripple, sense his godly magic, so much stronger than mine. And then he's gone, as though he never were. I glance around the meadow, making sure no human has seen us. It's deserted. Even better.

I give up on my hunt, and return to the important one. After all, I meant every word. And what Hades doesn't know is how close I am to this last lead…

The moment I push the bar door open, the smell of stale beer, sweat and rancid cigarette smoke hits my nostrils.

I wrinkle my nose. Mortals. How they've become so nasty-smelling is beyond me. I've never spent much time around them, not as much as my male counterparts in Olympus, but hell if I understand the appeal.

A quick glance around shows how I stand out. Everyone is dressed in what mortals call jeans and t-shirts—breeches and shirts of ungodly cheap material. In contrast, my leather outfit of boots, pants and a breast-bounding top stands out as much as my frizzy red hair.

As if to confirm the fact, a man in jeans pops in front of me, eyeing my outfit. "Where's the Halloween party, gorgeous?"

I frown. What is he on about? Halo-what?

Not that I'm that surprised at the attention. I've noticed mortal men have a propensity for getting up in my face. But if they expect me to cower in fear or plaster myself at their feet in adulation, they'll be sorely mistaken. I'm a goddess, and they can fucking deal with it.

My eyes are already scanning the area, looking

for a sign of *him*. His trail led me here, surely I can't have been wrong. Every deity has their own particular imprint, a hint in the air around them, a piece of them they leave behind when they lose control. Mortals call it magic. We call it primordial essence, and there's a lot more to it than potions and spells.

Which is why I know it can't be duplicated. Therefore, I must be in the right place. I've spent the last twenty years hunting him and there's no way he's getting off easy now that I found a more permanent trace.

*And I know he's here, in this building. Morrigan's immortal was right, after all.*

But where, exactly, is Fenrir hiding?

"Babe, did you hear me?"

I arch an eyebrow at the man. Imperiously, I wait. Either he moves or I'll move him, but I'd rather not cause a scene so soon.

After a beat, and another of staring in my eyes, he steps to the side. Mutters something under his breath. I let it go, and move instead closer to the barman—bartender. *I must remember to watch my words. Mortals may no longer believe in the existence of the old gods, but I might run into other creatures who'll be all too happy to take advantage. Me being in another realm doesn't mean I'm still as powerful. Quite the contrary, given how none of them believe in my existence anymore. No belief, no worship; less divine power for me.*

I take a deep breath, choking on more cigarette smoke and something spicy. The last person standing between me and the bar stands aside, moving to a table and some rowdy mortals.

Finally. I wave over the bartender, my mouth watering at the thought of ale. It tastes like crap these days, but it's still better than nothing. And after my long trek here, it's the least I deserve.

Unfortunately, the bartender seems to be avoiding me. I watch him serve a woman, then another. Wave my hand again. Still nothing. His profile is interesting—strong jaw, proud nose marked by a slightly uneven line that suggests it may have been broken, and shoulder-length blond hair. It's not quite the curly texture Apollo's has; rather, wavier. On any other male, it might have looked odd. Effeminate. But on him…

I lick my lips. He wears a shirt that shows a nice set of muscles, and jeans riding snugly on his hips. If he wasn't so blasted annoying right now, I would've considered having him warm my bed tonight.

As it is, I can feel my ire rising. The air around me crackles, and I temper it down. Control and patience will get me what I need.

"For the love of Thanatos, what do I have to do to get served around here?"

I curse myself the moment the words escape

me. So much for keeping a low profile. A quick glance around shows no one caught the odd cursing, which is one small mercy.

My gaze returns to the bartender. A woman's snapping her fingers in front of his face, but he seems not to notice her. And when he turns to me, I freeze. I'd noticed the rogue look from afar but this close, those eyes—that shade of onyx, with specks of something so *in*human—

"You."

I lean over the counter, grabbing a handful of his shirt.

"Do you know how long I've been searching for you, Fenrir?"

His nostrils flare.

**Fenrir**

Like everyone else, I caught sight of the redhead the moment she'd entered. It was hard to ignore her, given her outfit—showcasing everything to every drooling male in the vicinity.

And like an idiot, I stuck around. Hoped it was a trick, some woman in need of help. Many mortals, I've learned, have mental issues that tend to show in rather obvious ways on their person. Perhaps this was one such unlucky soul who'd mistaken today for an early Halloween.

Alas, such is not my luck.

No. Instead, who else but a goddess graces the steps of my establishment. And if I'm to listen to what my memory tells me, the red hair and archer outfit can only belong to one such goddess— Artemis herself.

Clusterfuck of clusterfucks, can I not catch a break?

Out of all the gods, it has to be Olympus' bounty hunter on my tail. Then again, perhaps I should be grateful. A flock of Valkyries sent by my grandfather would've been much more conspicuous.

I tear my gaze from Artemis' fiery emerald eyes—filled with a shine too godly to be human— and unhook her fingers from my shirt. "You have the wrong person."

She laughs, unamused. "You wish I did. I bet you wish I'd go right back out that door and never return."

My back tenses, but I refuse to give in to the rise she's trying to provoke. Instead, I focus on my female customer and the drink she'd ordered. Was it a Cosmo? A Bellini? Fuck, my mind seems to be disintegrating, panic seizing my chest. And something else. Something worse, rumbling in my chest, poking its unwanted nose.

*I can't let it win. If it wins, if my emotions get out of control—*

Closing my eyes, I take a deep, short breath. Then release. And do it again.

*This is my bar. My territory. And I will protect it at any cost. But for the moment, I've got mortals to serve, and appearances to maintain.*

I force a smile on my face, and thicken the Irish lilt I've perfected for the benefit of my customer and her American friends. "What was it again, gorgeous? Your radiant smile seems to have worked its charm over me—blown my mind, sure."

The compliment works, and a smile does, indeed, work its way onto her face, replacing the scowl. "A Bellini, please."

I nod, and start to fix the drink.

"You can ignore me all you want," Artemis says from her spot, "but I'm not leaving."

Clearly.

And it's what I was afraid of. How the hell did she find me, anyway? I've been careful—except these last few years. I should've been *more* careful. Then again, running does get old. As does living a life of solitude, constantly in fear of being exposed.

Once I'd finally stopped running, once I'd put my beast where he belonged—locked in a compartment of my mind—I was able to sort myself out. It took me a long time to make my way to Ireland, but I knew this seaside town was meant for me the moment I set foot in it. When I'd found this bar, the sea air and gleeful locals had hooked me. I couldn't have left if I'd tried.

*And now you're paying the price.*

I pass the drink to the American, then turn on to the next person. This coastal joint is packed tonight, and I wouldn't have it any other way. It might give me a chance to escape—if I play my cards right.

Even as I fix more drinks, and ignore Artemis—who throws a jab at me every time I head her way—I scan the crowd for Mary, my apprentice. Where is the damn child? Granted, nineteen is considered an adult in human years, but in my head, she's still a child. A damn good bartender, though. I don't know what I'd do on busy nights without her.

Finally, about ten minutes later, she pushes through the crowd—all five feet of her, clad in jeans, a top, and messy black hair in a pixie cut. She steps around Artemis, then behind the bar.

"So soooo sorry, Finn. Me mum, you know, she's—"

I wave away Mary's apology. "You're all right, just help me out with the crowd, yeah?"

She nods and scurries to take some orders. Movement out the corner of my eye draws my attention, and I turn—

Artemis copied Mary and flipped the end bit of the bar, entering my space. I clench my fists, forgetting all about orders as I take a step toward her.

"What do you think you're doing? Get out of here."

She tips her chin up, crossing her arms under her chest. I ignore the way her bodice strains against the movement, presenting the outline of her breasts to my eyes and every male in the vicinity. Now if only my dick was as good at ignoring it.

The man to my right flat-out leers at her. "You can serve me anytime, Red." When she doesn't answer, still focused on me, he reaches over the bar and grabs her arm.

Artemis whirls on him in a second, twisting his arm to the point of breaking. "Clearly, women here have not taught you how to behave." A crackle whips the air, and two mortals nearby turn, as though stung.

*Damn it all to hell, she's going to send him to the Underworld before his time if she's not careful.*

I might've been avoiding my godly powers for eons, but that doesn't mean I don't remember how fragile mortals are compared to us. Especially when faced with the full grasp of our powers.

"Art—" Fuck it, I can't call her by her real name.

Before I can warn her, the man yelps, his buddies getting halfway up out of their seats. I hurry to fill a glass of beer and push Artemis aside, forcing her to release him. I slam the glass on the bar. "Take it and go."

The man grumbles, but grabs the free drink and slouches away, his friends following in his wake.

Artemis scowls at me. "I had it under control."

"I could tell. But I can't have you disrupting my establishment. Please, leave."

Instead of listening, she takes a step closer to me. "I'm not going anywhere, Fenrir. I'll be right here, shadowing your every step. Because of the mortals, I won't haul you away now. But make no mistake—you *are* coming back with me to Olympus."

So. They've finally come for me. I've been waiting for this day for eons, it seems, and now that it's here, I'm weirdly unwilling to face my comeuppance.

"Do what you must," I growl at her. "But stay the hell out of my way, and out of my bar."

# CHAPTER 2

**Artemis**

*"Stay the hell out of my way, and out of my bar."*

I don't reel back at the anger in his tone, nor the flash of lighting in his eyes. Instead, I allow a smirk to tug at the corner of my lips. "Careful, Fenrir. Your *divine* is starting to show."

He freezes, something akin to panic flashing on his features. And then he schools them once again, takes in the mortals around us, before his eyes settle on me. "You need to go. I won't say it again."

"I'm not going anywhere. Hades sent me to find you and I intend to bring you back."

He waves at a mortal who's getting belligerent,

then fills a cup with a frothy drink, which he passes to him. On his way back, he tosses my way, "What the hell does Hades want me for?"

Is he playing dumb? Because that won't work with me, no matter how much he thinks it might.

"You know what for. You attacked him."

Fenrir tosses me another glare, his eyes even darker now. "That was eons ago. You're going to tell me he can't let something so mundane go?"

I lean against the bar, ignoring the look from the young mortal—Mary, he'd called her, and she's clearly not impressed I'm in her space. "In case you've forgotten, pantheons don't take kindly to attacks on each other. Especially not when they lead to gods going missing."

A low hiss escapes his throat. "Keep your voice low, dammit!"

"What, here?" I snort. "The noise here is enough to drown out my words, and your precious mortals are too busy getting drunk to listen in. Even if they do, they won't believe what they're hearing." At his surprised look, my smirk widens. "Yes, I did my research."

He mutters something under his breath, then turns his back to me. When he reaches for a bottle of golden liquor some moments later, coming back in proximity, I haven't budged.

"What's your master plan, hmm, Fenrir?"

"It's Finn here."

I arch an eyebrow. "Creative." He doesn't an-swer, so I nag him again. "Truly. Do you hope to stay here and forget all about the past, about who you are?"

"Yes."

When I still don't budge, he moves closer and grabs my arm. "Listen, Artemis, you have to go. Be-fore you bring the rest of them here."

This close, I notice his eyes aren't obsidian like I'd thought, but a dark blue the color of a stormy sky near nighttime. So dark, it's easy to mistake them for black.

Then his words sink in. What in Hades' balls does he mean, *bring the rest of them here*?

That tension is all around him again. It amazes me that he doesn't get it—I'm not going anywhere, not unless he comes with me.

Still. We *are* attracting a few too many interested glances, and I'm not in a mood to deal with more mortals. Perhaps if I mollify him, pretend to leave, then he'll drop his guard and I can find out what, exactly, he's doing here. And what he's hiding.

*No. Bad idea. You're here for a mission, and that's all you'll do. No investigating, no second chances. Grab, go, and disappear to Olympus, at the first opportunity.*

I can't allow myself to get embroiled again. Duty first, nothing else second. No more. Not after last time.

I force a smile past my tightly-pressed lips. "I'll be back at closing. And when I return, you had best be ready to follow."

Shrugging myself out of his hold, I chug the rest of my drink, wipe my mouth with the back of my hand, and walk out of the bar.

**Fenrir**

"Who *was* that?"

I turn to Mary. Her eager tone tells me this'll be a conversation she won't drop easily. Her youth can be so grating on my nerves sometimes.

"No one."

"Finn, come on. She was hot as hell! Is she your ex? You got some kinky costume cosplay thing going?"

I frown, trying to place her words—I might've been on this realm for a long time, but the latest slang still escapes me. Assuming *cosplay* has something to do with costumes, I shake my head. "Something like that, but it's not important. And no, she's not my ex. Just someone I know."

She jabs her elbow in my side. "So, where'd you meet her? And are there any more of her?"

I roll my eyes, forcing a smile. "Mary, drop it."

She looks at me—really looks at me—and her smile fades. Not sure what she must see in my expression, but it does the trick and she shrugs, backing off. Leaving me to my dark thoughts, and the invading goddess in them.

*Artemis.*

Mary's right, she is good-looking, much as I'm loath to admit it. *Doesn't take away from the fact she's here to drag me back to Olympus.* I shake my head. I need to leave, go somewhere she won't find me for the night, and then figure out what I'll do in the morning.

I don't want to drop everything I've worked hard for. A long time ago, when I was still hopping through realms and living on barely anything, leaving would've been easy. It was all about survival back then, which was why my beast had control. Now that I've made a life for myself, the idea of abandoning it pierces my heart, leaving me deflated and very unwilling to do so.

But I also can't risk returning to Olympus, or anywhere near the gods. Not with this darkness inside me.

An hour or so later, there's an odd break in the busyness of the night. Mary moves closer to me, so she can be heard above the loud music and some raucous guys playing pool in the corner.

"So, I know it's none of my business…"

I focus on cleaning the glasses by the sink before we run out of them. "And yet I'm sure you're going to make it yours. Am I right?"

"Well…"

The way she drags out the word makes me glance at her. Big mistake. Her dark, short-cut hair, big green eyes full of mischief and pouting mouth easily make her look like an elfin creature. One who is up to no good.

"Don't start," I warn her.

"But I so rarely get to tease you, Finn. This is my one chance." She nudges me, her sharp elbow in my side making me grunt.

I roll my eyes, and go back to cleaning the glasses. "Go on then, get it over with."

"Eek!" She claps her hands—Mary's never been one to be subtle. "So, where'd you meet her?"

"I don't remember."

She gasps, slapping my shoulder in the next breath. "You dog, tell me you didn't!"

I pull out of her reach, bringing a soapy glass with me. "Would you quit it with the smacking me about, girl?"

It's Mary's turn to roll her eyes. "You've got enough muscle to take it." Then she places her hands on her hips. "Now please tell me you didn't sleep with her and forget her name!"

"I—what—" Images of Artemis' creamy skin, splayed on a bed, my body over hers, crash into my brain with burning intensity. I shake my head to get rid of them, cursing my overactive imagination. I may have needs, but that doesn't mean I need to satisfy them with the bounty hunter who's on my tail. "*No*, Mary. Feck sake, where did you even get that idea? Out of all the bloody stupid things to say…"

Mary shrugs, an innocent look on her features. "Well, it's where my mind went."

"Yeah, right in the gutter, I see."

Her devilish grin completely disarms me. "But you already knew that, after all this time."

*All this time* being the last two years that she's worked for me. And, true enough, I've gotten used to her lexicon that could make a sailor blush. Still.

"You won't drop it, will you?" I ask her.

"Nope, not even a little bit."

I sigh, dry the glass I'd rinsed and set it on the counter next to the rest. "In a past life, I owed a debt. I figured it'd been written off, but she was sent here to collect." It's the closest thing to the truth I can give her. Unfortunately, it does the exact opposite to getting her off my back.

Mary's mouth drops, her eyes widening. "She's a bounty hunter!?"

I wince. *Way too close to the truth, now.*

"Something like that, yeah."

A low whistle escapes her next. "Wowza. They sure don't make them like they used to."

I roll my eyes again and push her aside, retaking my spot in front of the sink.

"Do you reckon she'd take, you know, some other form of payment from you?"

I reach into the soapy water and toss a handful at Mary. She squeals, stepping away and sputtering as she wipes her face. Then she bursts out laughing, further attracting the attention and indulgent smiles of our nearby customers.

Someone yells an order at the end of the bar. Mary grabs a rag and wipes at her shirt, then passes by me. "You're a right dick, sometimes," she tosses over her shoulder with a grin. Then throws the rag in my face.

I grab it, shaking my head and chuckling. Still, her words flip and flop through my head. Even more so after a client has me do shots with her. *In your dreams, Fenrir. In your fecking dreams.*

The rest of the busy night passes by in a blur of meaningless conversation, flirts I'm in no mood for, and breaking off two fights. By the time last call rolls around, I'm ready to drag myself under the bar and sleep right there. If it wasn't for the threat of Artemis returning, I would do exactly that.

One question, as I wrap up, keeps going on a loop in my head. Why would Hades have sent Artemis after me now, of all times?

## Artemis

Hours after I'd been waiting outside, Mary leaves the bar. Which means Fenrir is in there, alone. *He better not be thinking of escaping me.*

But as I peek around one of the windows, I see he's doing exactly that. Stuffing paper bills—what mortals call money, around here—into a small leather bag, which he then tosses over his back. He looks around, regret etched in every angled feature.

By the dim light, he almost looks like the god I've come here to hunt. And less like the mortal-wannabe he's been pretending to be.

Then he turns the light off, and exits the bar, locking the door.

I could take him now, but instead I choose to see what he'll do. Much as it would be easy to open a portal, a few things stop me. Mainly because he's from a different pantheon, and if I force him to come with me, the energy I'll be expanding will be worse. It gets worse the farther away from home we are—my home, that is.

But Hades' request was urgent, meaning I can't waste time, either. If I can convince Fenrir to follow me to the spot I landed in, where it'll be easier to open a portal because of the existing energy, then so be it. And if I can't… I'll drag him by his balls, if I have to.

Footsteps echoing in the distance get me moving. I might've let him walk away, but there's no way he's getting out of my sight. Sticking to the shadows, I follow him, making sure to keep my steps light. We pass street after street and the uncaring wind carries his mutters to my ears.

Does he make a habit of talking to himself?

"…Olympus…should've known better…" Some of the Irish lilt is gone from his words now, replaced by a harsher accent. His real inflections. I take some pride in knowing I've gotten under his skin. Thanatos knows he's been under mine for long enough!

We finally emerge out of the colorful side streets onto a main thoroughfare, with a port right beyond it. Tourist boats are docked, but Fenrir pays them no attention. Instead, he makes his way toward a boat farther down the line.

A tiny piece, anchored and swaying on the turbulent waves. *Leave it to the Norse gods to go for the less flashy versions of everything. They sure love to live it rough, don't they? Even when they could have better.*

Fenrir goes inside, still muttering to himself. I listen intently—no other noises follow.

*Good. This should be easy enough, then.*

**Fenrir**

Fool, fool, fool. I should've moved along three years ago, like I always do. But no, I stuck around. I'd been tired, wanting a break. And enchanted by this little piece of heaven I'd found. While it lasted.

And now, I'm paying for that mistake.

Artemis may be gone, but she'll be back. I know her reputation only too well; she's like a dog with a bone. It's a small miracle that she didn't drag me into a portal right then and there, in full view of the mortals at the pub.

Which means I have little time. If she found me, so will others. And if Odin sends the Valkyries after me… I shudder. I'm in no condition to fight them off. Nor to answer to my grandfather about my escape and what possessed me to attack a ruling god of another pantheon.

I toss the duffle bag filled with tonight's sales on the bed, and glance around the place I've called home for nearly ten years. Tears prick my eyes—of rage. Of helplessness.

I drop on a small chair by the table etched into the wall. My gaze lingers on a bottle of some liquor or other I'd brought home and never drank. But instead of reaching for it, I tense—a memory rises to the surface, playing out in the murky reflection of the bottle.

*I'm in my beast form. A wolf, three times the size of the type seen on Midgard. I pace agitatedly, in a cavern.*

*Underneath Asgard, my home. Above me, I can hear a feast. My uncle Thor's booming laugh echoes through the stone walls. Music enchants the stone. Asgard is filled with life, with joy.*

*Longing bursts in my chest. I wish I could join them, without seeing the fear in their eyes. The prophecy they all dread, of me bringing about Ragnarök—the end of the world.*

*And yet here I am, stuck underneath, a charmed chain tying me to the wall. I wish… I wish…*

*"Tsk."*

*I turn, facing my father, Loki. He's dressed in full regalia, in armour and a dark green cloak. His black hair reaches his shoulders, his onyx eyes meeting mine with maliciousness.*

*"They really shouldn't be keeping you down here," he says, coming closer, touching the chain binding me. A flare of hope bursts in my chest—will he free me? Quickly squashed when he lets go and moves away. "Alas, they don't listen to me. I keep telling them you're not a threat, but you know how they are. They see us as outsiders. As less than." He looks at me again, a mask of disappointment on his features. "And your little outburst with Tyr, biting his hand when he put that chain on you? Tsk. My son, I do wish you could at least try to act more human. Staying in this beastly form is so…. unseemly."*

*I want to tell him that I tried, but my beast refuses to listen. To relinquish power. And something in the dark-*

*ness seems to agree with it. Even as he speaks, I seek it, my gaze darting to the corners. But there is nothing.*

*Loki kneels in front of me, grabbing my muzzle with both hands. "Don't think about escaping, Fenrir. You don't have the intelligence required to pull something like that off, and you'll only embarrass us both."*

*He stands then, and leaves. And when he's gone, the darkness from the shadows starts inching toward me.* Let me soothe you…. Give you power…

*I snarl, then cower away with a whine. Close my eyes and hope for it to go away. But it doesn't. It never did.*

I open my eyes. My head feels tense, like the memory was enough to bring on a headache. I rub the back of my neck, forcing myself to let go of some tension. Then I stand. There's no point dwelling on the past, what was and what could've been changed. Only the now matters. And the *now* tells me I need to get my ass in gear.

So I pull a gym bag from a corner and start preparing. First thing I toss in is the money, shoving a few wayward bills in my wallet for easy access. Then jeans, shirts, and a few small tokens— memories—get tossed in, as well. I'll have to travel light, and leave immediately if I'm to make it out of here before she finds me again.

Midway through packing, a creak above tells me I have a visitor. I grab the nearest filleting knife and hide behind the door.

A breath. Two. More footsteps. A shadow passes and someone pushes the door open—

I jump, pulling them against me, knife at their throat. Only to find myself on my back and with an arrow pointed at my face within seconds.

I look up into sparkling emerald fire.

"Skipping town, Fenrir? Why am I not surprised?"

Artemis tosses my knife on the bed and lets me stand. I rub my backside, wincing at the bruise I feel developing. Wishing I had my healing abilities, or at the very least wasn't afraid of using them.

"What are you playing at, using human weapons on a goddess? If I didn't know better, I'd say you want to get caught."

*It's not like I can use my powers without consequences.* But speaking is useless. Especially now that my plan is thwarted, and I have no other options.

"Maybe it's better... Then I wouldn't have to keep running."

She watches me closely, then plops on my bed. Seeing her there unnerves me, and I've no idea why. "Get off."

"Why?"

"Just—get off."

I move to her, intending to drag her off the bed myself, but a zap of electricity hits me when my arm brushes against hers. I try to ignore it, instead focusing on why the hell she hasn't opened a portal yet.

Even I know Artemis doesn't fuck around with her bounties. So why is she humoring me?

I turn to her. "You've yet to drag me to Olympus."

All I get is another shrug. "I found you. I'm not losing you. Besides, if you can come without fighting me, it'll be less expanded energy for me." She stops as if she's just told me something she shouldn't have.

"And… are you here on orders to not expend said energy?"

She scowls, and in that one movement the air becomes static all over again. "My orders are to bring you with me. So, keep packing, and let's go."

I hold up a hand. "One day. Let me end things properly here, so no one asks questions."

"I don't care about human nonsense."

"But I do! One day, and we can leave. I'll come quietly. I swear it. Just… Let me speak to Hades when we get there, that's all I ask. To explain myself. Then you can call my pantheon."

I've given too much away and she has no reason to listen. Still, I hope.

She tilts her head to the side. "These mortals mean so much to you?"

I hesitate, then nod.

Artemis looks away. "As you wish. But one day only, Fenrir. No games. And I sleep with you tonight."

"I—you—*what*?"

She blushes at my sputter and her eyes crackle all over again. "Mind out of the gutter. I mean *here*. Around you. To make sure you don't sneak away." She sets her bow next to her. "And, Fenrir? Don't even try. I'm a very light sleeper."

I continue packing, feeling her eyes on me the entire time. But she says nothing else. So I give in and get ready for sleep, knowing the next day is the end of life as I know it. The past never stays hidden for long, but I'd hoped…

I sigh deeply as my eyes close and my thoughts drift. One more day, one more chance to escape the darkness. And *his* control.

# CHAPTER 3

## Artemis

*The grass is soft under my back, the sky bathed in shades of violet and pink. And the sound of water nearby, so close by…*

*A shadow blocks the sun. White wings, soft as silk, flap in the air. Hooves touch the grass with barely a sound. The beautiful white horse neighs, fluttering his wings, once, twice. The breeze hits me, making me smile. I curl onto my side and watch him.*

*A moment later, light envelops him. And the magnificent creature gives way to one equally as magnificent. Azure eyes land on mine, and already, Pegasus is moving toward me.*

*Kneels by my side, tugs on a lock of my red hair.*

*Drops his mouth to mine, a deep groan making its way through his body. "When will we stop hiding, Artemis?"*

*I tug him on top of me, ignoring his question. And instead try to distract him with more kisses, my hands reaching behind him, under his tunic, for the muscle they crave to touch.*

*Pegasus pulls away, holding himself on his elbows atop me. "I mean it."*

*I turn my head away. "Pegasus—"*

*"What are you so afraid of? Your father's reaction?"*

*I scowl at him. "Zeus wouldn't care."*

*"Wouldn't he?"*

*I don't want to admit the truth. That of course he would, because it would interfere with my worth to him. If I'm a goddess in love, I'm no longer his prized bounty hunter. And having seen the way he deals with those who offend him, I have no wish to be on his wrong side.*

*"I…"*

*Pegasus shakes his head, and drops to the grass by my side. "I don't understand your reticence."*

*"Then maybe this should stop."*

*He frowns, watching me as I stand, refusing to be there a second longer.*

*"Artemis, wait—"*

*But already, I'm shimmering, and disappearing.*

I jerk awake from the memory. That was the last time I'd seen him… At least, until Hades told me he'd been killed.

My chest aches, and I lift a hand to rub it, letting out a soft sigh. Then it hits me—the room is too quiet.

I jump to my feet, looking around—Fenrir is nowhere to be found.

"Damn you, Norse god!"

On a growl, I dematerialize my bow into the ether—can't be running through a mortal city with it, after all—and take off.

**Fenrir**

Mary looks at me, her eyes wide and uncomprehending. "What… I don't understand, Finn. What are you saying? You're *leaving*?"

"I have to, Mary. And I'm leaving the bar, everything, to you. Do with it as you will—sell it, run it, it's up to you. I just didn't want to disappear without telling you."

"But…why?"

I shake my head, knowing I'm already running out of time. Artemis will wake up soon, and she won't be impressed when she notices that I'm not there. Especially when she made it clear she needs to be by my side no matter what.

But I couldn't have done this with her here, not with the distraction.

"It's time for me to go, that's all it is."

"I call bullshit, Finn. Does it have anything to do with that redhead?"

"What? No, she's got nothing to do with this."

Her gaze narrows on me. "You said she's a bounty hunter, here for you."

Fuck. I did say that, and I forgot. This is why I try never to lie.

"That's a different matter, it—"

"Why are you lying to me?" This time, her eyes fill with tears. "We're friends, aren't we?"

I let out a sigh. "Of course we are, Mary." I pull her into a hug, and she rests her cheek against my chest, sniffling. "I promise, nothing bad is going on. I just need to leave, and I don't want this place to go to anyone but you." I push her away a little until our gazes lock. "You've always wanted your own bar, you've said so yourself."

A small smile tugs at her lips. "I did, that's true."

"So, take it. Make it your own. Be happy here." *Be happy, because I'll never be happy again.* "I'll send you my forwarding address when I get settled, and you can tell me all about it."

"Promise?"

"I promise."

She smiles at me, seemingly more settled. Then her gaze goes over my shoulder, to the entrance. And all smiling mood falls aside. "You said the redhead has nothing to do with you leaving?"

"Yeah, why—"

"Might want to tell her that."

I follow her gaze, groaning when Artemis bursts through the doors of my bar. Her divine energy's crackling all around her, affecting the air itself as she moves for me.

"For someone trying to escape, you sure aren't very bright."

I move to intercept her, dropping my voice. "Watch yourself. Mary doesn't need a show of Olympian power."

Artemis gets even closer in my face, until all I can see is the crackle of emerald fire in her gaze. "You've got some nerve, making demands. Which part of last night didn't you understand?"

"Finn—"

Artemis turns her scowl to the little mortal. "Back off, this is private business."

I nearly let out another groan. Mary's pretty sweet, but when her friends are threatened, she tends to—

"*Excuse me*?"

*That.* This is not going my way at all.

I angle myself differently, interposing myself between the two. "Ladies, let's take a moment. Mary, read over the transfer deed to make sure I didn't miss anything." To Artemis, I add, "Come with me at the back."

She follows, waiting until the door closes behind us. Her energy skyrockets, sending me flying in the chair. "What games are you playing, Fenrir?"

A jolt of panic hits me. *Her energy! If she doesn't watch it, she'll bring them straight to my door.* I force myself to exhale and keep calm as I answer. "No games. I just wanted to have a conversation with Mary without you around, so I could explain."

"Explain what? That you're a god on the run, and I'm here to bring you to face justice?"

I scowl at her. "No. That I'm leaving, and she's inheriting my possessions, including this bar. That takes time. It's why I left early, while you were sleeping."

She bristles, annoyed at the reminder that I got one over her. In all fairness, it had been easier than I'd thought—though I'd envied her the dream she seemed to be in the throes of. Mine tend to linger more on the darker side these days.

"We both know you could have left a note."

I shrug. "I don't write love letters."

Artemis takes another step toward me, but I'm already standing. The movement puts us chest to chest, nose to nose, barely a hair's breadth between us. A tendril of her hair flies in my face, and I notice for the first time the specks of gold and indigo in her emerald gaze.

I gulp, forcing myself to focus. "Now, you can let me finish up, and then we can leave. But I won't take a step out of here without being done with what I need to do. So you can either drag me out, and waste all the energy you're not supposed to, or fucking wait, for once in your life."

"You have no idea what my life has been about."

"Oh, but I do. Asgard may be less *fun* than Olympus, but tales of you and your brother reached even *my* pantheon, long ago. Zeus' golden twins, breaking hearts everywhere." I lean into her, determined to show her I won't cower in front of an Olympian. "I don't know where the mortals got their idea of you being the virgin huntress, but it sure gave me a laugh when I found out."

Her gaze grows more incendiary, if possible. I walk around her, heading for the door.

Artemis isn't done, though. "What is your problem!"

"My—" I stop a few feet away, fists clenching, fuming. Then I turn, walking back toward her just as quickly as I'd stomped away. "*MY PROBLEM!* My problem is I had a life. For the first time in over twenty years, I'd stopped looking over my shoulder and seeking things I didn't understand. And then you showed up. Fucked it all up. That's my Olympus-given problem, in an Olympus-sized package."

She scowls at me. "You could've just said so."

My lips part, not quite believing what I'm hearing. Then I scoff, toss my hands up in the air, and take a few steps over to the door again. Frustration like I've never felt fills me, making me want to wring her neck.

*Yes…. Olympian blood tastes sweet…*

The voice is a reminder I'm on the precipice of something bad. And if I let it happen, I'll lose the little control I have left. And I can't do that, not now, not ever. I close my eyes, let out a breath, and force the tension out of me.

"You could start by telling me what you're hiding," Artemis says.

I open my eyes and find her watching me, seeing more than she should.

I'm quiet for the longest time. When I finally speak, my tone is barely above a whisper. "You wouldn't believe me if I tried." Then I shake my head. "Give me another half an hour, then we can leave. I swear it on my honor."

Instead of making another jab, Artemis nods. I guess Olympians still trust the word of a Norse god. *That's something, at least.*

I walk out of the office, and back into the main area of the bar. Mary's tapping its surface, staring at the transfer deed as though it's a snake ready to bite.

"Did you read it?"

"I did."

"And? Did I miss something?"

She shakes her head. "It's all in order."

"Good, then. All you need to do is sign."

"Are you sure this is what you want, Finn?"

I nod, giving her a small smile. "It is."

She sighs, then pulls up a pen and flips through the pages, signing where appropriate. I'd already added my signature before giving her the papers, so I pace the ground behind her, taking in everything I've built over the years. Everything I now have to say goodbye to, forever.

The granite bar top, painfully paid for by doing labour work at one of the local quarries. The worn wooden chairs I'd refurbished with my own hands. It had taken me six months to learn how to do it, and another six to prepare everything. But in the end, I'd had the satisfaction of working toward something, and eventually enjoying the fruit of my labours.

Artemis steps out of the office, but leans against the wall, doing nothing. Not yet, anyway. Small mercies.

Mary finishes signing the last paper, then tosses the pen on the bar and walks to me. She hugs me, holding on tight. "I'm going to miss you, so much."

"I know, kid. I'll miss you, too."

Out of the corner of my eye, I see Artemis moving. I turn, still holding onto Mary, to find she's materialized her bow, and has an arrow notched.

"What the—"

Mary pulls away from me, looking at Artemis

like she's just grown two heads. "What are you—is that a *bow*?"

It takes me an extra moment to realize Artemis isn't aiming it at us. Instead, she's aiming at something over my head. "Watch it!" she yells.

When I don't move, she lets loose the arrow, shattering the window of the bar as it goes to meet its target. A screech—blood-curdling—is the answer we get.

That screech has fed my nightmares for eons.

And now…

"No…"

My whisper is drowned in the chaos. Artemis tackles me, dropping me to the ground. To my left, where Mary stands, something bursts through the window…and the wall. Half of the bar breaks apart, massive bricks falling everywhere.

"I call upon the earth…" Artemis whispers in my ear, still atop me. A golden globe of light rises from the ground, surrounding and protecting us from the debris falling everywhere.

I try to shove her off me, but she clamps her knees around my thighs. "Stay the fuck down. We're under attack, can't you see?"

"Mary!" is all I can scream.

Artemis looks to the crumbled side of the bar—where Mary had been standing. "There's nothing we can do. We have to leave, now."

"No!" Bucking my hips, I shove her off me, and burst past her barrier.

Even as I reach the mountain of debris, I know it's a lost cause. I shove away stones, ignoring Artemis' yells, and finally, find Mary. Crushed under everything, her features ashen, blood surrounding her head like a halo.

"No…"

Something hits my gut, slamming into me. I welcome the physical pain, a distraction from the emotional.

"We have to *go!*"

She shoots two more arrows into the sky, then drags me with her, out of what's left of the bar, and down the street. The entire time, she's got the bow in her hand, and she's scanning the skies for more attacks. A trail of blood tells me her arrows have found *some* targets.

Then more screeches fill the sky.

"Above…" I clear my throat, forcing my voice to be louder. "They're above, hiding in the clouds."

"I know." Artemis's jaw is tight, her entire body as taut as the bow in her hand.

It's then that it hits me—she saved me. She could've easily left me to die, but she saved me. Probably because she can't go back to Olympus without me, but still. The effort doesn't go unnoticed.

When the screeches seem to head farther down, toward the bar, toward more innocents, I yank on her hand. "We can't just leave the mortals!"

Artemis turns on me, grabs me by my shirt, and shoves me against the wall of a house with surprising strength. "Are you going to use your powers to save them?"

My mouth opens, shuts, opens again...but no words come out.

"I didn't think so. I don't know what the hell is going on around here, but clearly they're after you. If we go into hiding, they will disappear. They have to."

"They won't!" I push against her hold, feeling desperate like I never have before. Mary...dead. Many more...dead. All because of me. Because I stayed too long. "These people worshipped you, eons ago."

"They worship no one now."

My anger flares, and I manage to flip us around, pushing her against the wall instead.

Artemis gapes at me, incensed that I've dared touch her. Her nostrils flare, and she draws in a big gulp of air, as though she's getting ready to scream at me. I beat her to it.

"You're a damned goddess, *do your job and protect them!*"

Only afterward do I realize I've put myself way

too close to her. And the crackle of her power reverberates through her skin, into my fingertips, and underneath my skin. Lightning licks up my spine, then down my chest—a warning.

Then, Artemis bursts out laughing. "Why, so you can run away from me when I'm exhausted from it? I don't think so, Fenrir. For all I know, you orchestrated this whole thing."

My fist slams into the wall next to her head, knuckles splitting open. The scent of blood fills the air. I barely wince at the pain, my eyes on her the entire time.

"I did no such thing."

She looks at me, at my fist, and back at me. Something seems to work behind her gaze, then it widens in realization. "I thought it was odd, but now I see there's definitely more going on here. You aren't using your divine powers. Why?"

I push away from her, running a hand over my face. "Please, just… I'll tell you. But help them. Help them, because I can't."

Artemis stares at me a moment longer. Then she backs away from me, her bow angled to the skies. She notches three arrows, and for the first time, lets loose her entire energy. Light suffuses the arrows, the bow itself, her own being. Her red hair crackles in the wind, her skin becomes golden, almost impossibly bright.

She looks…like a goddess. Intimidating. Powerful. Invincible.

She lets loose the arrows, watching as they disappear into the clouds. Moments later, another screech sounds. And another. Nothing falls out, but a flash of light flips behind the clouds, like someone turned on the lights, and then turned them off.

Artemis waits, and waits. Finally, she turns to me. "They've portalled out of here. And we should do the same, if we're smart."

I gulp, trying not to fall at her feet to express my gratitude. "I have a better idea."

# CHAPTER 4

**Artemis**

We go to a hotel for a night. Or what Fenrir calls a hotel. I call it a cesspool of crap. It's a far sight from the marbled halls of Olympus and, I imagine, Asgard. Which once again begs the question of why the hell Fenrir refuses to go back to his people.

I let him deal with getting us a room, paying the shifty-eyed hotel manager with money from the small bag he retrieved at his boat on our way here. Since I'm not about to let him out of my sight, I tell him to make sure we share a room.

While he does that, I inspect our surroundings, trying to make sure there's no more creatures. That's when I notice the crowd of people around us give *me* a weird look. As if my leather outfit is any worse than their multiple-piercings-jeans-sagging-barely-there-shirts.

Finally, Fenrir signals me, a plastic card in his hand. The elevator ride up is silent, filled with tension. I want answers. He's mourning the loss of his mortal. It couldn't be more awkward if we tried.

When the doors open, we try to exit at the same time, and bump into each other. A shot of electricity runs up my arm where it touches his. We both pull away at the same time, gazes locking in mutual confusion.

Then Fenrir gulps, gesturing for me to go first. I do, making sure I don't touch him again. A few feet later, we stop in front of a door that's seen better days. He unlocks it, and I step in after him. Go straight to the window, my eyes stuck on the skies. Nothing. The clouds have given way to a beautiful day, and the sun's shining everywhere.

Why do I feel so cold, then?

"What were they, Fenrir?" I can practically feel him freezing behind me. Slowly, I turn. "I gave you your day. And all it did was land us into shit. And get your little mortal killed."

Pain flickers on his features, echoed by the haunted look in his eyes. A flash of guilt runs through me, but I stomp it down before it can emerge. I'm not doing anything wrong, pointing out that what happened was his fault. And I need answers. Otherwise, I'm flying into this blind.

"You're right." He drops onto the bed, burying his head in his hands. "I should've fucking left years ago. Or at least the moment you came, and faced whatever the hell awaits me. Delaying it, for my own selfish needs, only cost me."

I didn't think Norse gods wore their emotions on their sleeves. Most of them, anyway. Unlike us. My mind drifts to Pegasus, his easy smile, his quick anger—just as easily thwarted by a simple kiss. I shake my head to free it of him, and instead focus on the Norse god mere feet away. Sitting dejectedly, as though he's got the weight of the world on his shoulders—he'd give Atlas a run for his money.

"You can have your moment to mourn, Fenrir, but I need to know what we're facing."

He lifts his head from his hands, shoulders drooping even further. "I wish I knew."

I stomp over to him in a flash, planting myself right across him. "I'm going to need more than that, Fenrir. You know something. I know you do."

When he doesn't answer, I reach for his chin, lifting it. His gaze hooks onto mine, and all of a sudden the touch feels too heated—the proximity, too intimate. I let go and back off another step. *What the hell is going on with me?*

Fenrir lets out a breath, runs a hand through his hair, and finally nods, as if to himself. "You're right. You are, but I don't know *what* I know."

"What does that mean?"

"I'll answer, but first, a question of my own: what do you know of Hades' attack?"

I narrow my eyes on him. "That he was in this realm, and he was attacked. By you. Hermes saved him. And much later, a second attack happened—one that killed his best friend, Pegasus." I clear my throat of the hoarseness his name alone evokes. After all this time, I should be more put together when it comes to him. "And with you having gone missing, your pantheon making excuses, your immortals found dead… It was concluded that you were behind that, too."

"Immortals? I—I never had any! Nor was I responsible for their deaths, whoever they were."

Fenrir jumps to his feet, putting us precariously close yet again. Heat emanates off him, a heat that seems to curl around my own body, demanding I lean into it more. I give myself a mental shake, trying to focus on his words instead of the closeness of his hard-coiled body.

"I left, after that first attack," he's saying. "And even that, it wasn't me."

"You're making no sense."

He grabs my arm, shaking me. "I know I'm not, but you have to listen."

More jolts of electricity run up and down my skin, but this time, I seem to be the only one aware of them. I wrench myself free, taking a step closer, jabbing my index in his face. "Don't be so loose with your hands, else you *will* lose them. And I don't have to listen to anything you say, I simply have to bring you back to Olympus."

"Artemis, please." Palms raised, facing me, he tries to catch my gaze. "I wasn't behind that second attack. The first one, I didn't… I didn't mean to. I was lost to—to something, and it led everything that happened." When I say nothing, he adds, almost desperately, "Please. The creatures that killed Mary today, they're the same. Same as those who attacked Hades."

That pulls my attention. "How do you know that?"

"Because—" He seems to realize he's dug himself into a hole, because he drops to the bed again, deflated once more. "I know it sounds bad. But I've seen them before. There's a reason I keep running from place to place, every few years. They know where I am, they hunt me down."

A scoff leaves my lips. "Because you're so important to them?"

"I—" He looks at me, and his features do a complete flip. "Fine, don't fucking believe me. But they hunt me, and this time around, you led them straight to me. It's my fault I delayed leaving with you, but Mary would've still been alive if you hadn't used your damn divine powers every chance you got!"

With that outburst, he gets up and heads to the bathroom, slamming the door behind him. I could follow him, demand he explain himself, but I don't. Instead, I force myself into cool-headed Artemis and head back by the window, thinking through things.

Hades had given an account of the first attack on him alone and, later on, the second attack when both Pegasus and his immortal guards had been present. He'd never once linked it to Fenrir, but Zeus had. Odin couldn't—or wouldn't—defend his grandson, going so far as to call him a *friend* rather than remind everyone of their familial link. But over time, most forgot about it. Until Hades returned to Olympus, eons later, with news that Tartarus had been breached. And if it'd happened once, it would happen again.

I like to plan. To know things in advance, avoid all obstacles, and have smooth sailings. This mission has been nothing but a headache since it started. And now…

*Mary would've still been alive if you hadn't used your damn divine powers every chance you got!*

Of course, she's not the first mortal to die by my hand, or because of it. Many have, over the eons, either from worshipping me, or simply playing with things they didn't understand. I wasn't able to save most of them.

But Mary *was* an innocent. And her death could've been avoided, if I hadn't been so focused on Fenrir, on making sure he didn't get hurt. *Because I need him to come back to Olympus, with me. To prove to Zeus I've still got it. Nothing else.*

So if that's the truth, then why is his pain tugging at my heartstrings? If I move closer to the bathroom door, I'll feel it emanating. Does he even realize that his divine powers are very much on display?

Hang on… *If you hadn't used your damn divine powers every chance you got!* Fenrir accused my powers of having led the creatures to him. Does that mean they can track divine energy, from any and all pantheons? If so, skills like that... Who could've come up with it?

I think back on the Council meetings from back then. It takes a moment to sort through all the eons, go back to the time Hades still lived in Olympus, before he was relegated to the Underworld.

The first time, when the news of Fenrir attacking Hades spread… Odin had been shady, even for his ancient being. He'd said, *"We cannot find him. In fact, we fear something worse has happened."*

And something worse *did* happen.

Odin soon came to report they'd found Fenrir's immortals—the guardians assigned to him—dead.

*"Their throats were slashed by a blade that seemingly has no issues affecting a supernatural."*

I remember listening with growing dread to the account. And to Zeus' edict that no one was to leave Olympus. We were prisoners for millennia, lacking the freedom we once had. Even the immortal guardians assigned to us were losing their minds, restricted as they were from moving across pantheons, visiting each other.

And then Hades seemed capable of handling Tartarus, and all the evil the various pantheons had dumped within it. At least…up until twenty years ago. When he came pleading for help in Olympus, warning about Tartarus and Cronus escaping. Hades skimmed over the details of how he'd gotten the Titan back—probably in an effort not to remind everyone he speaks the Old Tongue—but I'd always wondered…

Not that my uncle was deceitful. Only, I believe he's always known more than he lets on. And I don't blame him for not being willing to share, given how he's been treated.

But when it comes to Fenrir, what the hell does it all mean? That there's more going on? That *he* wasn't the one who'd killed his immortals? And if not him, then who?

The door to the bathroom opens, but he doesn't come out just yet. Instead, I hear him moving about.

I try for another approach. "How is it a god of the Norse lands in this…hell?"

The tap water turns off.

"Not all pantheons need the finery Olympus is used to. Some of us are perfectly fine with the bare minimum."

I snort. "Right, because Asgard is so minimal."

"How would you know?"

I roll my eyes, glad he can't see me lose my composure. "Because I was there, when I first started hunting you."

He pops his head out of the bathroom, mouth gaping. "You were allowed entrance?"

"Don't be silly. As if Olympians would be welcomed with open arms. I had the pleasure of running into Heimdall, is all. And seeing Asgard from afar. Didn't look very minimal to me."

"Maybe not, from afar. But I assure you, we're all used to simple meats and ale, same as the mortals who worship us. No luxuries or fancy trimmings."

I snort, and he goes back inside the bathroom. The need to poke him some more is too strong to resist. "So, is that why you picked Earth to stay on?"

"You really don't quit, do you?" A moment later, he walks out, the only thing on his hips a towel. "I'm not saying anything more. Not until I see her."

I scan the length of his torso, the ripped muscles,

tattoo on his left bicep, and the fine line of light hair leading into the towel. Something tightens in my core, and I force myself to take a breath. It doesn't help. The hotel washing stuff might be cheap, but on him, it smells like…the chaos of turbulent waters. Which is exactly what he is.

And then his words penetrate. "Her? Who's her?"

"My sister, Hel."

"Why?" Much like Hades, she presides over her own Underworld realm where she greets some of the dead. Smaller realm, but still impressive.

"Because she might have some answers."

I arch an eyebrow. "Give me something, Fenrir, or else we're heading to Olympus."

A faint smirk tugs at his lips. "Forcing me will only exhaust your energy, remember? And if we get attacked again, that won't look too good, will it?"

"It won't, because you refuse to use your divine powers." I can tell I've struck a nerve by the clenching of his jaw. "What kind of Asgardian backs down from a fight, hmm?"

He jabs a finger in the air between us. "Don't push me, Artemis. You have no understanding of our way of life. Olympians have always had it way too easy."

I roll my eyes. This is an old taunt. "Tell me something new." Much as I hate to admit it, though, he's right. I can't force him. With a sigh, I offer, "All right. Tell me what Hel can do for you, and I'll try to get to her once we're back in Olympus."

"No. Before."

"That's impossible. It's not that easy to get an audience with another pantheon. Especially for an Olympian like me. And *most especially* now."

Fenrir tilts his head to the side. "Why not?"

"Because of you. Attacking Hades."

Darkness fills his eyes and he shakes his head. "I told you, I didn't mean to."

"So you say. But you've spent millennia on the run, living around mortals… And I've spent the last twenty years on the hunt for you. I haven't chased you across all these realms in order to give up now and head home without you."

"Then I suppose that leaves us at a standstill."

I scowl at him. "You're impossible, you know that?"

He shrugs, walks to the bed, and tosses himself on top of the covers. The towel's precariously close to slipping off him. Instead of ogling him some more, I lie down on the opposite bed, by the door.

**Fenrir**

I close my eyes, but I can hear her moving, until she finally settles on the bed. Her obvious discomfort with being in such shitty quarters is a source of amusement, I can't lie. It must suck for an Olympian used to the best, to slum it down like this.

Well, she'd better get used to it. Until she promises me a meeting with Hel, *before* we go to Olympus, I'm not budging. The immortals she'd mentioned, the ones I'm also meant to have killed—they died inside the Norse pantheon delineations. Meaning, their souls would've gone into Hel's domain, not Hades' or anyone else's. Speaking to them, if Hel can find them, means clearing my name.

Souls... Mary. My eyes shoot open, their vision blurring on the ceiling. I blink, and blink again, trying to fight off tears. It hurts, knowing I'm responsible for her death. It's another weight I'll carry around for the remainder of my existence.

*Even when you try to do something nice, you hurt people.*

I shove aside the voice, and the grief. Pack it all up in a neat little box in my mind, to be set aside. Until I have a moment to deal with it. A moment where I'm not being watched.

I let a breath out slowly, forcing my thoughts back to Hel. If she could speak to the dead immortals, she could shine the truth on that one attack. And then it might cast doubt on my involvement with everything else...perhaps?

*Or perhaps you're an idyllic fool.*

Maybe. But at least it's worth a shot.

At first, I'd fully intended to head on, give myself up to Olympus. But after this attack? No. Someone's hunting me, aside from Artemis. And they're using her to track me down, because she doesn't shy away from using her divine energy.

The question is, what use am I to whomever it is?

And is it worth telling Artemis my full doubts, or will she just use it against me, trying to figure out a way to take me to Olympus regardless?

I turn my head to the side, watching her for a moment. Her red hair is spread on the pillowcase, and she's shifting left and right, trying to find a comfortable spot on the mattress. Her leather outfit clings to her body, drawing my attention on curves I'd much rather forget about.

I rub my chin, recalling her touching me, earlier. It had felt like a branding of my skin.

*She's shown me kindness, when she didn't need to. Is it worth trusting her?*

I clear my throat. Her fidgeting stops. "Eons ago, my father Loki had a crazy plan. To overthrow the Vanir deities, and place himself as the new All-Father."

Artemis snorts. "Isn't that what he always does?"

"Pretty much. But this time around, he blamed it on me."

A gasp is her only reply. I'm surprised she even

cares, given she's not of my pantheon, and has only been around me for the better part of two days, now. Nor do I know why I'm telling her this. Maybe because I need someone to finally believe me, to reassure myself that I'm not crazy.

"I was imprisoned. See, my pantheon already didn't trust me because of the role I'm supposed to play in Ragnarök—the apocalypse."

"Right... A bit morbid, no? Especially since it never happened, and you've been around for eons."

I let out a sigh, forcing myself to keep cool. "Olympians may turn their nose up at darker events being foretold, but in Asgard...we call it as we see it. And, truthfully, my pantheon *does* still believe in Ragnarök. Nothing will ever teach them otherwise."

Artemis turns to her side. For a long time, she's quiet. When she finally speaks, her tone is less flippant, more pensive. "I suppose it is hard to change our tune, considering how long we've all been alive."

I take it as good enough, and continue with my story. "Well, my grandfather, much as he does occasionally bestow his favor on me, is still very much self-serving. When the opportunity presented itself, he knew it was his one and only chance to get me out of the way. So he got the dwarves to create a chain that would forever bind me. Tyr—he's the bringer of order and justice, in our realm; sort of like your Athena—was the one in charge of tying me up, and he... The moment he did, the moment the chain touched me, darkness the likes of which I've never felt before entered me. I chomped off Tyr's arm, fought the rest of them, freed myself. They never truly trusted me again after that." I clear my dry throat, trying to find the words for the next bit. "You mentioned immortals, something else I'm accused of killing. I don't remember much after that initial attack on Tyr, only flashes. What I *do* remember is that I was under watch, but it was by Valkyries, not immortals. I... The next thing I recall is that one day, after a fight with Loki, I snapped. I must have hurt him, perhaps others. I had blood on my hands. And then... I disappeared through the first portal I could find." I take a deep breath. "That portal led me to this realm, and my attack on Hades. I didn't know who he was, in my mind. Not then. In between realms, my true self—my wolf—took over. I reverted to my beastly state. Darkness ruled me, and darkness wanted to attack anything of the divine pantheons." I close my eyes. "Improbable as it might sound, I didn't *mean* any of what happened. And I swear I didn't have anything to do with that second attack that killed Hades' best friend."

A moment goes by, and another. Finally, Artemis says, "You really expect me to believe that?"

I turn her way. Instead of understanding, I find anger in her eyes. "I've just confided to you the truth—"

"And I don't believe a word of it. Everyone knows the Vanir deities are powerful. Your Asgard has barriers around it that even Olympus hasn't been able to duplicate. Yet some kind of mystical darkness could've entered, and forced you to do things you didn't want to? A bit convenient, no?" She shakes her head. "And to blame your pantheon? I knew you Norse gods were all about drama and dark themes and shit, but this is pushing it. So, we all have issues with our parents. They're still our parents. I doubt they'd have betrayed you to the extent you make it seem they did. They're still your pantheon."

"Asgard isn't Olympus, and your way of living isn't ours. Duty rules most of us and—"

"Stop, Fenrir. Just stop. You're trying to make me feel bad for you." She flops back down on the bed, scoffing. "I'll try to get you your audience with Hel, but not because I believe any of this. Only because it'll be the easiest way to get you back to Olympus, to face the consequences for your actions."

My stomach curls into a pit of despair. I tried, and all I got back for my efforts was scorn. Fuck. If Artemis won't believe me, away from her pantheon, who's to say anyone else will?

Olympus is known for refusing to see the harsh truth. They don't want the bad stuff. The negative. The darkness. They'd rather pretend it doesn't exist the same way they've always refused to see the apocalypse. Nothing about that has changed. Zeus will condemn me the moment he sets eyes on me. Father will let me take the fall—again.

The painful reality is that I'm alone, and I've got no way out of this mess.

## Artemis

On some level, I'm aware of the lumpy bed under me, of the smell of stale air around me. But the memory tugs me under again...

*I return to my quarters inside Olympus, feeling decidedly satisfied. Another mission accomplished, and none too soon. Father will be pleased.*

*A knock on the door sounds, and I wave it open. Apollo bursts in, his sunny disposition all but gone. I immediately run to him.*

*"Brother, what is it? You look like death."*

*He shakes his head, holding my shoulders. Then he pulls me into his arms, in a forceful hug. I let him hold me for a few seconds, confusion racing through my mind.*

*Finally, I push him away. "What is it? What's happened?"*

*He shakes his head, eyes shining with tears. "I'm so sorry. It's Pegasus... He's gone."*

*"What?" I let out a shocked laugh. "Gone, how?"*

*"Dead, sister. He's...dead."*

*My knees give way, and I physically feel my heart breaking.* "N-no. No! Apollo, tell me it's not true…. Please…"

*He lets us both drop to the floor, even as he nods.* "I'm sorry. They were attacked—Hades barely survived."

*Agony spreads through me, fire and ice filling my veins. And the most agonizing scream bursts from me, echoing over, and over, and over…*

I jerk awake, trembling, my cheeks bathed in tears. I wipe at them, trying with the same movement to wipe at the memory of the pain.

And then I realize the room is too quiet. *Not again!* Sure enough, Fenrir isn't anywhere to be found.

"Argh!"

Fenrir may be elusive, but his primordial essence is all too easy to track down this time. It's filled with grief, probably for the mortal girl. And it's a grief I understand. But, selfishly, am also glad for, since it provides a direct path to him.

My feet dig into the sand, and the smell of seaweed and mortal shores fills my nostrils. I push away the annoyance at having, once more, lost him. And instead focus on the lonely figure on the beach in the distance.

The copper tinge to his blond hair clues me in to his identity. Cursing under my breath, I check everywhere to make sure no mortals see me, then snap my fingers and rematerialize next to him.

"You could've left a note."

A sobering sigh escapes him. He turns to me. The rising sun behind him blinds me, concealing his features.

"Would it have mattered?"

"It would've made me not chase you halfway across the city, yes."

"Sorry to inconvenience you." He sounds anything but remorseful.

"Is this about me not believing your crazy story? Because your attitude won't make me magically change my mind."

He shakes his head. "You don't get it, do you? I had a life. Why couldn't you just pretend you'd never found me?"

"Because I can't. I'm bound by my promise and I've wasted too much time on you already. My reputation is on the line."

A humorless chuckle escapes him. "Yes, we wouldn't want that."

"What's that supposed to mean?" But I know what he means. Of course I do. I've heard it my entire life. So it's not even much of a surprise when the words move past his lips.

"The Virgin Goddess. The pureness incarnate."

His derisive tone raises my hackles. "Don't test me, Fenrir. This isn't the time."

But already he's moving. I prepare to swipe at him but he tackles me to the ground—and then I catch his hissed, "Stay down!"

A moment later, I hear it—screeches. Otherworldly screeches that could only come from the worst of nightmares. And then shadows. The sky goes fully dark, mist rises from the water to our left. And still, Fenrir doesn't move.

Following his initial tackle, he's almost frozen on top of me. A strand of his hair tickles my face. His body feels a lot heavier than I'd given it credit. And when my hands touch his shoulders—to push him off me—the same hint of electricity from before runs through me.

The screeches get louder. Not as loud as Fenrir's whispered words.

"Control… Stay.. present. Don't let go. Don't let go. Don't. Listen. To. Him."

Instead of shoving him away, I tap him. "Fenrir?"

I pull back as much as I can. Sand fills my hair, and the back of my neck, sticking to everywhere there's bare skin. I shove against Fenrir again, but…nothing. It's like he's frozen.

*A big block of frozen, yummy granite.* Ugh. The thought intrudes too close to home.

I grip his shoulders, wrap my legs around his hips, and with a perfectly aimed flip, I'm straddling him. I only have a moment to catch the darkness in his eyes—what the *hell*—before another screech hits. Too close. Way too fucking close.

I jump off Fenrir, hold my hand out and materialize my bow and quiver. Its smooth wooden handle lands in palm as though magnetically attracted to it. With my free hand, I yank an arrow out of the quiver and notch it, flipping to my back, preparing to shoot.

The skies open above me, and a big cloud of dark dives toward me. No, not me. *Fenrir.*

I want to shoot, but I'm too frozen by what I'm seeing. The creature is half-horse, half something…else. A reptile? Head the shape of a horse, with scales. A tail with spikes, bat-like wings and red eyes. And when it shifts toward its true target, the rider atop it appears. Dressed in a dark cloak and knight helm, I can see nothing of his features. Yet the blade in his hand is all too real.

I calm the brief tremble in my arms and regain a firm grip on the bow. Deep breath in—I let loose the arrow. It flies off the mark, missing. Another one takes its place, and it still doesn't hit the mark. Nor does the third.

*Shit.*

I've never missed so many in a row. But then

again, I can't say I've ever faced a creature the likes of this one.

I take another deep breath, steadying my aim. My entire being begins to vibrate, glowing, until the glow imbues the arrow itself with my intention. I let it loose—it captures the tip of a wing, earning me some spittle and more roaring.

*I've got to get Fenrir out of here.* It's clear they don't care about mortals that might be nearby. Or anything else, other than him. I've never run into creatures that look like them, but maybe now's not the time to figure them out.

With one last look, I kneel next to the still-frozen Fenrir—now seeming more unconscious than anything—grip his wrist, and close my eyes. Blazing light engulfs us, and then Dingle's beach fades from sight. As do we.

# CHAPTER 5

**Fenrir**

*Someone's singing a lullaby. It's soothing… a rough voice, but with dulcet tones. I open my eyes—I'm in human form. Curled up against someone.*

*"There, there, my boy."*

*My body aches. So much. My back—when I move, agony fills me. Like licks of fire on my skin.*

*"It's all right," the voice says.*

*I look up, into my father's eyes. The onyx glimmer has a glint of madness in it.*

*"Father…. It hurts."*

*"I know it does. But what did I tell you? You have to learn to morph, over and over. Faster. Much faster than you do now."*

*"But the beast... We both hurt. So much."*

*His features harden to stone. "It's for your own good. It'll make you stronger, so that when they hurt you, when they beat you because they fear you, you'll be protected." He pushes away a lock of my hair. His fingers are stained with blood. Blood from the wolf form that was torn, when he forced me to morph again. "You'll be all right. The wounds will heal. And your spirit will be stronger. It's all for your own good, my boy."*

*And the lullaby begins again. Inside me, a beast—my beast—growls in anger.*

I slowly come to. First, warmth hits me. Second, the sea. Unfamiliar. A breeze unlike what I'm used to. I wriggle to a standing position, holding my head. A splitting headache crams its way into my skull, demanding all my attention.

It takes me a good moment to breathe through it, enough so my blurry vision refocuses. It's then I realize I'm not alone—Artemis is standing a few feet away, her back to me, the bow held loosely by her side. She's at the edge of a cliff, looking out into the horizon.

My groan must've clued her in to me being awake, as she turns her head toward me. A scratch is healing on her cheek. Where she got it, under what circumstances—all that escapes me when I try to remember.

She says nothing, instead watches me.

"What?" I finally ask.

That gets a reaction out of her. "What do you mean, *what*? Are you seriously going to ignore what just happened?"

"I don't know what you're talking about."

She frowns, clearly trying to figure out if I'm lying.

"The last thing I remember is the beach. The sunset. You coming after me, us fighting." Me bringing up her reputation.

She shakes her head. "We were *attacked*, Fenrir. Creatures unlike any I've seen before. And they wanted *you*." Her grip tightens on the bow. "You said before, after your mortal died, that you thought the creatures after you were the same as those who attacked Hades—you meant in the second attack? Where—" Her voice trails off. She closes her eyes, takes a deep breath. Opens them again. "Where another god was killed."

"Yes. I had nothing to do with that, like I said. These creatures did."

"Then what the hell is going on? What are they? And why are they *after you*?"

A shudder runs through me. Like broken images of a movie, snippets hit me. Blocks of darkness, horse-like heads with scales, wings like bats, a glimmer of something… dark clouds.

I shake the images away, clenching my fists to hide their tremble. "No one knew I was there."

"Someone did."

"Yeah, *you*."

Her eyes flash emerald fire. "I did not call those creatures in."

"So you say."

"You've got some nerve, accusing me of what all of Olympus knows you did!"

I scowl at her. "I told you my version. You refuse to believe me, refuse to believe there's more to the story than simply what you've been told. Because it would mean for once admitting that there's something dark out there, something not even Olympus can protect itself against. And that would go against your carefully constructed reality, wouldn't it?"

She glares at me, the fire in her eyes more intense than ever. "Maybe I would believe you more if you'd stop trying to feed me tales!"

I stand, wobbly at first, but my anger fuses my spine together. "Tales? Explain to me how I don't remember any of what just happened, then, if I'm so good at telling *tales*."

"You clearly have issues, I never denied it."

A low growl leaves me. It's a reminder of my darker side, the one I refuse to let out. The god I've pretended to no longer be. The one she keeps baiting, even as her eyes spit flames and the energy between us crackles, tightening to snakes of tension.

"If I'm the one lying, then why were those creatures coming after me, hmm?"

She says nothing, instead twiddling with the end of the bow. All I can see is her profile, so I don't know if she's actually thinking things through, or refusing to see the truth. And I sure as hell don't understand why it matters to me whether she believes me or not.

In the end, Artemis shakes her head. "I think I'm done. We go to Olympus, now. No more trying to get your shit together. No more time to say goodbye. No more excuses or appeals about going to see your sister first."

I open my mouth to argue, to fight back. Then an image of Mary, her lifeless body, the blood pooling under her head, hits me. And all fight drains out of me.

A weight the likes of the world presses on my shoulder, and my head. The headache intensifies. And instead of fighting Artemis, all I want right now is to give up. Maybe it's better we do go to Olympus, at least that way the creatures won't follow me. Or if they do, we'll have backup. And I won't have to be responsible for another death.

I shrug, defeated. "What do you want me to say? Rebel?" I hold out my hands. "Shackle me up and let's go, already."

Artemis scowls, turns away from me, and snaps her fingers. I'd expected a flash of brightness, some kind of…something. A portal. Instead, nothing happens.

I arch an eyebrow. "Did my argumentative side already drain you? I said I'm ready to go. That should count as enough permission to override any barriers of consent between gods."

"Shut up. I need to focus."

I can see the tension in her shoulders, the way her knuckles are whitening over the bow.

"Mind that grip—any tighter, and you're bound to break your bow."

She glares over her shoulder. "It cannot be broken. Hephaistos, our blacksmith, had it forged from unbreakable material. Now *shut it.*"

I look away, leaving her to do her thing. Take a few steps away, then turn in a circle. My head is still pounding, but the beauty of the landscape is too impossible to ignore. Mossy green grass under my feet. Hills of a similar color, in the distance. A cloudy, yet beautiful sky. And underneath the cliffs, frothy waves smashing against the rocks, reminding mortals that nature always wins.

"You brought me to the southern tip of Ireland? Why?"

"Living around mortals for so long must've wiped your memories, or something," she mutters.

"What's that supposed to mean?"

She drops her hands, whirling on me with a huff. "Do you not recall the theory of portals? Certain points of any realm are easier to open conduits. Hades' balls, but it was you Asgardians who suggested it! You buried crystals deep inside each chosen location, to harness the powers of the energy."

I give her a blank look. "I must've missed that lesson."

Or, more than likely, wasn't told. Because being Loki's son automatically meant I'd use such knowledge for nefarious deeds. My thoughts roam, weirdly heading down memory lane. To Asgard, and its magnificence. One I never got a chance to see. I was kept apart, in a cavern, with the seas as my only companion. Loki only came by when it suited him—usually when Uncle Thor or Grandad Odin fucked with his plans. And then he would spend the night petting me—I was still in my wolf form, then—and telling me all about how we would one day rule together.

Those were the good times. The bad times were when he chose to strengthen my character…. like that memory that woke me up. Centuries forcing my transformation, of putting me through the agony of it day in and day out, coupled with verbal lashings that only stopped when I got to a certain age. Then, even Loki seemed afraid of my power. Or perhaps he was just afraid of the beast that greeted him.

It took me the better part of some eons where I tried to get this approval, his validation, for me to realize what a load of shit that all was. *What a joke my so-called family has turned out to be.* It wasn't enough they'd kept me imprisoned for the better part of my existence. And then when they did pretend to release me, it was only so Tyr could leash me up like a fucking dog. The betrayal makes me shudder again, rising my hackles.

Granted, I'd taken Tyr's hand as payment for that. But, still. He'd fed me. Spoken to me. I'd trusted him. Trust, in Asgard, is overrated.

And probably everywhere else.

Artemis rolls her eyes, then turns her back on me again. She mutters under her breath some more, and I can practically sense the amount of energy she's raising, trying to create the way home.

But…nothing happens.

Back uptight, she turns to me with a stricken expression. "I…I can't go home."

"What do you mean, you can't go home?" It's my turn to narrow my eyes on her. "Just flick your fingers. It's easy."

"You fucking try it, if it's so easy! I'm telling you, it's not working."

I lean back on the grass and shrug, feigning as much indifference as I can. "Your problem, Olympian. Deal with it." I can't let her see my fear. *The longer I'm here, the greater the likelihood is of the creatures coming back. Fuck. And with the amount of divine energy Artemis is using…*

An angry huff, and a moment later she crosses over to me, blocking the sun. "Fenrir! Do you want those things to hunt you down?"

"Them, you, Zeus… What's the difference, in the end? Might as well wait it out."

Artemis kicks me, another angry huff escaping her.

"Ow, that was my shin!"

She bends over, still towering over me. Electricity crackles in the air. Clearly, the issue isn't her powers. "I'm not messing around, Fenrir. Use your damned powers, and let's get out of here."

I say nothing. We glare at each other for long moments. When she lifts her foot again, aiming for another kick, I get up.

"Fine, fine. Just…cool those heels."

I stand, straightening to my full height. Only then do I realize how close we are. How her lips are a mere inch from mine. And her angry huffing keeps raising her breasts, drawing my attention to—

*Enough.*

I walk around her, roll my shoulders, then make

a show of pretending to use my powers. Add a couple groans, mutters, and annoyed sounds. Then I shrug, facing her once more. "Guess whatever it is, it affects me, too."

Her narrowed eyes warn me I'm toeing a very tight line. "Why are you lying?"

"Lying?"

"Yeah. *Lying.* Why the hell are you lying to me?" She takes a step closer. "You didn't even try. I would've felt it."

"Pantheons can't feel each other using divine powers."

"Bullshit. I've been in enough Council meetings to know that's not true."

Fuck. Fuckity-fuck-fuck-fuck. That's what happens when you're kept out of any important business for your entire existence. You miss out on shit.

Is there any way to get around this? Not really. Nor can I tell her the truth—that if I use any of my godly powers, it gives whoever the hell is in my head the power to take control over me. I don't want that shit spreading around, especially in Olympus. The only person I'll tell is Hades…if I ever get to him. Outcast to outcast.

To Artemis, I shrug. "What can I say? It's the truth."

"No, it's—"

She stops, her eyes going over my shoulder. They widen, and she takes a step back. And another.

I turn, expecting to see those creatures appear out of nowhere again. But…nope. Not even close.

Instead, I'm faced with a vision. Of the female variety. The woman has long, wavy brown hair cascading down to her waist. She wears a robe of flowers, and when the brightness surrounding her dims, I'm ensnared by her eyes. Color of the sun.

"Who—"

Artemis seems to shake off her stupor, stepping closer to me until we're shoulder to shoulder. "Ileana, is it?"

The woman nods. A slow smile spreads on her face, and it has a weird effect on me. Like a blanket of reassurance, saying everything will be all right.

"What are you doing here?"

I almost want to tell Artemis to shut it so I can keep basking in the woman's warmth. But she doesn't seem to mind, addressing Artemis in a voice soft as honey.

"Things have changed since you left, Goddess of the Hunt. Zeus has shuttered all portals that give easy access to Olympus."

Artemis gasps. "How the hell are we to return, then? I found my bounty."

Ileana's eyes fall on me. "Yes, so I see."

I shift under her gaze, not wanting her to see too much. But even when I look away, I can tell she's watching me.

"Who are you, exactly?" I ask, in an effort to distract her.

"I am a protector of the gods."

I snort at the elusive answer.

To my side, Artemis whispers, "She's Hades' guard. Well, past guard. It's a long story. Her and another, Frumos, they're immortals. Remember the other attack you're accused of? Killing two immortals? That's Ileana's kin. They come from an academy specially designed to protect us."

Great. I wonder if this woman hates me, too, then. I see no obvious sign of it on her features, though. If anything, she watches me with something akin to amusement. That, more than anything, drives me to ask, out of curiosity, "So, you're a bit like Odin's Valkyries?"

Ileana snorts. "No, not like that at all. Though if it eases your mind to make that comparison, you may choose to do so." She gives a light shrug, and her hair moves around her shoulders like waves, swaying from side to side. "We are immortals, born of the purest energy."

"That explains it." In the vaguest way possible.

She gives a chuckle at my sarcasm, then settles a warning gaze on me. "I know you are both hunted by creatures untold. You cannot bring them to Olympus' gates."

"We wouldn't!" Artemis says.

"They follow your energy, goddess. And they will every time you open a portal, or do anything to protect yourself. That energy will lead them to your home."

"Told you so," I mutter.

An actual growl leaves Artemis. And something stirs in my loins when I hear it. *Something's got to be seriously fucked with my head for me to find her aggressive side remotely intriguing.*

Artemis shoves me lightly aside, and steps even closer to the immortal. "Who are they, Ileana? Surely you must know."

"I do not. Your companion might, though."

"If I did, my troubles would be over."

Ileana glances between me and Artemis, and back to me. "You remember nothing of the attacks?" Without waiting for an answer, she moves—almost floating—closer to me. Reaches for my head.

I jerk back, afraid of what she'll find—or what might happen—if she touches me.

Ileana smiles, and that reassurance, that sense of warmth, washes over me again. "Allow me, Fenrir of Asgard. Perhaps I can be of aid."

Not like I got much more to lose…

Sighing, I lean closer, dropping my head and stooping my shoulders so I'm lowered to her height. "Do your worst, then."

Her fingers touch my temples, as though to

massage them. A soft light escapes them, permeating into my skin, washing away the dark recesses of my mind, and the headache with it. All that's left is warmth, and peace, and light... So much light...

I close my eyes, breathing it in, allowing it to infuse every aspect of my body.

Something clenches in my gut, a foreboding sense, out of nowhere. *No—*

Too late. I open my eyes to see Ileana flying backward, past Artemis, nearly to the edge of the cliff. She lands in the grass, one knee on the ground, her hair covering her features. Slowly, she stands, and takes a deep breath.

When her eyes open again, the gaze that lands on me is reproachful—and filled with pity. "Your body is no longer your own, is it?"

I gulp. Artemis turns to me, gaping, but I ignore her gaze.

Ileana inches closer once more, but there's a wariness to her stance now. "Whoever has control of you, they are powerful. Too powerful, for such an evil energy."

I keep staring at the grass. "He feeds off my divine energy. It's why I can't use it."

I don't know how much of my mutter she hears, but her next words are not what I expected. "Do you wish to escape his hold?"

I look up, meeting her sunny gaze. "Of course!"

"How badly do you wish it?"

"With every fiber of my being."

She nods. "It will be necessary, this passion of yours. Do not lose sight of it when the road ahead becomes hard."

"Harder than it's been?"

She smiles, then, wistfully.

"Do you know how to get rid of him?" I ask.

"Not I, no." Disappointment spreads through me, but doesn't have a chance to spread too much. "But there is one who might… She lives in the Hoia-Baciu woods, and she alone can shed some light on who holds you in their sway. And, potentially, help you find a way back home."

"Hoia-Baciu?" Artemis groans. "Where is that, even?"

"Romania," Ileana says.

"Are you saying whatever's got Fenrir in his or her clutches, that's who's controlling the creatures after us? And if we can get rid of both, then I can come back home?"

Ileana nods. "I will open a secure portal, and get you in directly to Hades himself."

I wonder if Artemis noticed her hesitation, just before she nodded.

"Fine." Artemis sighs. "I don't suppose you can—"

"Scuze, but I cannot portal you to the oracle."

"Oracle?" I shudder. "In my pantheon, they don't mean anything good."

Ileana smiles. "She is…peculiar. But she will not lead you astray."

"Good to know," I mutter. Louder, I add, "We can take a flight."

Artemis whirls on me. "You expect me to *fly* on a *human* flight to these woods?"

I arch an eyebrow. "You got a better idea?"

Behind her, Ileana waves and disappears in a shower of flowers.

# CHAPTER 6

**Artemis**

This is just great. Now not only am I unable to go home, but I'm also stuck with a secretive, infuriating god for much longer than I'd expected. And I have to interact with mortals. Sigh.

Add to that the fact I owe Fenrir an apology for not believing his crazy story of there being more to his attack, and, well, this'll be the most fun I've had in years.

Not.

"You're not afraid of flying, are you?"

I look up from the contraption around my waist, startled to find Fenrir so close. It's not like these seats are big, by any means. I try to stretch my legs, and fail. It was bad enough going through what mortals call airport security, and having someone touch me. I thought I'd singe the man's hands—only Fenrir's warning gaze calmed me down. He'd been able to get me the paperwork necessary to hop on a flight, though all these hoops and idiotic things are enough to drive me crazy.

And then to enter the metal bird, and realize I would be strapped down the entire time?

I throw Fenrir a dark glare. "How would I know if I am?"

He chuckles and waves over someone. A woman in a tight skirt and bright smile comes.

"How may I help you, sir?"

"Could we get two glasses of whiskey, please? Make them doubles."

She giggles, but stops when she notices my dark look, and scurries away.

Not that it helps my mood any. I thought Ileana's apparition would be the end of my troubles, not the beginning. But the fact the immortal seems to believe Fenrir's allegations has me...off-balance. How can someone be inside a god? Control him? And why?

I cringe internally at how I'd reacted to Fenrir's story. Not my best moment. At the time, I thought I was in the right. I mean, my pantheon doesn't really believe in darkness and apocalyptic things. At least, my father doesn't. Therefore, I don't. And while Hades opened my eyes to things outside of our control, it didn't make believing them any easier.

Fenrir, though, he's lived with this stuff his entire existence. Had it drilled into him, by the sounds of it. It's like he wasn't even surprised by what Ileana said.

Which is why my mission has now evolved. At the end of the day, what matters is returning to Olympus. *That* is what I care about. Home. My reputation upheld. And a chance to breathe, to recover from the last twenty years. To see my brother again, go to one of Dionysus' parties, let loose with some nymphs and dance and play and be merry.

But that doesn't mean I should discard the truth, and forego this opportunity to find out more about what's going on, if given the chance. Might as well return to Olympus with the full story, rather than half of it.

Fenrir clears his throat, arching an eyebrow at me. "You could work on your customer service skills."

"My what?"

He rolls his eyes. "Never mind."

A moment later, the woman returns with the drinks. While she hands me mine without preamble, Fenrir's, she lingers with. Her sultry voice reaches my ears and makes me want to throttle her.

"Anything else, sir?"

"No… At least, not yet."

I glare at him until she's gone. He turns to me, arching an eyebrow. "What?"

"Could you at least pretend to… Ugh, never mind."

I toss back into my seat, only to get a kick in my back from the mortal spawn sitting behind me. *This is going to be a long flight.*

**Fenrir**

I can't tell why in all hells Artemis is so annoyed. But she sure downs her drink and settles in fast… at least, until the plane gets moving. Then her eyes fly open, and I catch her startled gasp.

"You okay?"

She makes a sound that could be acquiescence, or something else.

And then she grips the handles of her seat, her breathing coming in short pants.

"Artemis—"

I stop, knowing it's useless. The first time I flew in one of these contraptions, I'd been deathly afraid, too. So instead of trying to rationalize it, I reach for her hand, and intertwine our fingers together.

Her wide eyes fly to mine. Vulnerable.

I force a smile. "We'll be okay. This is all normal."

Her hold on my hand tightens. Her eyes shut tightly. The plane takes off, and my stomach tumbles right along with it.

When it finally levels out, Artemis opens her eyes again. Takes a deep breath, and turns to me. "I owe you an apology."

I stare at my hand. The breath she'd taken pressed her breast against the back of my hand, and the heat emanating from her is a magnet demanding I reach out.

With a deep breath of my own, I let go of her hand, and down the rest of my drink in one shot. "No, you don't."

"But I do. You tried to tell me there was more going on with Hades' attack—"

"Shh." I look at the mortal across the aisle from me, then give Artemis a warning look. "Watch what you say."

"It's not like they'd believe it."

"No, but they could make this journey uncomfortable for us."

She sighs, rolls her eyes, then nods. "Fine. I am sorry, though."

I wave it away. "You couldn't have known."

"But I could have. I—"

She bites her lip, and this close to me, I can see its plumpness. A rising part of me wonders what it'd be like to touch it, to have one taste. I force it away.

"When I saw what happened to Ileana, I realized the truth of what you'd said." She pauses for a beat. "I don't think going to your sister will do anything to help your case. But I do think Hades will be open to hearing you out."

"Why?"

"Because he's...different."

I'd heard as much. The black sheep of Olympus, they called him—back when I was among other gods. But his antics never landed him in any kind of purgatory, so I've always assumed he was an outcast with power. And that makes all the difference, at least to me. If anyone would believe me, it would be him. Olympians in general may turn their nose up at the truth but an outcast who's been faced with darkness will understand. I hope...

"I mean, granted, he was banished to the Underworld and made to watch over Tartarus because of that incident with the kid—"

I grip my drink tighter. "What?"

Artemis pauses. I can practically see the wheels turning behind her eyes, then realization dawns on her. "You disappeared from your pantheon way before that. So you don't know." She sips the last of her drink, and tucks a lock of hair behind her ear. "During the second attack—the one you were also meant to be behind—Hades was accused of showing his godly self to a human child. As a result, he was tossed out of Olympus and given his own realm. The Underworld, to watch over souls and, well, Tartarus."

I shake my head. "I only know of Tartarus from the mortal mythology books. What is it, truly?"

"Well, it's a barren land that existed since the beginning of time itself. It was always tied to the Underworld—ours, that is—but there were rumors it was linked to various versions of hell/purgatory in other pantheons. Anyway, after you attacked Hades that first time, Zeus put a ban on Olympus, refusing to allow gods to leave, for fear they would also get attacked. He insisted other pantheons follow suit. When Hades was banished, the pantheons migrated their worst evils—villains, if you will—into Tartarus, and reinforced it with barriers. It worked, and we all resumed our regular existences. But..." Her eyes cloud over.

"But, what?"

"Twenty years ago, Hades called a Council meeting. Said Tartarus had been breached, and my great-grandfather Cronus nearly escaped. He'd gotten the situation under control, but it was worrying. And it affected all pantheons."

I shake my head. "This is crazy. Cronus was a Titan, right?"

That much, I remember. I might have been kept apart from my pantheon, but Loki talked. A lot. And when he didn't talk, I heard rumors. Some gaps in my knowledge were reinforced by human books, once I made a home on Earth. I may not know all, but I know *some*.

Same as our giants and old gods, the Greeks have theirs. The children of the Originals—the eldest of gods—who were later overthrown by the new generation. Odin did the same with our Originals and became the All-Father. If memory serves, Zeus was equally in charge of getting rid of theirs.

Artemis nods. "Yes. And though Hades re-imprisoned him, he believed Tartarus was no longer as safe as it was. I was tasked to find you, then."

"I don't see the link."

"When you attacked Hades, there were rumors. Even the Celtic goddess Morrigan said she'd felt an undercurrent of darkness. I'd run into Osiris, and even Taweret—their goddess of rebirth—a few times, and both said nothing was running as smoothly as it once had on the Egyptian side. And you know how precious they are about balancing souls and all."

"Right..." Only vaguely, but that's beside the point.

She pauses again. Glances at her drink. It's empty, so she sets it next to mine on the little plastic top. "Anyway, that second attack on Hades? Because Odin couldn't find you after, only your dead immortals—or what we'd been told were your dead immortals—it was strongly believed that you'd had something to do with it, same as with the first."

"Yeah, you mentioned that before."

She throws me a look. "And I'm sorry I didn't believe your explanation. When Tartarus was breached, it had the same feeling of…abnormality…as the other two attacks did. So, conclusions were drawn."

My hands clench into fists, even as I feel a lick of darkness. "Of course. Because it's so easy for you Olympians to find the easiest surface-level explanation. Heavens forbid you go digging for the ugly truth."

Artemis narrows her eyes on me, probably sensing my mounting anger. Then her expression clears. "You're right. I'm not denying we're not set in our ways, same as you are in yours. But the fact of the matter is, your connection to these two events was never disproved. Hades went to the Underworld, Tartarus was reinforced, and that was that. Forgotten."

Something in her tone warns me there's more here. "Forgotten…conveniently?"

She hesitates, then says, "I believe so, anyway. My father is very one-sided, when it comes to things.

And he always wanted control of Olympus, so getting Hades out of the way served his purpose. I think there was more going on then, that he didn't share with us. But either way, it was *forgotten*. Until twenty years ago, when Cronus escaped. And Hades came back, warning us all there's more going on."

It dawns on me. "I'm the easy scapegoat. Same as Hades was, back then. But…why help me, then?"

Artemis bites her lip, chewing on it for a long moment. Eventually, she nods. "You have to understand, these are theories. And they change nothing. My allegiance is still to Olympus, and I *will* bring you back to face punishment if you're guilty. But…I also can't ignore what Ileana said. I'm a huntress. I hunt bounties, but also the truth."

Something she said a while back dawns on me. "You said you'd chased me across different realms…"

Artemis nods. "And I did. Burned a few bridges along the way, too. First with Heimdall—"

My eyes widen. "You actually met him?"

"It was the first place I looked. I thought your pantheon was hiding you."

I shake my head. "They weren't. I mean, I doubt they would have. I don't even remember where I went, after I lost control that first time. Everything is a blur of sleeping under various moons, stars, and surviving."

"So you were never in the Duat, then?" At my

blank look, Artemis winces. "Noted. Bastet got me good."

"The Egyptian goddess?"

"Mm. She told me your trace was found there, and long story short, it led to some misunderstandings between her kin and me, and the reason why I saw fit to breach the entrance to their pantheon."

"Wow. You weren't kidding when you said you'd hunted me across realms, then." More than anyone, I know how taxing that can be on our bodies. Because each godly realm function on a slightly different energy level, one of us entering in a pantheon we don't belong is seen as an abnormality. More often than not, our powers are muted, and our essence is drained for the entirety of the stay. "How did you find me, in the end?"

Artemis shrugs. "It wasn't easy. After the Duat debacle, I spent some time roaming, until one of the Asian Lóngshén came to me."

"The what, now?" Like I said, *some* gaps were filled. Not all. Which means a lot of stuff in other pantheons still escapes me.

As though being reminded of the fact, Artemis pauses. Tilts her head to the side, and some of her hair brushes my shoulder, then my arm. The strands feel so silky, their touch as soft as a lover's caress. I clench my grip on the glass so I don't reach out and touch them, see if they're truly as soft as they feel.

"The Lóngshén are a set of four dragon gods, representing the four cardinal points—you know, north, south, east, west. Because they're always roaming their pantheon, restless, they'd caught a scent they weren't familiar with. And when they'd heard I was chasing you, they offered me entrance to see if it was you."

"And, was it?"

"You don't remember that bit, either?"

"Maybe… I know there was a point I was in my beast form, and was chased by something. But I don't know if it was the creatures, or something else." I tap my chin. "I do seem to recall a lot of wind at the time, though. To be frank, I have no doubt you did follow my trace. You're too good a bounty hunter to not have. But my beast was always good at keeping me…safe."

The moment I bring him up, I know it was a stupid thing to say. Because at the back of my mind, his voice rumbles. *Then why keep me locked up, deny me? Over and over?*

I ignore him. The last thing I need while up in the air in a human plane is to morph into my ferocious primal self. So, I let out a breath slowly, then shake my head. "Wish I could be more help, but I've done my best to block the past out of my mind. All I can tell you is that I travelled…a lot. My beast ran for survival. I was aware of time passing by, but vaguely. But little by little, I lost all awareness and my beast refused to give it back." I shrug. "In a way, I suppose he was trying to keep me safe. But it took landing here, on Earth, for him to relinquish the hold on me. And to let me morph once more, for good this time. We found balance, I suppose. For as long as it lasted."

Our gazes meet and lock, holding for a long moment.

Artemis is the first to break it, looking back at her glass. "He did well, in a sense. Keeping you safe. Either way, if you did pass through the Lóngshén's territory, you were long gone when I arrived. And by the time I exited, years had passed, and your trail was even colder. I managed to pick it up here and there, but I was always a few steps behind. Eventually, I got some help from Ix Chel—the Mayan Moon Goddess. She appeared one night when I was feeling rather, ah, dejected. Said something about how the stars were telling her of darker times to come, of obstacles to face. And that the constellation of the huntress and the wolf kept coming up in her interpretations."

I frown. "I'm pretty sure there's no such constellation."

"That's what I said. Ix Chel was adamant. So, I asked if I could visit their heavens—where the Mayan gods reside—and talk to a few of her kin."

"What did you hope to find?"

She bites her lip, avoiding my gaze. "I don't know. A clue, I told myself at the time. Now, I think her talk of darker things spoke to my own doubts. And I just wanted the truth behind the curtain."

"And, did you find it?"

She laughs. "Ah, let's just say if anyone dislikes the Olympians more than the Egyptians, it's got to be the Mayans. I don't think they appreciated that the mortals who worshipped them didn't attribute to them, um, immortality. Not in the sense worshippers of the Greek gods did, for example."

I rack my brain, trying to think through the little mythology I'd tried to keep up with in my tiny library. "Right... Mayan gods were recorded in history without 'godly' characteristics; they could be tricked and killed by mortals. Basically, they were only meant to be supernatural entities. Powerful, but not all-powerful."

Artemis shares a complicit grin with me. "Don't let them ever hear you say that. They've developed quite a complex from it. And my outbursts of power when my temper flared didn't make me any friends." She grows pensive again. "I did talk a lot with Ix Chel about her prophecies, and what else she saw. She kept mentioning darkness and change. At the time, it didn't make much sense. Now, of course, I understand it a lot better."

"Mm."

She shrugs. "In the end, it was the Celts who put me on your trail on Earth."

"Fitting," I mutter.

Silence falls between us. Artemis glances out the window of the airplane, and I notice she seems a bit less edgy about flying now. Her shudder, a moment later, dispels that notion. Guess I'm not the only one good at hiding things.

"I don't get how you trust these metal birds to keep you safe." She turns back to me. "Anyway, that, in a nutshell, is a longer way of explaining why I'm here, going along with what Ileana said. I've put too much into this quest. And it's the only way to gain the full truth, to figure out what's missing. It's also why I think getting to Hades is more important than your sister."

"A moot point now, anyway. Not like we can get to him."

Still, everything she's said only serves to make me look at her differently. She was sent here for one thing, and at first she'd seemed so rigid in that mission. But now, she's on a flight, heading to the middle of freaking nowhere to uncover hidden truths that might even put her own pantheon in a bad light. I'd never expected such understanding, or…support? And I'm not sure how I feel about it.

Artemis leans back in her seat, gazing out the

window again. "If Ileana thinks whoever has you in their clutches is powerful, we're in shit. With no option for help from any of our kin."

"Mm." I'd been trying to point this out to her since the beginning, but saying *I told you so* seems irrelevant now.

I signal for another drink. Artemis' expression darkens again.

"You got an issue with the flight attendant?"

She scoffs. "No." A slight pause. "But does she have to be so needy? She'd all but crawl onto your lap if you let her."

I can't quite pinpoint her tone. But something about it has me chuckle. Which only gets Artemis' energy crackling.

I grip her hand again, tightly. She lets out a hiss, which I ignore. "Watch your reactions," I mutter. "If you crackle the wrong way" —I bend closer to her, my lips a hair's breadth from her ear— "this entire plane will go down. Human contraptions can't withstand interference from divine energy."

Artemis shivers, then nods. I pull back, trying to ignore the potency of her scent now filling my nostrils.

The flight attendant returns with my drink, her smile stretching when our eyes lock. I take the drink, make a little small talk, then she leaves.

The moment she's gone, Artemis pulls my attention again. "I wasn't listening before, but I am now. More than once, you said the creatures found you because of me."

A sigh escapes me. "For years, I haven't used my divine energy. Because it attracts them."

"So this happened before?"

"Not to this extent. Remember when I said I spent a lot of time running in my beast form?" She nods. "Well, whenever I morph from one form to the other, that also requires tapping into my divine power. On the few occasions I could no longer handle being in the background; when I felt I'd lose my mind completely…. I emerged in human form. And within hours, something would come. I never got to see them, not clearly. Just shadows, a sense of darkness. My beast would always take over, and then we'd run again." I force my fist to unclench. "Traveling through portals did the same. So, when I first came here, they also followed. But I morphed back to my human form and hid. I've…been hiding ever since."

"And your beast?"

I meet her gaze. "Not a problem to concern yourself with."

"But is he—"

"We're fine."

Artemis seems to get the hint, as she quickly angles the conversation in a different way. "So the bit about attracting the creatures… Does that cover *all* divine powers?"

I shrug. "I never had a chance to test it."

"You just…stopped using them?"

I nod. Her stricken expression confuses me. "Why do you seem so heartbroken?"

"Because I can't imagine not using mine. It'd be akin to cutting off a part of me."

"That's because you Olympians love to show off. In Asgard, we prefer subtlety."

"Did you tell your father that?"

"Touché." It takes me a moment to realize the surprised laugh I'm hearing is mine. Then I sigh, adding, "Still, it's easier to cut off said part when it's one you already hate."

She throws me a look, waiting for more. I'm not sure if I want to give her more… but the words tumble past my lips, though I keep my voice low.

"All my life, being Loki's son, having the powers I did—that was enough to mark me as the potential bad guy. I was doomed before I had a chance to truly grow into my own. Losing the powers that caused this for me was more a blessing."

She reaches for my hand this time, squeezing it. "I'm sorry."

I look at her hand, the drink buzzing through me. Our normal divine energy cleans our systems on autopilot, should we choose to, and I could technically avoid the buzz. But it's the only thing keeping me calm, after what Ileana said. After everything she confirmed.

"Thanks." I down the rest of the drink again, and it weaves a fiery path into my stomach. Artemis' touch on my hand is a branding, reaching to my very soul. Stirring me. Breathing life into parts of me I'd forever thought gone. I've had plenty of easy fucks, but I can't remember the last time I had someone who cared.

*Mary.* I close my eyes at the reminder of the innocent mortal who'd looked up at me in awe, and how easily her precious life was snuffed out. We'd only ever been friends, but I had cared for her. Deeply. *That's why should never let anyone care for me nor allow myself to care for them. Because I'll always lose them.*

I pull my hand out from under Artemis', run it through my hair, and ignore her look. "You should try to get some rest. You won't be able to use your divine energy to refresh, so might as well take advantage of regular sleep while you can."

She stares at me for long moments after, but eventually does as I tell her.

**Artemis**

The moment the plane comes to a standstill, I'm out of my seat and out the door, ignoring the cries of the offended flight attendants. No way I'm spending any more seconds in that death contraption!

Outside, the signs confuse me. Throngs of people move toward what seems like an exit. But the moment I head there, I see them flashing pieces of paper. Fenrir said what he got me would hold up to the scrutiny to get on the plane, but not necessarily when we land.

Fenrir pulls up next to me, the small carry-on bag in his hand. "This is customs. You have no papers to enter properly, so you'll have to use your powers and meet me on the other end."

"But—" I think back to the creatures. To what he'd told me on the plane.

Instead of seeming afraid, he's cool and collected, shrugging. "We'll have to take the risk."

A big difference from the man who was begging me a few hours ago to stop using my divine energy.

"What gives? You're no longer afraid?"

He looks around, takes a step closer to me, latches on to my gaze. "I've *been* afraid. For too long. And I'm tired. Yes, we'll be careful, because I don't want more innocents to suffer. But what you mentioned about *all* types of energy being tracked… Perhaps we can experiment."

"With what, exactly?"

"Various things that do and don't leave an imprint strong enough to track us. Like I said, it's a risk. But a necessary one."

Ugh. I don't take risks. I think things through, plan them to the nth degree, and make sure nothing will go wrong. How has he survived for so long on this cursed world with this attitude?

Fenrir points behind me. "Washrooms should do it. Meet me outside, by the car rental."

Somehow, that doesn't sound any more fun than being in a metal bird.

Instead of flat-out dematerializing and rematerializing outside of the compound, I study the schematic of the floor. And notice an emergency exit nearby.

"Let's see if this works." I check around to make sure no mortals are here, and place my hand on the wall. It shimmers, then I step through it—effectively walking through a few walls—until I come out the other side.

Technically, all I did was alter the fabric of the material in front of me, rather than dispend energy in dematerializing myself and rematerializing myself. Perhaps that'll be enough to keep the creatures off our tail? Only time will tell.

A big sign points to car rentals. Right where Fenrir said he'd be.

It takes me only a few moments to find his mop

of blond hair. He's exiting a little cubicle, a man following behind him. They shake hands, and he hands him something small.

Soon, Fenrir's heading to another death contraption, this one on four wheels. Though I'd lived in the wilderness for the last six months, I'd still seen them rolling around. Impossible not to. They're noisy and polluting and I curse the person who came up with them. The idea of being in one is enough to make me shudder.

At my groan, Fenrir looks over his shoulder. "Problem?"

"Will this make me sick, too?"

He chuckles. "Let's hope not. The rental agreement didn't cover cleaning vomit."

### Fenrir

Finally, something I'm in control of. I may not know anything else, but the human world? I've gotten used to it. And I do take a perverse pleasure in seeing Artemis completely off-kilter.

Whatever she did to get out of the airport doesn't seem to have had the creatures descend on us—a small mercy.

"I'm guessing, judging by our lack of a tail, that you didn't dematerialize."

"Not even close. I changed the fabric of the

walls, and stepped out that way."

I keep one hand on the wheel, using the other to rub my chin. "Hmm. So that means anything similar would be equally safe. But materializing by my side always got them coming, which means…" I throw her a look. "You'll have to call forth your bow, and keep it by your side. No longer in and out of the ether."

She scowls. "The bow is fueled by divine energy. Like your batteries here, it needs to return to the ether to recharge, so that my aim will be strong and true."

"Well, you might have to get used to having something less strong and true for a bit."

Moments later, I pull up in front of a hotel and check us in. Thankfully, the receptionist is more than happy to accept cash, and doesn't ask a lot of questions. Right as I pick the key for the room—Artemis was adamant at sharing a room so I don't run off—the woman says, "Not sure if you find it of interest, but there is a fair down the street. Good music. Good food."

"Oh, uh…thanks."

I turn to Artemis, finding her arching an eyebrow. "What's a fair?"

"A festival, of sorts. Did you…would you…" Wow, that sounds way more awkward than I gave it credit. "Never mind." I don't know why I even asked. She's a bounty hunter, for fuck's sake.

"Wait. Are we going to these woods tonight?"

I shake my head, with a meaningful look to the receptionist. We're far away that she can't hear, but I'm still paranoid. "It's too dark. Unless we want to be using you-know-what which will attract you-know-who within seconds."

Her eyes widen. "Right… So, then why not see this festival? I need sustenance. And if I need it, you must, too. You've been on this realm a lot longer than I."

I hesitate, then pocket the hotel key and lead the way.

The fair is in full swing. Tents are set up on either side of a small street, with various craftsmen and women selling their wares. Bracelets in one area. Clothes in another. Artemis is drawn to the fabrics, spending some time going through them. I pull out some cash, and she purchases a few items—fitting, since she has nothing to wear.

Then we head farther down to the stalls offering food. The smells remind my stomach to growl, and suddenly I'm reaching for everything. A bit of lamb kebobs. Sausages and mashed potatoes. Another area serves sarmale—cabbage rolls filled a mixture of meat and rice and spices.

Yet another merchant pushes a plate filled with something small and meaty at me—mici, he says they call them. He adds a copious amount of mustard on my plate and waits. I dip the meat in it and take one bite…then wave at him for another plate. It tastes like a mix of beef and other meats, grilled to perfection. And fuck if it's not amazing.

We make our way through various merchants, drinking from some—the local eau-de-vie is insanely strong, making even Artemis cough—and eating from others. It's by no means a vacation, but it is a nice break.

It's also a reminder of Dingle, and similar fairs I'd visited. And that brings back Mary's memory, and my good humor vanishes. The food tastes like ash, and I give the remainder to a little scruffy-looking boy.

Artemis watches me, then hands him her plate, too. "What's going on?"

I shake my head. "Just thinking of home." At her look, I amend, "What I left behind in Dingle, I mean."

"And Mary?"

I nod. "And Mary."

She's silent, and we walk for a bit longer. Then the tunes of a flute player drift on the wind. I'm drawn to the music, recalling many times when Tyr had used flutes to lull me into calmness. And then fed me. Coached me into being more aware than beastly. I'd learned to be human through him. At least, for a time.

*I've spoken to your father,* Tyr had said once. *The All-Father has, too. As of now, his cruel and unrelenting torments upon you shall cease. You may be our doom, but you are still an Asgardian.*

How hopeful I'd been. That the torture would stop, that Loki would magically morph into the father I wished for. But while he never forced me to morph again, he did find other ways to test my boundaries. Taking me on trips to Midgard designed to find my weaknesses. He even let me make a friend once… Then embarrassed me so much with his insults, my beast took over. He had no knowledge of the friend, and therefore killed him. I woke up with his blood drying on my hands.

After that, I learned not to care. Not to wish for anything. And to finally stop hoping.

Mortals, for all their faults, still have hope. It's something I envy them.

Noticing our attention, the old man playing stops and smiles. Says something in Romanian, something I can't understand. I shrug helplessly and return the smile. Then he places the flute back to his lips and a happier tune plays.

I turn to Artemis, holding out my hand. She stares at me, uncomprehending for a bit.

"You *are* Apollo's sister, are you not?" I grin. "And I used to hear he's the life of every party."

That seems to do the trick. Artemis smiles, and the smile is like a ray of sunshine to my beaten, lonely heart. The beat of the flute picks up, in tune with our footsteps. We dance, swinging, laughing, until he finishes his tune and we come together.

Close. So close.

I can see every speck of gold in her emerald-green eyes. Count every eyelash. Even though we've stopped dancing, my heartbeat only seems to increase its rhythm.

And then, someone laughs. A glass breaks. And out of the corner of my eye, a shadow falls on me. I jerk my gaze up, but it's only a raven.

*A raven.* Odin's messenger.

Muscles tense, I wait, watching it fly above us. But it doesn't seem interested in the fair, or me in particular. Instead, it disappears around a bend.

Nonetheless, the spell is broken. I step back from Artemis, clearing my throat.

In silence, as though by muted agreement, we walk back to the hotel, and I lead her to the room.

Some of the tension seems to leave her when we enter, and she doesn't see any dangers. "Finally…" She drops on the bed, stretching her arms. Then she sniffs under her armpit and makes a grimace.

I laugh, pointing at the shower. "It's all yours."

With a scowl, Artemis heads inside. Moments later, she calls out. "Umm, Fenrir?"

I step in. She's wearing a towel, covering herself. And pointing at the shower with another scowl. "How the hell does this work?"

"My, Olympus has spoiled you."

I pass by her, tap the handle and the hot water is soon pouring. "You can adjust it by this lever—"

She comes closer to see, the air behind me crackling. I start turning her way, wanting to show her how to work the lever. Her gasp clues me in—right before my body tightens, equally eager—that we're too close. I still force myself to face her, schooling my expression.

We're only an inch apart. The hand holding her towel together brushes against my shoulder. Electricity licks up my spine, shooting straight to my groin.

"How do you do all this?"

I try to say something smart, but it dies on my lips. My eyes instead are glued to the globes of her breasts, right above the towel, and the way she's biting her lip again.

"I…uh…practice."

Before my gaze can linger lower than her breasts, I get up abruptly and leave.

# CHAPTER 7

**Fenrir**

I wake up with a foreboding feeling in the pit of my stomach. Last night, I'd been able to ignore it for a little bit. Until I'd seen that damned raven, and it reminded me of Odin. Of everywhere I should have belonged, but didn't. Don't.

As for the dread, well, it hasn't really left since Artemis was unable to open the portal—the way to Olympus. But this morning, the ache is almost unbearable.

I drag myself to the bathroom, groaning and holding my stomach. Fingers gripping the sink, I look up into my haggard reflection. Haunted dark eyes, stubble growing to a near-beard, hair disheveled. The rasp at the back of my throat warns me of the impeding avalanche moments before I lurch to the toilet and vomit the bare contents of my stomach.

Moments later, my heaving subsides. There's a tentative knock on the door.

"Fenrir? What's going on?"

"Nothing." I don't want her to see me like this. "Give me a few minutes to shower, then we can leave."

Another beat of hesitation answers me. "I can use—"

"No. I'll be fine with a regular shower."

We might've gotten away testing the boundaries of her divine energy and the hold it has on the creatures, but I don't want to test it more now with a healing spell—or whatever she'd planned. Not when we're so close to entering the woods, and getting some potential leads for what's been going on.

Without waiting for Artemis' answer, I open the curtain and step in, letting the torrent of hot water wash the ache of my muscles and return some semblance of vigor to my limbs. Something tells me I'll need that. And that sensation only intensifies when I sense the pull of the darkness at the corners of my mind.

Gritting my teeth against it, I focus on the water. And let my thoughts run rampant. Focus on anything, but the tug at the back of my mind, promising me everything I wish I could have, but never have, and never will.

Today, it's harder. Fighting against this pull isn't easy when I'm awake and aware, but even less so when I'm exhausted, at the end of my wits. Beaten down by grief, angered at the hand dealt to me.

I rest my palm on the wall, bowing my head. The jet of the shower hits my shoulder blades harshly, and I welcome the sting. Steam fills the bathroom, fogging everything. I close my eyes.

The first thing that pops in my mind is last night, and Artemis—smiling, laughing with me. Dancing so close. And then, in this same shower. I'd left her with a towel around her body, and had fallen asleep to the sound of her showering.

"Fenrir?"

I don't open my eyes, too afraid to realize it's a fantasy. But the shower door slides open, and a presence comes up behind me. Soft breasts press to my back, and seeking hands roam my chest, my abs, lower still… Until they grip me in their silky touch, tugging on my hardness.

A groan escapes me. My hand joins hers, adding pressure, rhythm. My free hand digs into the shower's walls, desperately trying to hold on to a semblance of sanity.

But there is no sanity. Not when her touch brings me so close to the brink… With a groan, I come, my eyes opening in time to see the evidence of my arousal now jetted onto the wall.

And when I look lower, there's no hand on me but my own.

*Fuck. Now I'm daydreaming of her.* As if I didn't have enough problems.

Half an hour later, I step into the room, a towel around my hips, trying to avoid looking at Artemis. It's increasingly hard to do so when I can feel her eyes on me.

"Can you turn around, so I can get changed?"

She arches an eyebrow at my request, but does as I ask and within moments I'm ready to go. It's only then that I take in Artemis' attire—full leather pants, something that masquerades as a crop top—also leather—and her bow in one hand, quiver of arrows hung over a shoulder.

"What?" she asks, noticing my gaze.

"You can't go out wearing that."

Her expression goes bemused, then angered, real fast.

"No, I mean mortals aren't used to…this." I gesture to her form, then slap my own forehead. There's no way I can explain this without digging myself into a hole. "I mean… It's, it'll attract attention. The only time they see full-on leather outfits and costumes is around Hallows Eve."

"What's Hallows Eve?"

"An old holiday that's been turned into a night of fantasy. Mortals dress in costumes, pretend to be everything they can't be on a daily basis." Flashes of how her imagined touch felt on me hit me, and I can sense my cheeks warming. *For fuck's sake, get a hold of yourself. You're a Norse god, eons old. Not a mortal teenager.* "Please, can you just…"

"Ok, ok. But I only had this, and the stuff you had me wear the other time. On the metal bird — plane. And that was *not* comfortable."

I can imagine, for an Olympian. "What about the stuff from the fair?"

Artemis glances at the chair in a corner, where she'd set the items we'd bought from the fair. She shrugs and heads toward it. Lifts her hand as if to use her power to dress herself, then recalls she's not supposed to and simply shimmies out of her outfit. Creamy skin is revealed to my eyes, and I quickly turn away, giving her the same privacy she'd given me. I'd forgotten how happy Olympians are with their nude bodies.

Artemis clears her throat. "How about now?"

I peek past my fingers. She's wearing a loose skirt, which is fine—maybe not for the woods, but decent. The problem is the top she's wearing, and that it attracts attention just as bad as her other outfit did.

"Erm. What if you, uh, use some divine energy to change the fabric of what you're wearing to something matching me? Jeans. A t-shirt."

"You think because it worked at the airport, with the walls…"

"Yeah. It should be fine." I'll take the damn risk if it means her wearing anything that covers her body more. The fantasies in my head, I can live with. They'll be painful, but survivable. But something tells me Artemis won't take kindly to mortal males' attention, and judging by the growl in my chest, neither will I.

"Are you sure?"

I nod, somewhat impatiently, and Artemis shrugs. She snaps her fingers and a faint shimmering dust bathes her entire body. I blink at the luminescence, then open my eyes again. The skirt she was wearing is gone, replaced by jeans. And the top—I groan. She's got on a white t-shirt, same as me, except on her? It outlines her breasts, and everything else not covered. Including her nipples, standing to attention.

The heat in my cheeks intensifies. Yesterday, I'd

tossed her one of my shirts and she'd worn it over her crop top….bustier…whatever the hell she was wearing. For the plane. Obviously, her breasts were bound then. But how the hell am I going to explain *this* to her?

Artemis goes to move past me, and I automatically reach for her wrist. Touching her silken skin, I'm once again reminded of the shower. Of the feel of her, pressing against me.

I let go quickly, and clear my throat. "There's one more thing."

"What now?"

"Erm, your…" I gesture to her chest.

She looks down, then back at me. "What?"

"Yesterday, when I gave you my shirt, you had your…outfit…already on." She stares at me, the emerald gaze so unflinching. I take a deep breath and blurt out the rest, "Your breasts were bound. Mortalsarealsonotusedtobarebreasts."

"Huh?"

I let out the breath, and repeat, much slower, "Mortals are also not used to bare breasts, unless it's at nude beaches."

"Nude bea—"

"Never mind. The point is, could you wear something under, to cover your…breasts?"

Artemis arches an eyebrow. "Wear something like what?"

"Erm, mortal women use bras." I pull up my phone and do a quick Google search, then shove the screen in her face. "Something like this."

She takes one look at the image and scrunches her face. "I don't think so, Fenrir. If mortals are so offended, they can just look away."

I groan. "That's the problem. It's not... They won't be..." She only arches an eyebrow, waiting me out, so I try again. "Mortal men, though modern and intelligent, can still be complete cavemen. The sight of a woman's breasts will lead them to act like that asshole in my bar. The one whose ass you kicked."

"I *did* realize that on my own, thank you." Artemis' bottom lip juts out in a stubborn pout as she cocks a hip. "And I'm not the problem. *They* are. And their inability to understand boundaries."

"I'm not disagreeing. At all. But if we want to move around without attracting attention..."

Artemis rolls her eyes and turns to the chair where she'd tossed her bustier and pants. She pulls the t-shirt off, the bustier on, then the t-shirt back on over it. "Better?"

I nod, tearing my gaze away.

We finally exit the room, Artemis' bow slung over her shoulder. The girl at the counter takes one look at us, and at the bow and quiver full of arrows, and gives a bemused smile.

"We're looking to do some archery practice in

the woods," I say. "A good friend of mine is running a session in the Hoia-Baciu woods."

I don't miss the shudder that goes through her, though the fake smile stays plastered. "Weird spot for it, but sure. You need directions?"

I nod, and she's more than happy to point us to the woods, using a map to showcase the way there. It's not too far, but for the sake of expediency, I hail us a taxi the moment we're out of the hotel.

"Why aren't we using the other metal contraption, the one from the airport?" Artemis asks.

"Using it would mean leaving it abandoned on the side of the street and, well, who knows what kind of questions that would raise with mortals? Best to be safe."

She frowns. "So what was the point of getting it in the first place?"

"To torture you with more earthly contraptions."

I gesture to the inside of the taxi, trying to hold back my shit-eating grin.

**Artemis**

I don't understand why Fenrir has to pay the metal carriage driver for doing his duty. But then again, many things escape me about this realm. Maybe living in the wilderness for six months wasn't the best idea, after all.

When Fenrir's finally done, he walks up to me. We both stare at the foreboding woods. At the very least, they feel foreboding, with the mist rising from the ground, and the thickness of the air around them.

"Locals think they're haunted," Fenrir says.

I throw him a look. "And that should scare me, because…?"

"Just saying. In my realm, spirits of the undead are not to be trifled with."

I roll my eyes. "That's the Norse in you speaking. The dead can be perfectly polite, they don't have to be zombie-like and eager to devour souls as you all seem to think."

He mutters something under his breath about hopeful romantics.

I sling my bow off my back, and touch the side of my quiver, reassuring myself with the feel of its weight, filled with arrows. "Besides, my aim will be true for the living and the dead, believe me."

"Are you truly not afraid of anything?"

*I am. Of so many things.* Out loud, I say, "Nothing on this realm."

My gaze flicks back to the woods. Mist seems to cover the ground from the first line of trees onward. But on the outside, there's nothing. The sun seems to not pass through the canopy of trees, though it should—they're bare enough this time of year to let some light enter. Instead, there's barely any.

Trees of various sizes and shapes seem to lean toward each other, creating an archway. Almost inviting us to enter. The ground is covered with a mix of leaves, snow, and frost. It looks…desolate. I shiver.

"Ready?" Fenrir finally asks.

"No. But let us go anyway."

We step past the first trees, and the next. We're halfway down the archway, and still nothing has happened. I don't know what I'd expected. But it feels…normal.

I glance at Fenrir, noticing a similarly perplexed expression on his features.

"Not what we expected."

"No, it's not," he agrees.

Step by step, we go deeper in the woods. The archway finishes, instead giving way to even more perplexing trees. One has a trunk that's grown like a skeleton. Another looks four times my width, with a massive chunk missing, as though something took a bite out of it.

Despite the creepy structures, I feel more at ease. So much so, I relax my posture.

"Do you think Ileana was right?" Fenrir asks.

"I hope so, else that immortal will have much to answer for."

"How did they pop up, anyway?" I was much removed from the goings-on at Asgard, so to me they appeared from one day to the next.

I glance around, still expecting something—and still met by nothing. But I sense a tug deeper into the woods, so I trust my tracker instinct. We're meant to head in deeper, that much I'm sure of. The energy I'm picking up on, intuitively seeking, is clear enough.

"The immortals?" I rack my brain for what Pegasus told me. He was oddly fascinated with them, especially Hades' guards. "Well, no one knows for sure. You recall prior to them, we had the zmei protecting us?"

"The dragon shifters? Yes. Asgard never took them on, we had our Valkyries. But my grandfather considered them." He must notice my questioning look because he adds, "Loki complained about them for a bit. He'd hoped to get a zmeu, as they might've been easier to control for him."

"Ah." I look at the ground, letting out a sigh. "Perhaps that was for the best, considering how things ended. The zmei lost their minds and started in-fighting. We had to block their access to most pantheons."

"But they could still kill gods?"

"Yes…if they were alive. None have survived, save for the two Hades reported. They entered his realm, and helped him stave off Cronos when he exited Tartarus."

"But then…"

"I know. They're on our side, I suppose. But prior to that, while they were killing each other, an immortal school was set up by the inter-pantheon Council. Although, Peg—" I bite my tongue, and quickly rephrase, "Someone I trusted told me it wasn't the Council at all, but the Fates themselves who created them."

Fenrir stops walking. "For real? The Norns?"

I nod—Norns is what they call them in his pantheon. "No one knows for sure. Most gods refuse to truly believe in their existence. The idea that three sisters could have access to our destinies is, well…"

"Not very godly."

"Right."

His gaze grows heavier at this, as though he disagrees. But he says nothing.

"Whichever is the truth, once they were created and passed through their schooling, they were assigned to gods. Olympians received some, as did the Egyptians, even the Norse."

Fenrir frowns. "This was…"

"Shortly before your attack on Hades, yes." I meet his gaze. "For the longest time, Hades thought Zeus had purposefully assigned him his two guards to protect him against you. It wasn't until later he realized there might be more at stake."

"Such as?"

I shrug. "I'll let Hades explain the rest. If he ever figured it out, that is."

"But these immortals, they're...what, exactly? Ileana was very vague earlier."

"Beings of pure light. White magic, I suppose it's called here. But a lot more, as you've seen with Ileana."

He nods thoughtfully. "And they answer to...?"

"The god they are assigned to protect."

"And no one refused to accept them, as guardians?"

"The Mayans grumbled, but ended up agreeing. To be honest, I'm not sure if there's a single pantheon who didn't want them, given everything that was going on at the time. Fear is a powerful motivator." I tap my chin. "Although, if I'm to be perfectly honest, most of them got them for their main gods. It's why neither I nor Apollo have any. And in your pantheon's case. I suppose Odin didn't take on as many as the rest of us. I might be wrong, but I only ever heard of the two who were found dead."

"Who were supposed to be my immortals, by his account."

"Mm. Do you think they were meant to watch over Loki? Spy on him, as it were, at Odin's request?"

"If they were, it would've been with good reason. Still doesn't explain why Odin then implied their deaths were on me."

"No, it doesn't." I walk for a bit longer, lost in thought.

My openness isn't out of the goodness of my heart. I'm hoping, if I tell him enough, that it'll lead to a reciprocation. After last night, I'd love to get more into his head. Figure out how much of what he knows, that's locked up, could help us. How much we're missing, because he's too scared to face the truth.

"Now that I filled you in on what you missed, answer me one question."

Wariness immediately descends on him, but he says nothing.

"You said before that your beast drove you from pantheon to pantheon, to survive. Why didn't you let him take you away when I showed up? Is it really only because of the creatures hunting you?"

"Isn't that enough reason?"

I keep my gaze on him. "I feel like I'm missing something. That you're not telling me something."

"You said one question."

I glare at him, expecting more. When he doesn't give in, my frustration rises. "You are infuriating!"

He scowls, opens his mouth as though to say something, then shuts it again.

"What? Say it."

"No."

"Why not?"

"Because it's not worth it."

I reel back at the implied meaning. *You're not worth it.* I've had my share of things thrown at me over the centuries, but never this. And it stings. More than it should.

After going out of my way to help him, and putting my own reputation on the line.

*But is that so different from what I face at home?* I'd never once wanted to admit to myself that my worth rests solely in the capabilities my father sees in me. That by doing things for him, I am worthy of his attention, his praise, his love. Until I stop doing said things. And then... I'm just another goddess, among hundreds. Nothing special.

Fenrir's words bring the fear all back. And it's scary. Because only one person has ever been able to see through me like this before. And he'd ended up dead.

On a whim, I turn and stomp away. I only go a few feet before frustration takes the best out of me and I whirl around, yelling, "You're one to talk—"

My jaw drops. Fenrir is nowhere to be seen.

Instead, fog rises from the ground, surrounding me and blocking my vision. I immediately snap my fingers, pull an arrow out of the quiver and notch it on the bow. Aim, breathing steadily.

"What is this witchery?" My whisper comes out muffled, as though underwater. "Fenrir? Where the hell did you go?"

Did he play me and take off—again?

## Fenrir

The moment Artemis turns away, I know I fucked up. It's what I always do. Taking something that works, even something as simple as kindness or a second chance, and shitting on it.

Overcome with rage, I whirl on the nearest tree and punch it. The pain feels good against my knuckles, the bark of the tree scraping them until they're raw. So I punch it again. And again. At some point, the scraping turns into full-blown pain, but I relish it.

Finally, I let out a long breath and rest my head against the tree. *Maybe Loki's right. I'm a fuckup, same as him, and that's all I'll ever be.*

But…am I? Artemis was willing to believe me. Despite not being of my kin, of my pantheon, she alone was willing to give me the benefit of the doubt. The benefit of bringing me in front of someone who can give me answers.

*I can't do this without her.* The realization is sudden, shocking, but also—impossibly truthful. *I need to apologize.*

Only, when I raise my head, a thick fog surrounds me. And that foreboding feeling is back, clenching my gut.

"Artemis?" *Shit.*

I take a step toward where she'd disappeared, then look behind me. The tree is gone now, too. The sky above is gone. I'm surrounded by a mist so thick, I can't see anything besides it. And then, in the distance, a raven's croak. Enough to freeze me to the spot.

Is this a tactic of my pantheon to get me in line? Have they come for me, too?

And how the hell can I figure out where Artemis went...

*Your deeper self could. Your wolf. Let him take over. Let him rule you. Let him... Let him...*

My response is immediate. *No.*

Darkness is quick to suggest me reverting to my primal self, but I won't give in. I won't use the powers that will call those creatures to me.

But then how will I find Artemis?

# CHAPTER 8

**Fenrir**

It feels like I've been walking for hours. Not that I can tell, since my watch conveniently also stopped working when the mist rose. But press on, knowing I have no other option.

Thoughts of where Artemis might be—did she go back to Olympus, after all? Gave up on me? Can I blame her?—conflict with what I would say if she was here—I'm an idiot, an asshole? I always fuck things up?—and lead me to no answer, period.

As I'm wandering around, that damned raven's croak sounds again. Then, a slow clap starts around me. I turn in a circle, trying to figure out where it's coming from.

The mist shimmers before me, faint at first and then more brightly, before parting. And the last person I'd expected to see pops through.

"Father?"

"Fenrir, Fenrir. You always were a troublesome boy," Loki says.

He's a full head smaller than me, but what he lacks in stature, Loki makes up for in attitude. His thin lips are curled in a smirk, and with his dark hair, dark eyes and angular face, he's the picture of judgement.

*As he's been all my life.*

"What are you doing here? Asgard run out of mischief for you?"

He shrugs, and walks around me in a circle. "Living on this realm has aged you, son."

"Didn't peg you for one to care."

"Mm, true." He faces me. "Quite the trouble you've caused for me, you know?"

I stay quiet, knowing it's no use arguing with him. Loki's always right. Period.

"What, nothing to say?"

"You wouldn't care even if I did have something to say."

"True." A nasty look appears in his eyes. "Matter of fact, I would be surprised. If you *for once* lived up to your so-called reputation."

"Like you constantly do, you mean? No, thanks." I turn and walk away, but his next words stop me.

"You always were a disappointment."

"Same could be said for you, *Father*. Or have you forgotten you're only second-best next to the mighty Thor?"

His rage is physical, a force of winds and energy that hits me from the back, slamming me into a tree. My bones rattle, but something else does, inside me—something darker.

*Not now.*

"Thor will get his comeuppance, mark my words." Loki's feet inch closer, even as I'm shaking my head. "But you… you were supposed to be my secret weapon."

Secret weapon. It's all I've ever been to him. A means to an end, a sword of Damocles he could wave over his family's head, over and over. So they would forever live in fear of what would come. And I would forever live in the shadow of that fear.

"You never saw past anything more," I mutter.

"More?" He laughs, bitter. "What more is there, when it comes to you? All my efforts to make something of you—useless! You shied away from the beatings. You feared the obstacles I'd toss your way. And by all the gods, were you a kind-hearted fool or what!" His eyes grow more intense. "I thought I could mold you into something better. What a waste."

Another wave of energy hits me, smacking me yet again into the tree. This time, it cracks a little.

I spit a gob of blood on the ground, then wipe at my mouth. With my divine powers tightly under wraps, my body *will* bleed and *will* hurt, same as any human's. But between that and the creatures, I'll take it.

*If only those were my only problems.* That darker sensation inside me intensifies, roaring in my gut like a living force. It was so easy, for so long, to ignore it. No temptations. No straight challenges. Since Artemis entered my life, though…Those temptations, those challenges, have only come into direct conflict with my primal self. The beast I was always meant to be claws at the surface of my conscience, demanding to be freed. Not just to be freed, though. To lash at him. To get payback for all the past. And I don't know how much longer I can hold it at bay.

A shudder runs through me, and I whisper, "Stop."

"Stop?" Loki laughs. "Pathetic. You will not even defend yourself? Some Norse god you are, shying from duty and battle like a poor and puny mortal."

It strikes me, then, that his use of divine energy is quite possibly attracting those creatures around me. Same as Artemis' did, twice already. The panic gripping my chest is unlike anything I've ever felt. The roaring in me grows, and grows. The beast claws, tearing at my insides.

"If I could disown you, I would've done it ages ago. You are a disgrace to your blood, to your lineage, to Asgard itself."

It's not the first time he says this to me. But it's the first time it hits me so hard. Hard enough that I bend over, and my nails dig into the earth.

*You know they laugh at you, above? You think they would fear you, but they laugh. Because they know how pitiful you are. How you'll never amount to anything. How you'll die here in this cavern....and your destiny with you.*

His words had always been shards of ice to my heart. But I'd managed to block them, set them aside. Refuse to entertain thoughts about the past. But now that he's here, the memories unfurl. Anchoring myself is useless. The dark beast inside of me roars at the injustice, wanting to escape. To tear me apart—to tear *him* apart.

My back arches, bones cracking. I grit my teeth, but an anguished groan escapes me.

Loki cackles. "What, will you turn, now? Attack your own father? Go on, then. *Try it.* And let us see who wins."

*I'm sick and tired of Thor gaining all the accolades. Thor, who does nothing. Meanwhile,* my *machinations,* my *scheming*, my *plans are cast aside. All because he's the favoured son. You were supposed to be my secret weapon. You were supposed to be my out. Why can't you live up to what you were meant to do! Why do you have to be so pathetic?*

I look at him, my view distorted in black and white. The past mixing with the present. The change...

*No. I need...*

A red haze descends over me, and my arms crack next. The bones twist into something distorted. The fingers snap next, bending at unnatural angles. The last bit of my spine splinters, and I howl. My wolf ripples under my mortal skin, wanting out. To be free. For the first time in forever.

I endure every agony, gritting my teeth until my jaw aches.

And then it's not my jaw.

It's not my nose.

It's not my hands.

Fur grows over the skin, and fire encompasses my entire being.

Fire...to burn.

Fire...to destroy.

Fire...to seek vengeance.

But then...light. An odd, flickering thought, in the midst of all the chaos. *Artemis. I was looking for her.*

The beast inside me pauses, sniffing. Seeking. Her scent is faint, as though the mist itself obscures it, but it's there.

*I'm better than this. She's my chance at redemption. At clearing my name.*

It's small, but unmistakable—restraint.

The bones are broken. The flesh is torn. Finding the will to pull myself from the brink of the abyss is nearly impossible. Nearly. But I grit my teeth against the pain, and will the flesh back together. The bones, too.

Loki watches me, jaw dropping. A roar of pain escapes me as I'm finally put together. Then I fall to my knees, shaking and panting.

When I look up again, Loki's gone.

*What the hell just happened?*

## Artemis

*Stupid, stupid, stupid. How many times are you going to let him play you, and run off? Three times!*

Ugh. It's no use. No amount of berating myself will fix the fact that Fenrir is gone, and I've yet to find him. This damn mist is everywhere, and not even my tracker instincts help.

I hold my bow taut by my side as I step through. For the last few moments, I've felt someone watching me. But they're not showing themselves.

"Fenrir, if this is you, I'm not in the mood for games."

A quiet chuckle answers me. I freeze as the mist parts, and a shape emerges.

Hair as dark as Hades', eyes as blue as Zeus', but taller than them both. He's twice Ares' bulk, and that's saying something, since he's the god of war. And his energy…

I shudder, then draw my bow tighter, preparing to let the arrow loose. "What the hell are *you* doing here, Cronus?"

I stare at the Titan. I'd heard of him, and Hades told us all of the last fight. The one involving the zmei. No one in all the pantheons understood how Cronus was able to break through Tartarus, but he'd been shoved back in. And I'd never expected to run into him. Not here. Not alone. Not away from Olympus.

Cronus smiles, showing a line of white teeth, filed like canines. "Granddaughter, imagine my surprise at finding you here."

"I don't understand. Why…how… You were in Tartarus!"

He shakes his head, tut-tutting as though I'm a child. "Really, to believe such tales?"

"They're not tales! You used the broken dragon shifters, the ones seduced by dark magic. You used their souls as spies, and broke out of Tartarus, scheming to get back at the gods—at your own sons!"

He snorts. "My sons, who imprisoned me in the first place."

"They had to. You were out of control, wanting to rule everything with an iron fist and—"

"Give it up, huntress. Olympus is gone."

My tirade cuts off immediately. Dread bubbles in the pit of my stomach. "W-what?"

"Yes." His smile widens, the glint of his canines even scarier.

"That's…not possible. Olympus is unbreachable."

"Not to me. They are all gone."

*All gone.* My heart sinks, my breath stops, coming in short pants. Olympus… Hades, Zeus— Apollo! All of them, lost?

But how? How did Cronus escape again? Hades said he'd clean up the Underworld. Figure out how Cronus escaped. Make sure no one else could help… And punish Charon, his ferryman, whose sole responsibility was to ferry the souls of the dead to the Underworld. Until he went above his station, beyond his duty, and betrayed his master. But Hades himself took care of that, tossing him into Tartarus. Cronus had no more outside help… How could he have escaped again?

I blink away my tears, scanning his form. Which seems to have become more tangible with each second of my suffering…

And then it hits me. There's no divine energy

coming off him. Nothing as powerful as Cronus should be displaying, anyway. But there *is* something. Something foreign.

My tracker instincts kick in. "You're not... You're not real."

"Want to bet?"

He's on me the moment after, hand on my throat, lifting me off the ground. His nails push into my throat, cutting off my breath. With his other hand, he digs into my shoulder—my fingers loosen on the bow, and it falls below, covered by the mist.

*It's not real. It can't be real. Cronus would've crushed me with his divine energy, not bothered getting his hands dirty.*

But no amount of reasoning helps me.

*He can't kill me. Not in this realm.*

When I look at him, Cronus' eyes flash. "I can, and I will."

It's like he can read my thoughts, my fears—and still, his form is even more tangible now. Solid rock, when I try to hit him. And with each second he's touching me, I feel more...mortal. At first, his grip on my throat was only uncomfortable. Now, it's draining my airway, and powers.

Out of the corner of my eye, something else parts from the mist. A shape dressed in dark gear—a dark great helm, black armor, and a sword. His appearance seems to distract Cronus—or whoever the hell he is—and the grip on my shoulder eases just a fraction.

Though my vision is blurry, my throat nearly closed with the force he's using to bruise it, I move my fingers. The bow jumps out of the mist and into my hands. I reach with my free hand to the quiver, using a small burst of the divine to call an arrow the last of the way to me.

It slides into my palm with such force, it nicks the skin, and a drop of blood falls. I ignore it, instead notching it into the bow, and shooting. This close together, I have only enough space to pull the bow a little. But the arrow does the rest, lodging itself into Cronus' gut.

He roars, dropping me. I fall to my knees, grasping another arrow and aiming it his way. "Fuck you. Olympus isn't gone, and you're not real. *What* are you?"

Cronus shimmers and disappears, into whatever hell he'd come out of. One thing I'm sure of— that wasn't my grandfather. If he was, I wouldn't be alive. It's hard to kill a god, harder still since any weapon who could do so was either given to a proper guardian or destroyed. But for a Titan? It's still very much a possibility.

My breath trembles out, and my attention turns to the dark rider. He stares at me a moment, and a shudder runs through me. Is he part of the illusion, of these forsaken woods' torture?

He takes one step toward me. Tilts his head. Then lifts his hand to his mouth, as if to blow me a kiss.

A gasp escapes me. "Pegasus?"

He's gone the moment after, disappearing into the mist. I run after him, screaming his name again, feeling like I'm losing my mind.

And then I stop dead in my tracks. Whoever it was—whatever it was—he's now vanished. *Pegasus is dead. He died in the second attack, and Hades' immortals couldn't save him. You know this.*

But why did my heart kick into overdrive when he did that thing with his hand, and his mouth? In the past, Pegasus had used it as a secret signal between us, a way of showing me attention, even from a distance. Back when everything was good, and light, and…

*You're losing it. Doubting your abilities, just because you lost track of Fenrir again. So what if the last time you did so was when Zeus forced you to spy on Hades himself, and you got distracted with Pegasus? Falling in love is not a crime, at least not according to Aphrodite. And she's the goddess of love, she should know.*

*But that's no excuse to be losing it. Keep your head in the game. You need to find Fenrir, get to this oracle, figure shit out, and then return to Olympus with your bounty. Whatever you think you saw, it wasn't Pegasus.*

I gulp, forcefully pulling myself together. With the dark knight's disappearance, the mist around me parts, too. Behind me, I hear a noise. I whirl around, expecting to see the dark rider. Instead, it's…Fenrir. He's on his knees, panting and shaking near a tree that looks ready to topple over.

"Fenrir!" I run to him, dropping to my knees by his side and pulling him into my arms.

It's an odd reaction, to say the least. I'm not even sure where it stems from. He's not the one I would have chosen for this quest, but the relief I'm no longer alone is way beyond what I expected.

It takes us long moments to catch our breath. Even longer for me to say, "Maybe those mortals knew a thing or two, after all. About these woods."

Fenrir lets out a strangled chuckle, then pushes away from my arms. Our gazes lock, so close together. I'm keenly aware of the heat of his body, the darkening of his gaze. The fact his lips are so close to mine.

And then he crawls backward, putting more distance between us, and runs a hand over his face. The moment is broken. His eyes are so wary and haunted, all I want is to pull him back into my arms. Because his closeness made me feel safe, too.

*Head in the game, Artemis. Your mission. Nothing else.*

"I'd say," he mutters. "Illusions, you think?"

"Probably. Or some type of magic. Who did you see?"

He shakes his head. "My father."

I open my mouth to say something, then close it. Finally say, "I saw Cronus."

"That's not possible. You said yourself he's back in Tartarus."

I nod, slowly. "I know. Which is why I'm leaning toward an illusion of some kind. It's just...for a moment there, I almost thought it was real, what he was saying. Even though I knew it couldn't be."

Fenrir says nothing, just watches me. It's on the tip of my tongue to mention the dark rider, but that would mean having to tell him about my idiotic, half-cooked thought that he could be linked to Pegasus. Could *be* Pegasus. Which is insane. *Besides, Fenrir doesn't need to know about him. He's not...it doesn't matter. One has nothing to do with the other.*

"Want to get back on the road?" is all I say instead.

Fenrir nods and we stand, then walk away. Within moments and after passing a few more trees, a cabin emerges from the woods, like it was waiting for us all along. A fire flickers inside. As we watch it, mesmerized that we got to it in the end, shapes move inside.

I notch another arrow on my bow and we approach slowly. Fenrir picks up a log of wood, holding it like a weapon. He grips the faded, wooden door handle, looks at me, and nods. I lift the bow. Then he yanks the door open.

There's a blast of something that smells like sulfur and an entitled voice rings out. "Who the fuck are you?"

# CHAPTER 9

**Artemis**

A woman emerges from the cabin. Everything about her is hostile, from her pursed lips to the menacing glare she levels at us from blue eyes the shade of a midnight sky. She has auburn hair, pale skin, and a scar running the length of her left cheek.

And she's not alone.

Behind her, a shadow moves, soon manifesting into a big bear of a man. Facial hair fills the lower part of his jaw, offset by the shaved head. He wears faded jeans and a shirt, similar to Fenrir but in different colors. A worn leather jacket finishes his attire.

It's a contrast to the woman's flowy dress with

an exploding cleavage and knee-length boots.

But what strikes me the most about the pair is when the man levels a blank stare onto me. It takes a moment for it to sink in—he cannot see. And yet one of them used magic, for that's what the sulfur smell was. Question is, which one?

Fenrir moves between us, his nostrils flaring. "I've heard of your kind. Undead."

His posture is defensive, almost aggressive—the most I've seen out of him. And it's all focused on the woman.

She arches an imperious eyebrow, chin tilted in the air like we're her servants. "Spare me. Again, who the fuck are you?"

"How about you answer that?" I bite back.

Our gazes meet, clashing. Mutually assured hate.

My hackles rise at the hostility in her, and the Olympian in me wants nothing more than to display the kind of power that'll put her in her place.

Then I remember our purpose here, and force myself to grit my teeth against the urge to throttle her. "Are you the woman living in this cabin?"

"And if I am, what's it to you?"

The man behind her shifts. He hasn't said anything yet, but his attention is a tangible force upon us.

I take a step forward. The woman opens her arms wide, effectively blocking the entrance to the cabin.

"We don't have time to waste," I hiss at her. "So either answer my question, or I'll—"

"What, poke me with the little arrow? Try it." Her eyes flash at the dare.

Oh, I'm tempted. But not if she's the one we seek. *Please, by Hera's ever-mercurial mercy, let it not be her. I don't think I can be civil enough to ensure she answers our questions.*

"Don't bother," Fenrir says behind me. He's so close, I hadn't realized he'd moved in, as though ready to attack—to defend me? Cute, but unnecessary. "Mortal folklore says you're all gone from this realm. What are you doing here?"

She simply stares at us. I feel like I'm missing something, a rather big piece that explains why she's not scared of us.

I glance at Fenrir questioningly, and he mutters, "She's a vampire. They're dead mortals, who live off the blood of other living mortals." Lower still, he adds, "Short of using your powers, nothing else will scare her off. And that's not a risk we can afford, after the woods."

I nod in silent agreement, then turn my attention back to the woman. Our whole exchange took only seconds, but I can tell she was listening to every bit of it. *Clearly, her being undead means enhanced senses. I'll have to keep that in mind.*

"He's right, you know. Nothing you do or

threaten to do will scare me."

Someone clears their throat. My eyes go to the man with her.

"I'm Ştefan, a Dacian warlock," he says, in a voice as smooth as honey. "This is my companion, Elizabeta Ţepeş, of the House of Dracul. We're here seeking—"

"Would you shut *the fuck up*?" Elizabeta says. Her tone still rankles me. "I want to hear what *they're* here for."

Ah. So my instincts were right, and she doesn't belong here. Neither does he.

I arch an eyebrow at her. "You first."

Moments pass as we stare at each other. My annoyance rises, the air around me crackling. The man behind her—Ştefan—lets out a small noise—half gasp, half grunt. It draws my attention to him; did he feel it? How could he have, if he cannot see me?

Elizabeta rolls her eyes and turns to him, hand on her hip. "What is it now, Dacian?"

He grabs her wrist and pulls her farther into the cabin, leaving the way open for us to follow. Be it on purpose or not, I don't care. I move past the threshold, Fenrir following in my wake. And stop dead.

If I'd expected order, I'm sorely disappointed. The entire cabin is in upheaval.

I whirl on the duo. "Did you do this? Because I swear if—"

Elizabeta snarls my way, but Ștefan tugs on her wrist again. She yanks it out of his grip, dropping her voice to an angry whisper, but I can tell she wants to come at me.

*Let her. I'll happily oblige, without my powers.*

My gaze roams around the house again. Jars and potions are scattered every which way and that. Scrolls, notebooks, papers of all kinds fill every surface. In a corner, on a small table, uneaten food has molded. And the smell—musty, like it hasn't been aired in a while. Which, judging by the two windows—each of which has a latch on, and some sticky stuff around it—is accurate.

A larger table is filled to the brim with more books, more old parchments, maps, and small bowls filled with powdery substances. An imposing stone hearth holds the remnants of a dead fire. The rest of the surfaces have shelves of all sizes, none that match. And in another corner, as though forgotten, is a small bed with what looks like a lumpy mattress.

"Hmm." Fenrir pulls up close to me. "I don't see the witch—"

"Shh."

In the corner, the other two have stopped speaking. Ștefan is angled once more toward us.

"You're here seeking the oracle?" he asks. "But how did you bypass the payment?"

"Payment?"

I hold back a groan. Too late. Fenrir clearly doesn't know the art of keeping our information close to our chest. Little as it is. *What the hell payment is he talking about, Ileana? And why didn't you know about this?*

The woman's—Elizabeta's—eyes sparkle with interest. "So you don't know—"

Ştefan pulls her behind him abruptly. Ignoring her stifled cry, he says, "As you must know, this is the cabin of the Hoia-Baciu oracle. She always asks for payment, and it is rumored the woods help her in collecting it. I'm not sure how or why you were able to get this far in without providing it, but there must be a reason." He pauses, then adds, "She left, shortly after we arrived. My sister is sick and the oracle alone can provide the help." He takes another deep breath, and a shudder wrecks his big body. "But you seem like you need it more. We will return later."

"No, we won't." Elizabeta moves fast, blurring from behind him, to me. "I'm not moving until that old hag returns. I don't take kindly to people playing games on my territory."

"Your territory?" I snort, crossing the last bit of distance that puts me right in front of her. "Don't make me laugh. This entire realm belongs to—"

Fenrir tugs on me, inserting himself between us until he forces Elizabeta to take a half-step back. "How about you two leave?"

More anger flashes in her eyes. "I said *I'm not.*"

"Elizabeta."

She turns to Ștefan. "Listen, Dacian. You may take it lying down, but I don't back away from a fight."

He bristles. "Need I remind you that you're the one who scared the oracle away?"

"I didn't!"

"Oi!" Fenrir yells, slamming his palm on the table. The Irish lilt is back in full swing. "Feck off out of here, before I make you."

Elizabeta snarls. "I'm not going to take a mutt's orders—"

Fenrir's rough threat, almost a growl, seems to be the deciding factor for Ștefan. "We're leaving, don't worry."

Something fills the air then—sulfur—and Fenrir flares his nostrils by my side again. Elizabeta freezes, as though immobilized into a magical hold. Without any preamble, Ștefan picks her up by her waist, tosses her over his shoulder, and walks away.

I watch them go, bemused as to why she's not moving. "Did he…enchant her?"

Fenrir lets go of a sharp exhale. "I believe so, but I don't like the way he did it."

"What do you mean?"

"I smelled…blood. Blood magic isn't a good thing, even in the mortal realms."

All magic, to some extent or the other, entered this realm from the gods. I'm not surprised that mortals found a way to sabotage it.

"How in hell does a blind man handle that much…attitude?" I shake my head. "Never mind. Thank you for that."

A grunt is his only answer.

When I next look at the woods, the other two have disappeared.

**Fenrir**

Vampires. I've seen it all, now. And to think mortals are so oblivious.

Too many smells in this cabin have me on edge. And those two… the bloodsucker. I thought Loki joked about their existence. All the made-up stories I heard in Dingle were just that—stories. Except…not.

I turn my attention back to the cabin, taking in the mess. The remnants of the fire remind me of hearths in the cold of winter, sacrifices to the gods, hanging around mortals. An odd memory.

It was my first run-in with mortals on this realm. I'd been young, and Father had once again brought me on Midgard, this time in human form. I didn't know it at the time, but we were there to witness a winter ritualistic sacrifice to the Norse gods. And what a ritual it had been…

For hours on end, I'd eaten good food and drank ale. By the end of the night, I'd been so sleepy. It was the one time I don't remember Loki ruining anything. He'd been talking to someone, a stranger in a cloak, the entire time. And by the end of it, we'd left. Nothing but a peaceful night…

I shake the remnants of the memory off, focusing instead on the present.

Can this so-called oracle really help? In my pantheon, they're not exactly to be trusted. I have a hard time imagining how this will magically answer all my problems. Yet… I also can't help but hope.

*You won't get rid of me so easily.*

I let out a slow exhale, forcing myself to block the voice. Artemis clears her throat, effectively distracting me from it.

"Some characters, those two."

"Mm."

I can feel her coming closer, the air itself changing. Here, she doesn't have to hide the full extent of her divine presence, and it shows. The air crackles with it, and it acts like a magnet for me, pulling me in.

"The woods fooled us."

I turn to her, then. There's an odd expression on her features. "Fooled us into thinking we were safe, sure." I run a hand over my face, trying to wipe away Loki's image—and his words.

"Do you think they manifest our darkest fears?"

I choke out a laugh. "No. If they did, my illusion would've been ten times worse." Although, it was weird how, for an illusion, that thing had known exactly what to say to me. Exactly how to push my buttons.

Too late, I realize my cryptic words once again drew Artemis' curiosity. She takes a step closer, touching my shoulder. A zap of electricity travels from the tips of her fingers into me, and our gazes latch on.

"What happened, Fenrir?"

For a long moment, all I can focus on is the light in her emerald gaze. I could tell her everything—how Loki taunted me, his hurtful words, the way it pushed me over the edge. How I nearly gave in to the dark beast, to what lies underneath it, and probably would've gone on another rampage. But if I do, will she look at me differently? Will she see me as a threat, just like all the other gods?

Only one way to find out.

"Loki, he… It's the same old. How I'm a disappointment, how I was his hidden weapon to begin Ragnarök, and so on. But he kept pushing and pushing and—" I close my eyes. "My true self, my wolf, took over. He's been…*I've* kept him at bay. For a long time. Purposefully. Because the last time, he hurt people. Yet I still nearly shifted today, fully and completely. I don't know if the illusion using fake divine energy would've attracted the creatures that hunt me, but my shift almost certainly did."

The soft touch on my shoulder turns into a firm grip. "But you didn't turn, Fenrir. You said you nearly shifted."

I open my eyes, meeting her gaze. The words are on the tip of my tongue—*Thanks to you*—but they never make it past my lips.

"I need to tell you something, too," Artemis whispers.

"Before you do, I owe you an apology."

She frowns. "For what?"

"Before we got separated, the things I said. They were uncalled for. I'm sorry."

She shakes her head. "It's forgotten. I'd say we both paid more than we should've with what those illusions made us go through."

I turn to her fully then, my hand going up to cup her cheek. That same zap of electricity fills my palm, radiating all through me. She's the light tugging me out of the darkness, out of my drowning despair. And I'm starting to realize, more and more, how much of a difference this makes when I've never had something so…beautiful. Something so…mine.

"Artemis, I—"

"My turn. Please. When Cronus—his illusion, whatever it was—appeared, I had a moment of… There was…" She struggles to find the words, trailing off. Her eyes shadow, filling with pain.

The door to the cabin opens then, and a short, stout woman walks in. She lifts her head, wrapped in a polka-dotted scarf, and shows wrinkled, leathery skin and intelligent black eyes.

She takes us in, and I drop my hand from Artemis' cheek at her perusing gaze. Then she looks around, as though verifying we're the only ones in here.

"Well, well, well. To what do I owe this pleasure, new visitors?"

# CHAPTER 10

**Fenrir**

The woman's wrinkled face takes us in, appraising. Her vibrant dark eyes settle on Artemis, and she cackles at her surprised expression. "Don't look so shocked, gorgeous. Age hits us all." Then she takes another look at her, me, her again. "Then again, perhaps not."

She moves to the center table and drops a basket filled with herbs on a quasi-non-existent corner of free space. Scents of rosemary, thyme and mint fill the air. I take a step back, offput by the mix, for some reason.

The woman—oracle—on the other hand, she

looks completely at home, moving about with an ease I wouldn't have expected given her stooped stature.

"So. You managed to get those two to leave. Good riddance." She turns to me. "Care to tell me what brings you to my door, Fenrisúlfr?"

I gape at her use of my official name. "You…you know who I am?"

Another cackle is my answer. "I know who everyone that steps in these woods is." She flicks her hand. "You all pay a price, see."

Something shimmers in the air, and a vial appears in her hand. The size of her index, made of glass with a wooden cork, it's inconspicuous. Except for the red liquid sloshing inside. My nostrils pick up the faint hint of copper escaping the cork.

*Blood. The damned hag is taking blood as payment for entering the woods. That's what the vampire's companion meant, about the price.*

Rage fills me. Out of all the violations, taking our blood is one of the worst. Not only can it be used against us, when bound with dark magic, but it's such an intricate part of us, it contains a little of our divine essence. This, no matter which pantheon one belongs to.

"Give that back!" I growl.

Her smile shows broken teeth. A second later, the vial disappears in a literal poof of air. "I don't think so." She goes to a corner and pulls out a bottle of a red liquid. Wine, if I were to guess. "Care for a drink?"

Her back is to us. I clench and unclench my fists, held immobile by my need to both correct her, but also not give in to the darkness. Already, I can feel its pull, pushing me to violence. Violence will unleash it, breaking my control, and I can't afford that.

Artemis shifts in my periphery. I turn to her, meeting her gaze. Emerald fire burns within it, and the thin set of her lips tells me she's equally infuriated. She may not have my olfactory senses, but she connected the dots.

The bow, which up to now she'd been resting against her hip, comes up. She notches an arrow, and gets into position. I shake my head at her, but her focus is on the old woman as she aims at the center of her back.

"I would think twice before you unleash that arrow, Goddess of the Hunt."

Artemis' shocked gaze flies to mine.

"I also have *your* vial of blood."

Artemis' grip tightens on her bow. Its quiver and whine is loud in the confined space. "Old hag, the gods' blood is not yours to harvest. Give it back."

Unworried, the woman turns around, glass in hand. She watches us and takes a sip. "No."

Artemis scowls. The air around her feels heavy again, crackling with her divine energy.

I take a step forward, pulling her attention. "Drop your bow."

"But we need—"

"She won't use it against us. Not yet, anyway. Isn't that right?"

The old hag nods, that smile still etched on her lips. I had a feeling oracles could be tricky, but even I didn't expect this. They normally see the future, not take it upon themselves to use weapons against those who seek them out.

This one, apparently, has different motivations. Now I just need to figure out how to use it against her, so we can get what we came here for. If that's even possible.

"You collect them, I suppose?"

Her smile widens into a grin. She waves to the wall behind her, and the air shimmers again. Where previously there had been a wooden panel, now it fades away, revealing its true contents. Shelves upon shelves, filled with thousands of vials of blood—if not more. "Precisely. Smart one, is he not?"

Artemis looks at the wall, then at me. Slowly, she drops the bow. "What do you want?"

The old hag smacks her lips. "I think the better question is, what do *you* want? You're the one who came to me, after all."

"No, I mean what do you want with the *blood*. Why keep it, if not to be used?"

Her eyes sparkle. "As payment. And insurance. Should anyone who comes to me wish to double-cross me, well… This ensures they cannot do so. One spell with the right type of magic, and I can turn their deepest desires, their darkest secrets, their most powerful weapons against them."

The brilliant eyes linger on me, then focus back on Artemis. "Now. I am Olga. Welcome to my abode, huntress. Let us not waste time, as I sense you are in a hurry. What is it you seek?"

Artemis looks at me. "My…friend has a problem. One that seems to extend to me."

The hag hides behind her glass. "You'll have to be more specific."

If looks could kill…

I intervene before Artemis raises her bow again. "Someone is after me."

The hag—Olga—opens her eyes wide in mock surprise. "You have Olympus' tracker with you. I should think that's obvious."

"No, I—" I press my thumb into my forehead, relishing the pressure that grounds me, and try again. "Someone besides Artemis."

"And what makes you think such is the case?"

"I've…" How to explain, without giving it all way? Clearly, she's aware of the pantheons. But I shouldn't be giving her more ammunition against me, such as the fact I'm wanted by Olympus and my own pantheon. "For years, I've chosen residence on this earthly realm. But whenever I've used my divine powers, creatures have come after me."

"What kind of creatures?"

"Winged ones," Artemis says. "Red eyes, horse-like heads, reptilian scales. Bat-like wings. Ridden by black riders."

"Ah. The Heka priests' favoured shifters."

That throws me for a spin. "The…what?" I glance at Artemis, but she seems equally clueless.

Olga heads to the paper-overloaded table and takes a seat—and another sip of her glass. With her free hand, she rummages through the paper load, until she emerges with a small booklet. Hands it over to Artemis. "Is this what you saw?"

She takes it, flipping through it one-handed. I'm about ready to offer to help, but she freezes. Then shows me the page. On it is the same type of creature she described. Except its skeletal jaw is open in a screech.

I can almost hear it, that hair-raising, blood-curdling scream…

"This is it," Artemis says.

I hand the book back to Olga, nodding. Then walk away, putting some distance between us until I can lean my back against a shelf.

"I thought as much." She pauses at that, sipping more wine.

I wait a beat. And another. Finally growl, "Will

you fucking tell me, already? What are they?"

"I just did. Heka priests' favored shifters."

I grind my teeth together so hard, I can feel the pressure in my brain. "Explain."

Olga rolls her eyes, as though we're massively inconveniencing her. "Heka priests were sorcerers in Ancient Egypt, circa four thousand years ago. Give or take. Pharaohs used them for everything— including syphoning off their gods' energy, when needed. Upon their deaths, the Heka priests were also buried with the pharaoh."

Artemis narrows her eyes. "And the creatures…"

"The Heka priests loved using dark magic. The ether that gave you all birth, housed both light and dark forces. Most gods channel the light. Some, a rare few, channel the dark. And throughout the ages, there have been humans desperate enough to worship those darker deities. In so doing, they gained access to dark magic, and passed it on through time and generations." She pauses for a moment to stare at her wine glass, before continuing. "Through dark magic, Heka priests were able to force a metamorphosis onto every creature they saw fit, save for a human. Shifter humans have nothing to do with them. But, it so happened one of their favorite creatures to force this upon were the pharaoh's horses."

"How…" I clear my throat. "Why do they look like that?"

"Like something straight out of hell? Because dark magic eats at the flesh of the living. In order for the horses to do what the priests wanted of them, it required energy. Dark magic thus ate at their flesh, creating skeletal-type beings. Unnatural. Abhorrent. A sin against nature itself."

A long silence extends between us, making the words linger in the air.

Artemis is the first to speak again. "If these priests were buried with the pharaohs, and there haven't been any pharaohs for a few thousand years... How are their creatures now out and about? And hounding Fenrir?"

Olga grins. "Now you're asking the right questions, huntress. Clearly, a Heka priest is creating them once more." She turns to me. "The interesting thing about these creatures is they hunt dark forces. Any reason why they would be interested in you?"

"No." My gut churns at the implication. I try to school my expression into a neutral mask, but something tells me Olga sees right through it.

"Hmm. Well, perhaps you've angered someone that you didn't realize."

"I would've known if I ran into a Heka priest." I may not have used my divine powers in ages, but that doesn't mean I'm immune to sensing powerful beings.

"Perhaps, perhaps not. So, you seek to find out

who it is that's sending these creatures after you?"

"Yes."

"Ah." Olga stands, groans, takes another sip of wine, and paces the length of the small cabin. She stares at the wall for a moment. Then turns to us. "You were correct in coming to me. I know who hunts you. And I can tell you—"

"Great," Artemis says. "Who is it?"

"—for a price."

"Name it."

"Have a cup of tea with me and spend the night here."

I share a look with Artemis. She's as bemused as I am. "That's it?" I finally ask.

"Yes. I'm an old woman in need of company. One cup. One night. Then, I'll tell you what I know."

It seems too easy. But do we really have a choice?

"Deal," Artemis says, sealing it.

A flash of something crosses Olga's eyes, then she sets about preparing a tea. I don't pay much attention to it, moving away from the strong aroma and instead toward Artemis. She leans in closer, too, and her much more palatable scent assails my senses.

"Heka priests," I mutter. "Do you think it could be one of the Egyptian pantheon, then, who's after us?"

She bites her lip. "Could be. But it feels too easy."

"What do you mean?"

"If someone framed you, wouldn't it stand to reason they could just as easily frame the Egyptians?"

"I suppose so." In fact, it makes too much sense.

Olga moves from her little stove, carrying two steaming mugs to the table. "Come, come. Take a seat."

I hesitate, but finally do as she asks, sitting at one end of the table. Artemis sits at the opposite, and Olga, between us. She passes each of us a mug. I take mine with both hands, careful not to spill onto the papers still strewn all over the table.

A quick glance tells me there's texts in every language I can think of, and then some. The illustrations on some look like priceless artefacts.

"How did you come upon all this?"

She shrugs. "Years of doing favors for people." She nods at my cup. "Drink, drink."

I take a sip, scalding my tongue in the process. A hit of jasmine, citrus, and something else slides down my throat. Olga watches me carefully, then glances at Artemis, who's also tasting her mug. Satisfied, she leans back into her chair.

"Now, tell me all about your travels here. And how Fenrir's troubles have affected you, my dear huntress."

Artemis hesitates. After a shared glance, she finally explains a toned-down version of the story—

sticking to how she came to seek me, but not saying why; explaining the attack, then the trip via flight here, but not Ileana's involvement. If Olga realizes we're omitting details, she says nothing.

By the time Artemis is done with her story, my mug is empty. And so is hers. Olga takes them both, then stands. She shuffles around, tossing them into the worn sink. Finally, she faces us again.

"Well, that'll be me for the night. I need to run a quick errand, but make yourselves at home." She gestures around, a wide grin on her features. "Please. Even gods need rest."

Artemis gives her a smile, which strikes me as odd. But then again, I'm feeling fairly mellow after the tea, too. Damned mortals and their herbal remedies. We might consider ourselves superior in some regards, but when it comes to it, we're just as prone to their effects as mortals are. Same as drugs, alcohol—unless we flush them out of our systems via our divine energy.

Still, Olga's drink seems to be more suited for relaxation, so I let it go.

By the time my attention focuses on her again, Olga's by the door. "Bye for now!" She waves once, then disappears through the door.

I look at Artemis. My throat feels parched, but all I can focus on are the contours of her face. Her smile. The light that seems to surround her like a halo.

Then I realize it's coming from the fire, and a chuckle escapes me. Artemis giggles with me, and soon, we're both full out laughing.

When we stop, oddly in sync, our eyes latch on. An undercurrent passes, something that tugs at emotions and urges I've been feeling around her for the last days. My gaze drops to her full lips.

What would it be like to kiss her, I wonder? Would it be a sweet kiss, or something more passionate? Would she melt in my arms, or try to take control?

My body tightens in response to the mental images. Even more so when I think of my morning daydream.

I tear my eyes from her lips and stand from the table abruptly. A wave of yearning rises within me, dismantling my carefully constructed defenses, leaving a path of lava in its wake. My knees nearly give way, and there's a tightness in my head—and in my pants. I turn from Artemis before she sees it, walking to the sink, resting my hands on the edge of it.

But instead of staying seated, Artemis stands. Her chair scrapes the floor behind me.

"Fenrir, I feel—"

I glance over my shoulder. She's staring at the empty mugs in the sink. Then her eyes lift to mine, but they're dark. The emerald is nearly swallowed by her dilated pupils.

"Artemis—"

In a daze, she walks to me. Rests her head on my shoulder. Wraps her arms around my waist from behind.

"It feels…good, though. Right?"

Her hands move. Up and down my torso. *Just like in your fantasy… Remember the shower?*

I clutch the edges of the sink harder, my fingers digging into the wood. With every fiber of my being, I try to focus my attention on the uneven surface under my fingers, the roughness of the wood.

Not her touch. And how it's igniting a fire under my skin. The kind of fire I haven't felt since Asgard. A fire only the freedom of lust, of giving in fully to passion can ignite. A freedom I've never allowed myself.

"Artemis—"

The strangled word dies on my lips when one of her hands moves lower. Resting right over my bulging erection.

"Mm." Her moan of appreciation is my undoing.

I whirl around, hand on her hip, the other tangling roughly in her hair. Pulling her head back.

She meets my gaze. Licks her lips. "This changes nothing. I'm still bringing you in to Ol—"

I crash my lips to hers, cutting her off. Her lips are the stuff of dreams. Soft. Plump. Made for me. She answers my kiss eagerly, feverishly.

And when I pull back, see the mussed look, the fire in her eyes, I know I won't stop. I push Artemis back, until her legs hit edge of the sink. One-handed, I hoist her onto it. Her legs spread, accommodating me. And then I'm pressing against her, groaning.

In a frenzy, I undo the top button of her jeans, slide the zipper down. Artemis squirms, panting, pleading. I push my hand inside, seeking—*that*.

"Fuck."

Her heat swallows my fingers whole, tightening around me. Artemis moans loudly as I add a second finger to the first, thrusting both inside of her tight heat. With one hand, she grips the back of my neck, nails digging into my flesh. Then she throws her head back, giving me access to her neck. I kiss, nibble, bite everywhere I can get my hands on. And when that's not enough, I tug the shirt off her, and move lower.

Artemis pushes me away, panting. Only to then pull me closer by the belt of my jeans, palming my erection again. She unzips the jeans, reaches inside, and touches me so—fucking—gently.

Something short-circuits in my brain, and I stop thinking. Not that I had, up until then, but I'm definitely not now. All I can do is feel the softness of her grip, stroking up and down my hardness.

I push more in her hand. She licks her lips, moves one leg to slide off the sink, then starts kneeling. I realize her intent, and my grip on her hip tightens, stopping her. Pulling her back up until she's straightened. And then I smash my lips to hers once more, plundering her mouth.

When she melts against me, I stop for a second, moving my lips to her ear. "If I feel your mouth on me, I'm going to lose all semblance of control."

She meets my gaze, grinning. "Isn't that the point?"

I groan, push the jeans off her hips and pull her legs back around my waist. This time, when my hardness rubs against her, Artemis gasps. She clutches my shoulders, begging, pleading in my ear.

I tease us both, my boxer-clad erection resting just at the apex of her thighs. Touching, but not quite, her heated center. Her underwear's the last barrier, and even that's soaked. And then, little by little, I rock forward. Once. Twice.

Artemis moans. Her mouth seeks mine desperately, feverishly. After a rougher kiss, she moves to nibble on my jaw, my earlobe—tugging on it, biting it.

Something changes in the air. So quickly, I have no way of stopping it.

The steady thrum of lust in my blood is replaced by something else. Something darker. An instinct to—

## Artemis

My senses are on overload. Fenrir, his touch, his passion, it's too much. There's a frenzied need inside me, to take him, let him take me, to consume myself within him. It's strong enough to obliterate even Pegasus' memory from my mind.

When the tip of Fenrir's cock grazes against my thighs, then my dripping center, I grind down on him. Kiss him roughly, biting everywhere I can reach. I need him, like an itch I need to scratch now, before I burn alive.

The yearning is so powerful—too powerful?—I don't realize until it's too late that Fenrir's no longer participating. Instead, he's completely frozen.

I stop what I'm doing. The craving in my blood is urgent, desperate, seeking satisfaction. But I'm not so far gone that I don't realize something's utterly wrong.

I drop my legs from around his waist, then pull back enough to meet his gaze. And then I jerk back, needing to put space between us.

The eyes meeting mine aren't his. There's a coldness to them, a glint of something so malicious, I can't—

I move around him, diving for my bow. Only, I never get to it. Instead, my feet are just as frozen to the ground as Fenrir's are. And then he speaks. Only, it's not his warm, soothing voice that comes out. This one is raspy, cavernous.

"Huntress… I will only say this once. Stay out of my way."

I force a gulp. "Are you the one hunting Fenrir?"

"I need not hunt what belongs to me."

"He doesn't!"

The cavernous voice laughs. "You do not know what you are dealing with. Stay out of my way. And remember, I can take over at any time. Any. Time." The glint in his eyes becomes more intense. "Is it his cock you wish for, or a stranger's?"

And then, he's gone. Fenrir falls to his knees, gasping, panting. The same way as he did in the woods, when I'd found him after we'd gotten separated.

I pull the bow's string, notching an arrow. My hand shakes. "Wake up, dammit!"

His panting subsides and, slowly, he glances up. Blinking wildly. Eyes widening when they fall on the arrow, and my undressed state. "What…what happened?"

"You don't remember?"

He slowly stands, but keeps his distance. "I…no. All I remember is kissing you, wanting to be inside you." He blanches. "What happened? Did I hurt you?"

I shake my head slowly. "No. But I think I just met whoever's after you. Only, I don't understand how he spoke *through you*."

For a long moment, all he does is stare at me. His mouth opens, then closes. And repeats. Then his shoulders drop. "I see."

I watch, confused, as he zips his jeans, buttons them, then heads to the corner farthest away from me. He grabs some rope he finds in Olga's supplies, then wraps it around his ankles. Another piece, he wraps around his wrists, binding them to the side of a shelf.

"What…what are you doing?"

He won't meet my gaze. He's so far removed from the passionate man who'd nearly made me come, I can't begin to rationalize his behaviour. And then, he speaks.

"For so long, I've tried to make sure he doesn't get the upper hand. For so long, I've…hoped. But it's a lost battle." This time, his eyes meet mine. Distant. Haunted.  "If I move, shoot me. Hades won't care if you bring me back dead or alive."

Fenrir tears his gaze from mine after, and stares at the ground instead. A muscle ticks in his jaw. Mouth agape, I can only stare, and try to make some sense of what's happened.

We'd been fine. OK, not fine; clearly, Olga put something in the tea. But I wasn't fighting it. It felt right.

And then… the voice. The warning.

Is this what Ileana meant, that his body isn't fully his anymore? It's one thing to hear it, another to experience it in person.

Slowly, I move about the cabin, picking up my clothes and getting dressed. I discard the shirt, in favor of only my regular leather top. And throughout it all, Fenrir doesn't budge. Doesn't ask for his shirt. Doesn't even glance my way.

By the time I sit back at the table, one thing is clear. Fenrir's right. Hades might not care if I bring him back dead or alive. But...I'm starting to.

# CHAPTER 11

**Artemis**

Minutes go by, turning into hours. And all through-out, Fenrir remains silent. I try to engage him in con-versation more than once, but he keeps his head bowed, his face turned away from me.

I know he's not sleeping. His muscles are tense, corded. Reminding me even more of the sweet sen-sations he had coursing through me mere hours ago. Of his taut body, pressing against mine.

In the end, I give up and close my eyes. Might as well get some sleep. And perhaps some quiet will help him work through whatever demons he's try-ing to rebury.

The door bangs closed loudly. My head snaps up. First, registering the old hag is back. Then going to Fenrir—he's still tied, still in his previous position. Slowly, he moves his head toward the door. His expression is haggard, with dark circles under his eyes.

"Well, well, well," Olga tsks. "I take it the evening didn't go as planned?"

"You old bitch—" I make a move on her.

Fenrir speaks, freezing me to the spot. "We did your bidding. Now tell us, who hunts me?"

Olga arches an eyebrow, taking a few more steps into her cabin. She looks from him, to me, then back to Fenrir. "Did you do this, huntress?"

My fingers itch on my bow. "No. He did it to himself."

"Interesting…" Olga flicks her fingers. Fenrir's careful knots fall apart, releasing both his wrists and feet. "Care to enlighten me why, wolf god?"

Fenrir stands, uncoiling his muscles slowly, as though aware of each movement he's making. "Not particularly. Does it matter?"

"Quite."

When his gaze turns to her, it's glazed over, unfeeling. "Whatever you drugged us with nearly did its purpose. But we had an uninvited guest."

Olga arches an eyebrow. "Not the bloodsucker again, surely."

"No. Whatever's inside me decided to make itself known."

"Ah…" Olga turns from him. Fenrir might not be able to see her expression, but I catch enough of it.

"You *planned* this?"

Fenrir freezes at my accusation. But I'm not nearly done, the connections working through my mind.

"The drug…the tea. It inhibited our senses. Caused an aphrodisiac effect."

Olga shrugs. "The tea only made what was already under the surface come up for air. Blame me not for your own impulses, huntress." Her gaze lands on Fenrir's shirt, still on the ground, with meaning.

Fenrir bends for his shirt. The muscles of his back and abs ripple as he pulls it back on. I won't lie, a part of me is sad at seeing everything hidden again. The other part? Happy for the distraction being removed.

*Eyes on the mission. The old hag just confirmed it, last night was all because of the teas.*

Only, another part of me eagerly points out, *She also said the teas only bring to light what's already under the surface.*

Olga's right, unfortunately. The tea couldn't have affected gods to the point of causing an attraction that wasn't there. But that's neither here nor there, and something for me and Fenrir to work on later—when we're alone. Not in front of someone who clearly knows more than she's let on.

"Fine. The impulses were all ours, but what happened after, wasn't." I pause. "And yet, it's what you'd expected. Tell me it's not true."

Olga faces me, her expression free of remorse. "You see through me, huntress. Not unexpected from Zeus' daughter, after all."

I scowl, taking another step closer. "Do you even know what you stirred? What I saw under the surface—he's—"

"Yes, I imagine he was something to behold." Olga turns her attention to Fenrir. "Do you remember anything of the incident?"

"No. Complete blackout."

"Hmm." She goes to her paper-filled table, hunts for something. After a moment, she emerges with a crystal ball.

"If you're about to play some trick that works on mortals—"

She cackles. "Relax, Fenrisúlfr. I need this to illustrate my point." She waves her hand over the crystal ball, and puffs of smoke emerge. By the dozens. They separate, floating over her head like an odd halo. "Let me explain something. Your pantheons, they give you strength. But your divine powers are rooted in something much deeper."

"We know," I growl. "Worshippers. The more we have, the more power we get."

"Artemis… Let her finish."

I glance at Fenrir, but he looks away. So much for addressing me directly.

Olga clears her throat. "Quite. Worshippers play a role. The fabric of each pantheon's realm plays another. It is why gods crossing into other gods' pantheons will find their powers nullified, or nearly inexistent. Because a version of them exists in that pantheon, worshipped by other humans, who do not recognize yours."

I roll my eyes. "Right. Like Isis and Hera, both goddesses of fertility, but one from the Egyptian pantheon, the other from the Greek."

"Very well, huntress." Olga's eyes shine. "Gods interacting with each other happens in safe spaces only."

I share a glance with Fenrir. *Like the Council created in Olympus.*

"But," Olga continues, "gods are also unaware that their divine energy can be tainted."

Fenrir freezes at this. "Are you saying—"

"The one who hunts you is a god, yes."

I jab a finger at her. "I *met him* last night. This

thing was *inside* Fenrir. Do you understand? It didn't just control him. It doesn't just hunt him. It's *inside of* him. No god can possess another!"

"And is that a law, huntress?"

My mouth opens, then closes. Racking my brain trying to find the answer, but unable to come up with anything.

"Quite." Olga makes the puffs of air around her move. As each one comes in full center-stage, she points. "You are only aware of your current pantheons. The Greeks. The Egyptians. The Norse. The Africans. The Asians. The Mayan. And so many more. But old gods, the ones who came before any of you younger ones…they had no rules around them. It's why Titans like Cronus were imprisoned."

I shake my head. "Still doesn't explain how—"

"I'm getting to it, huntress. A new god cannot touch another's mind because of the rules you subject yourselves to. A contract you all agreed to partake in, in order to maintain order and not risk complete annihilation. Though some gods would enjoy it, of course." Her gaze goes meaningfully to Fenrir. And I remember what he said about his father, Loki. "However, an old god can touch another's mind… if he has worshippers."

"But old gods, by definition, are forgotten," Fenrir whispers.

Olga shrugs, and the puffs of air disappear from

around her head. "I have given you your answer, wolf god. Whether you are satisfied with it or not, is of no concern to me."

My eyes narrow on her. "You better have more than that after the price you made us pay."

She shrugs again. "He's old. Of a much older generation. And, given he has to take over another's mind, he must be limited to some extent. Perhaps lost, perhaps imprisoned. And he belongs to a different pantheon. No older god could possess another of the same pantheon."

I wait for more. But all Olga does is stare at us.

"You—" This time, I bring my bow up, notch an arrow, and aim at her. "Old hag, we did not come here for cryptic riddles. We came for answers!"

"Stop," Fenrir says, in the same dead tone. "She followed the bargain."

"No, she didn't. First drugging us—"

"Artemis, let this go."

I watch, gaping as Fenrir simply moves to the door and opens it. He lingers in the doorway, as though it takes too much to move. I drop my bow, letting the arrow dissolve, and move toward him.

"I could find out more," Olga says behind me.

I stop, facing her. The glint of victory in her eyes tells me it's exactly what she wanted, but I don't care. I want to know. For Fenrir, for myself. Because this isn't right, and nothing about this should've ever come to pass. Existing in a world where it *can* pass, where another god can possess another, is unthinkable.

"How?" I ask her.

"You could spend another night—"

"No!" This, from both of us.

"Then, you can get something for me. An itty bitty thing. And when you return, I will find out exactly who hunts you. And how you can get back home."

I scowl at her. So she was busy all night, finding out more about our weaknesses. Including that we can't return to Olympus.

I glance at Fenrir, but he seems detached. Ready to get this over with. *Hades won't care if you bring me back dead or alive.*

A flare of something rises within me, and I face Olga again. "Fine. What do you want us to get?"

She walks to her table and pulls out an old parchment. The paper is yellow, its edges frayed. On it is a design. "This."

Despite myself, I move closer. The image depicts a shield made of gold, its edges seemingly dulled by age. On it is a creature with a horrifying visage and hair made of living, venomous snakes—a Gorgon's head.

I jerk my gaze to Olga. "The aegis? Athena's shield? *That* is what you seek?"

Olga grins. "Yes. I am sure your sister will not miss it."

Athena would probably disagree, but who am I to argue with this crazy old hag?

"Only one problem. The aegis is probably in Olympus, and I can't enter, as you well know."

Olga's grin doesn't waver. "That would be a problem…*if* the aegis was there."

"I don't understand."

"Love makes one do terrible things, huntress. When Athena endorsed Odysseus in the war against Troy, she cared for him."

"Yes, we all know the story."

"But do you know that upon his old age, she gifted him her aegis, and asked him to hide it somewhere no mortal or god could ever get to?"

I shake my head at her. "Athena wouldn't—"

"But she did. As I said, love makes one do terrible things. And it so happens that this hiding spot is nearby. Nestled within a mountain that my woods will lead you to."

I roll my eyes. "Give me the location, and we will bring it to you."

Fenrir clears his throat at the door. "Why do you need this…aegis?"

Olga smirks. "I'm a collector, remember?" She then hands me another parchment—a map. "This should get you where you need to go. That, and my woods."

I turn my back on her, and follow Fenrir out the door. This should be even more fun than being cooped up for hours on end inside the flying metal contraption mortals inexplicably love.

# CHAPTER 12

**Artemis**

As the tracker, I lead the way. Which suits me fine, giving me a moment to collect my thoughts. Fenrir's need to give up is rankling at me more and more, and I'm not exactly sure why.

Maybe it's because of the stereotype I have, that all Norse gods are like Thor and Odin. Big-bodied, loud-mouthed, and opinionated. Never back down from anything.

To be fair, so are the women. I recall a long ago fight at a Council meeting, with Freyja and Aphrodite. Both goddesses of love in their respective pantheon, they were casting their vote upon something, alongside other goddesses of love of other pantheons.

Freyja insisted her vote should have more weight in the matter since it involved a woman's future. Aphrodite got mad, saying she cared much for women's future. But Freyja was quick to point out that while Aphrodite might care, she had a shitty way of showing up for what she believed in. Given she'd submitted to everyone's pressure and married Hephaestus, the forger god, despite not wanting to. And had then proceeded to cheat on him. Freyja, faced with a similar situation in her pantheon, had stood her ground and refused to submit to the pressure. Needless to say, it turned into quite a cat fight.

So, yes, I have preconceived notions of Fenrir's pantheon. Just like he has of mine, I suppose.

I glance down at the parchment, choosing to focus on a different puzzle instead. The map is enchanted, I'm assuming, since a little dot shows us moving, and the path lights up ahead of the little dot. The woods around us don't look that much different—though, there are no more hallucinations.

"How do you think she controls the hallucinations—illusions—whatever they are?" I ask Fenrir over my shoulder.

Nothing.

"I'm guessing she figured out how to bind earth magic, and she's using it to her advantage. Though how in hell she did that…" My mutter trails off, to more silence.

I don't like his sullenness. Not when I know there's fire underneath that façade. I felt that fire, and even now my body heats at the memory. I've never been one to shy from the truth, and the truth is I wanted him, last night. And I still do, like an itch I need to scratch.

We keep traipsing through the woods, though I can't resist baiting him some more. "Cat got your tongue?" When he doesn't answer me, I whirl around, stopping his advance. "Fenrir."

He stops. Looks at me. And there's so much anguish in that gaze, my will to pester him goes to dust.

"I'm sorry," I whisper.

"You have nothing to be sorry for. I'm the one who behaved like a brute."

I frown. Before I can argue, he moves past me and keeps walking. "Why do you suppose she needs this artefact? I don't buy her story about being a collector."

I sigh at his obvious change of subject. "Who knows? Old hag's crazy. At least she gave us some clue to what's going on."

"Mm."

"Why, you have another theory?"

He shrugs. "In my pantheon, we also have an aegis-shield. Their mythical properties are well-known, after all. To protect a god from all attacks?

To never falter, and enhance the god's powers if need be?" He shakes his head. "I remember Loki telling me about ours. The last time the dwarf Fafnir bore an aegis-helm on his forehead, he was sought out and killed for it. Of course, he'd used his dragon form to piss off quite a few strong personalities, so the man who killed him—Sigurðr—had no choice but to do so."

"And…?" He stops, tosses me a surprised glance over his shoulder. I shrug. "I'm guessing there's more to the story. The Norse pantheon doesn't just pick a fight for no reason."

Fenrir seems to realize I'm the one with the map, as he takes a step back and gestures for me to continue leading the way. After a quick glance at the map, I adjust our course.

A beat later, he continues, "This particular aegis wasn't the one we seek now. But there seems to be a form of it in every pantheon, to some extent. And it always causes problems to its owner. For the Egyptians, Bastet carried hers—a small, bronze amulet with her image as the goddess etched on it—on her person, as a symbol of her divinity. Some say her sister, Sekhmet, carried it. At some point, it made its way into the hands of a prominent pharaoh, who gifted it to his wife. And she to her daughter, and so on…" He kneels on the ground, glances at a frozen leaf with interest, then stands once more. "Mortal mythology books may not have *all* the answers, but they have some."

"You're saying some people see more than just some shield—or whatever form it takes—in this thing?"

When he doesn't immediately answer, I pause again. He hesitates a beat, then nods.

A sigh escapes me. "If that's the case, it makes figuring out what Olga wants with Athena's aegis even more important."

"Perhaps she needs it to protect herself."

"From what? That vampire creature?"

Fenrir simply gives me a look.

I'm about to argue some more, but when I turn and take my next step, the air ripples. And then we're no longer in the same woods. The air is lighter, the mist is gone, and the trees are…straight, reaching for the sky, their foliage bright. The heaviness of the Hoia-Baciu woods simply vanished.

"That witch and her tricks," I mutter, slowly turning to take in our surroundings.

Fenrir's quiet. Whatever seems to have given him some fuel, is now gone, and he's reverted back into silence. I glance at the map, noticing we're all of a sudden much, much closer—a third of the way there.

I get back to moving. After a beat, the crunching of leaves tells me Fenrir has followed.

"There's one thing I don't understand," I end up saying. "Why won't you go back even to your own kin? You're so eager to give in to Olympus, but we both know you didn't really try using your divine powers. You probably could vanish, and I'd be hard pressed to come get you from Asgard."

When he says nothing after a few moments, I pause again. Glance over my shoulder. He's a few feet away, the most peculiar expression on his features.

**Fenrir**

"What does it matter?" When she doesn't answer, I jerk my chin at the map. "Let's just move. The sooner we get this over with, the better."

"But, why?"

I shake my head at her. She won't budge off the topic, and I'm annoyed as hell. I stomp over to her and try to reach for the map, but she only pulls it out of my reach. The movement makes me go off balance, tipping into her. My breath gets caught in my throat. Our gazes catch and hold, emerald fire in hers.

A shot of something goes straight to my groin, and I step back as if I've been scorched. Already, I can see Artemis shifting gears, preparing to bring up last night. *Distract her. Fast.*

"Because there's no point, all right?" I end up

saying. "I wouldn't be welcome with open arms. Not after what I did, how I left."

She frowns, and I can practically see her other train of thought disintegrate. "Fenrir, it's your pantheon. Not all of them will agree with whatever lies your father spread. Or even any lies Odin might've spread."

I snort. "Why wouldn't they?" When all I get is a blank look, I sigh. "What do you know of Ragnarök, Artemis?"

"That it's meant to be the end of the world, or at least of Asgard, as prophesized by your witches."

I nod. "Right. Do you know the specifics?" She shakes her head. "I'm to bring it about. My birth was what sealed Ragnarök into existence, turned it from mere potential to certainty. And I was—am—at its center. I'm to devour the sun, bring eternal darkness, and kill my grandfather, Odin, in my wolf form. I was never more than a menace, to any of them." I wait a beat. "Now, do you understand? None of them give a flying fuck about me, and they never will. Believing I'm responsible for the worst of the worst comes second nature to them. As does blaming me for shit they can't explain clearly. Hell, they're probably happy I disappeared."

"I—" She purses her lips. "But even so."

"Even so?"

Her eyes glitter. "Yes, *even so*. They are still your

pantheon. They can distrust you as much as they want when it comes to affairs of Asgard, but they should still be there to protect you against other pantheons."

A short laugh escapes me. "Oh, is that all?"

"Yes."

"And you'd expect Zeus and the others to do the same for you?"

"Unequivocally."

I scowl. Her assurance that they would is even more of a stab to my gut. But, it's not like this is news. I've always felt alone, and today's no different. "Well, sorry to destroy your fairy-tale picture of the world, but not all pantheons work that way. And like it or not, mine is well acquainted with betrayal and despair. Hell, they feed on it. Fighting for the strong—like Thor—comes naturally to them. Fighting for someone like me, an outcast? Less so." I gesture at the map. "I've answered your question, Artemis. Can we get on with this pointless quest already?"

She marches to me, shoving against my chest. "It's not *pointless*! I'm trying to save your damn idiotic ass, can't you see?"

"And I didn't ask you to!" I roar. "You tracked me here so I can meet my punishment. Do your fucking job!"

I've felt the darkness at bay since last night. But now? Now, it's a force of its own, demanding I give in. Pressing at my head. I hiss, turning away from Artemis. A buzz, like a bee swarm, starts in one ear, moves to the next. Before I know it, I'm disoriented.

It rises within me, a snake ready to strike. A taint, on my very soul. A darkness that obliterates my will, my control, my...everything.

"Fenrir!"

I whirl on Artemis. Her wide eyes clue me in that something's wrong. Something worse than the darkness demanding my submission. This is an entity I can't deny, because it's my beast, dug into every fiber of my being.

Claws push past my fingers, dislodging the nails. The fur, breaking skin. The transformation's upon me, and I can do nothing to stop it.

"Artemis...run."

She takes a step toward me, hand reaching—

"RUN!"

She stops at my bellow. I drop to the ground, in a vain effort to hold on to my wolf. It's no use... Not this time. It's like he's angry at having been suppressed before, with Loki in the woods. And this time, he's out for blood.

Doesn't help that our argument had me thinking of home, of what's expected of me, and brought him to the forefront of my mind. And that he's always, *always* been the strongest of us whenever I've been in danger.

My spine snaps. I scream. Fire rings down my body. The fingers digging into the earth break, one by one. Each snap is sickening, turning my stomach. But I don't get a chance to throw up.

No, my wolf's already clawing his way out of me, shedding my human skin, which disintegrates the moment it touches the ground. And then he's running, running, running. Paws pounding the ground. I'm relegated to the background, a mere passenger in what used to be my body.

And with each meter he crosses, Artemis' scent becomes stronger. And stronger. And stronger.

*Run, Artemis, fucking RUN!*

She can't use a portal to get the hell out of here—away from me—which makes it all the harder for her to escape.

Satisfaction courses through my wolf. He's enjoying this a little too much. We run through trees, up small indents of hills, hop over fallen logs. Everything is vibrant, freeing. In some ways, I missed this. In others...I dreaded it. Knowing that when it happened, it would bring about more hurt. More pain.

A memory slides through. It takes me a moment to realize my beast is pushing it toward me.

*We're running, running, running. Large mountains tipped with snow surround us. Except, the snow is...pink? No, it's not pink. The color reflects the sky, and the beautiful sunset—a myriad of rainbow colors in shades of pinks and violets and burgundy. The ground underneath me isn't ground, not really. It's too fine.*

*Sand. We're running on sand. And that's sand dunes all around us, not mountains.*

*My beast tosses its head back and howls, long and loud. When he stops, an answering howl comes. We pause, panting. The air is growing cooler, but the sand under our paws is hot. And in the distance, on a dune, a black animal pops. Its ears are thin, larger than ours. It takes me a moment to find the word—jackal.*

*Anubis?*

*I'm in the Egyptian pantheon!*

*And then we're running again. Only this time, the jackal gives chase. In the distance, a portal opens. And through it we go….and away.*

I come to. We're still chasing Artemis' scent. *Stop, please,* I beg the beast.

*She hurt you.*

*No, she didn't. We were arguing—*

He shoves another memory at me. I try to resist it, but I can't. And this time, it's less pleasant.

*"Fenrir!"*

*I turn my gaze from the beautiful valley beneath me, to my father. He's looking mighty pleased with himself.*

*The man by his side smirks. "You sure your boy can do this?"*

*"Yes, he can." Loki's eyes glint maliciously. "If he*

*gets his focus back on track like we discussed."*

*The man passes him a small bag. Loki looks inside—
a light emerges. He's grinning like a maniac when he
closes the bag, and the light disappears.*

*Then Loki says to me, "Go on, son. Morph."*

*So, I do. When I'm fully wolf, I follow the man down
and into the valley. He runs like the wind. We get to a
castle shortly after, and he shows me a picture of something. An object, fuzzy to my memory. Then he points inside. I nod and dash forward, seeking whatever he'd meant
for me to get.*

With all my might, I force myself out of the
memory. *I don't want to see more of the quests Father
made us do, all for his little machinations. Enough.*

*For now…* the beast says. *You need to remember
the pain. Remember why we try not to trust.*

Then he catches Artemis' scent again. We're too
close. Before I can even try to rein him in, to take control again, we emerge out of a cluster of trees. Artemis is standing in the middle, bow and arrow
pointed at us. My wolf growls, snarls, snaps his jaws
toward her.

*Shoot me,* I try to tell her, knowing full well she
can't hear me.

"I don't want to do this, Fenrir," Artemis says.
"Please, change back."

I couldn't even if I wanted to. Only one of us can
exist at a time in this body, and when he takes over,

I'm relegated to the back until he sleeps. Which is usually after a hunt. Such is my curse.

My wolf's body grows taut—he's ready to jump. Artemis seems to realize the same thing, as she adjusts her stance, firing the arrow. It misses.

*She's had the bow with her for too long, it never recharged in the ether. Her aim is no longer spot-on.*

Surprise fills her eyes at the same realization, then she adjusts once again, preparing another arrow.

But already, we're moving. My beast lunges in the air, and only some sixth sense saves her. She drops to the ground, and my claws rake her left upper shoulder only.

The smell of blood fills the air. Artemis hisses, moans low at the pain, then grits her teeth. I can pick up on the smallest noise she makes.

She stands once more, the bow aimed at us. Shoots.

The arrow misses again.

"Dammit!"

My wolf zig-zags, coming at her again. And this time, she doesn't see us coming. Not until we're on top of her.

**Artemis**

The wolf smacks into me, and we roll onto the ground.

My bow flies out of my reach, as does my quiver of arrows.

I'd always thought wolves were adorable, from a distance. Many times, I'd loved seeing little pups play with their parents.

But this beast, up close, is anything but cute. Three times my size, he's filled in the chest, which only serves to show him as bulkier than he is. His massive jaws are open, canines ready to sink into me. His paws, one on each of my shoulders, are easily five times the size of my hands.

And his eyes—gone is the warm, dark hue, replaced by a deep red, the color of blood. The color of *rage*.

I'd known when I missed the second time that it would cost me, but I didn't realize how open I'd made myself. Gaping jaws hover over me, and his sheer bulk pressing me into the earth, trapping me. I can't budge him. Not unless I use divine energy to throw him off me, which would only bring about those damned creatures again.

Fenrir's wolf self is a thing to fear, that much is certain. I've seen my share of monsters, but underneath all that, he's still the man who'd kissed me, who'd melted me last night.

And I want that man back!

I pull my legs to my chest, using them to shove at the wolf's chest, but it makes no difference. He's too strong. And those spine-chilling canines inch closer.

I cast about for anything I can use, anything within reach. And then I see it. An arrow, a few inches next to my right hand. If I could just reach it, distract him with a flesh wound, it might buy me time.

But the snarling teeth come closer still. His weight presses down more on me. It's almost like he's enjoying the anticipation of the feast I'll become.

With a groan of pain—pushing against his weight is no small feat—I reach the arrow. Then I angle it just right, stabbing him—not center-chest, as I should've, but to the side. Enough to distract him.

Fenrir whines, growls, then howls. He moves off me, pawing the ground.

"I know," I cry. "I'm sorry! I had no choice." Taking a deep breath, I press my free hand into my bleeding shoulder from his earlier attack. "Come back for me. Please."

The wolf meets my gaze. All red irises, no feeling. I can practically sense his wrath filling the air. But then the red flickers, replaced by dark blue. And then red again.

Fenrir. He's trying to fight back.

*Quick. What can get through to him?*

I think back to last night. "I want to kiss you again. Fenrir, remember the feel of me in your arms. Please. I can't have been the only one that kiss affected such." A short laugh escapes me. "You were right. My reputation's full of shit. But I can tell you one truth—I've never ached so much for anyone. In all my eons of existence, nothing has been so…"

The irises change. The wolf opens his mouth. And the growl that comes out turns into a single word. "…per...fe…ct."

I gasp. But then the wolf falls to the ground, howling as though in excruciating pain. A gash cuts into his belly, like from an invisible sword. I open my mouth in horror—but it's only Fenrir. He emerges from the now-dead wolf. The moment he's fully out, bloody and naked, the wolf disintegrates. A faint light covers Fenrir, then leaves him clean and dressed on the ground.

I rush to him. He's panting so hard, I'm half-worried he'll cough up a lung. "Are you okay?"

He shakes his head. "Thank you…for getting me back. He never…lets me…regain control. Until it's too late."

I rub his back in soothing circles, relief spreading through me. Fenrir looks up then, and he's so close. I couldn't hold back if I tried. I press my lips against his, enjoying the taste of him—the feel of the man under my hands.

He lets the kiss go for a moment, then pulls away, avoiding my gaze.

"Is this why you don't want to return?" I ask. "Because you have no control over your wolf?" When he doesn't answer, I rush on, "It's all right, Fenrir. I can help. If this is your fear, I can show you—"

He finally meets my gaze. "I've never been able to fight my wolf's hold. Until now. You've given me something worth fighting for." He takes another breath. "But no, it's not just that I have no control over my wolf, huntress. It's that someone else controls him."

"Who—" Then it dawns on me. "You mean whoever controls you. He has access to *both* sides of you…" Horror fills me, and I bring my hand to my mouth. "Which means he could use you to bring about whatever he sees fit. Ragnarök. Or the destruction of any other pantheon…including Olympus."

Fenrir only nods.

I force his chin up, meeting his gaze. "You're missing one thing. You told me you never attacked Hades, and it took me a while to believe you. Now I understand why. Even when I came to terms with the fact that someone is inside you, I always thought they didn't control your wolf. That they'd controlled you and forced you to shift, knowing the wolf would do whatever it wanted. But if *you* cannot control your wolf, and this god can…"

Before I can say anything else, a shadow covers us. And another. I look up, into the largest, whitest wings I've seen. At first, I fear it's the creatures. But nope. It's—

"Fuck," Fenrir groans. "The Valkyries found us."

# CHAPTER 13

**Fenrir**

They descend upon us in perfect formation. Nine Valkyries, guardians of the Norse gods. Blonde hair in a tight braid, either pinned on their head or swinging in the wind. Steel-colored armor covering their torso and top right shoulder. Blades in their hands. And beneath them, the sturdy steeds.

In their midst, another rider pops out. A tenth person. One whose hammer immediately clues me in to their identity, despite the distance—my uncle, Thor.

"Artemis, go!"

She throws me a look like I'm crazy. "I'm not going anywhere."

"If you fight against them—"

"I know. Let us both be guilty, then. See what they make of it."

She pulls up her bow, notching an arrow into it. I've barely had enough time to recover from the shift, from being back in my body, and the Valkyries are closer than ever. I bend low at the knees, then jump as high as I can go—which isn't much, without my divine powers. But with the Valkyries' descending momentum, it's enough.

I latch on to the reins underneath the closest horse, using the extra momentum to swing and come up behind the Valkyrie. Steely eyes meet mine over her shoulder, then she tries to elbow me in the gut. I avoid the shot, nearly tossing myself off the horse in the process.

Then I reach for her blade, battling with her. Fortunately for me, Valkyries never liked me. They hated my existence since my early youth because of the danger I posed. Which means whenever Loki embroiled me in one of his schemes, I got a lot of practice fighting them, and learning their maneuvers.

In eons of being away from home, those maneuvers haven't changed much.

And yes, it gives me a perverse kind of pleasure to best the Valkyrie, take her sword, and hop off the horse, back onto the ground. *At least now I'm armed.*

Artemis' arrows fly around me, striking their

targets—unlike with my wolf. Horses whine in pain, though I can tell from the angle of the arrows that she's given them flesh wounds only. Wounds the Valkyries will easily be able to heal.

Doesn't mean it makes the Amazonian warriors any less angry toward me.

Three land, hop off their respective horses and charge at me. I pull the blade up, weighing it, getting used to its weight again. Not that I have much time... I scan the skies again, but Thor seems to have disappeared. Unless I dreamt him, like I did my father?

I shake my head. *No time for this shit.*

The first Valkyrie strikes, and I par her attack just in time. Then push back, kick at her leg, and duck under her arm. Use the momentum to grip her blade arm, twist it—getting rid of the weapon. Toss her into her companion.

I whirl to the third Valkyrie in time to stop her blade from embedding into my stomach. The angle I'm holding mine at is weird, and pain reverberates up my arm. I look into the Valkyrie's eyes, but all I read is contempt.

A whoosh splits the air, then a knife embeds itself into the Valkyrie's forearm. She cries out in pain, dropping her blade. I catch it with my foot, kicking it up and into my free hand. Turn to Artemis, and toss it at her. Only then do I notice the knife had come from her.

She nods, gripping the blade, and leaving the knives. Then she faces off against her own duo of Valkyries.

Movement out of the corner of my eye shows the three I'd dealt with recovering. The other four keep circling above us. And once more, I see another rider in their midst. This time, he's close enough to the ground that I can make out his determined posture.

*What the hell are they waiting for?*

Doesn't matter. Whatever it is, I need to put an end to it.

*Use your powers. Call the dark creatures to you.*

That *would* be easy. But also counterintuitive.

*Pitch them against each other. Watch chaos unfold.*

I can't. No matter what the voice suggests—what *he* wants to make happen—I can't give in.

But then the earth shakes—Thor has landed.

I turn, slowly, gripping the blade tighter in my hand. "Hello, Uncle."

His expression is—what else?—thunderous. I'm told him and Zeus don't get along for a reason. "Fenrir, it's time to stop the foolishness and return home. To Asgard."

"For what purpose, exactly?"

He scowls. "You know what purpose."

"Ah." I touch the blade, fingering it. Behind me, the sound of the fight continues, and I know Artemis won't last long. She's powerful, yes, but I've muzzled her with the same weakness as me—holding back on her divine powers. These people, though, won't.

*Perhaps it's time to switch things up, after all.* I look up at Thor. "Imprisonment, then?"

"I wish it were different."

"No, you really don't." Over my shoulder, I yell, "Forget about the limitations. Just use whatever you've got!"

Artemis' startled gaze flies to mine. "Fenrir—"

"Just do it!" I refuse to be imprisoned again. At least, by my kin. I'll gladly take Olympus' punishment, because at least I'll have one person willing to hear my side of the story. Maybe two, with Hades.

Then I crouch lower, raising my blade. "Come then, Uncle. Let's see who will win."

Thor swings his hammer, then charges at me. He's twice my bulk, at ease with his inner divine strength. He's fought more wars. He's had more training. And he has a way better weapon. His hammer—glinting with symbols and vibrating with power—twists the fabric of the air itself. Its power shifts the air around me, pushing me backward before he's even halfway to me.

Thor jumps. I grip the handle of my sword tighter, only this time, I empty my mind. Trying to ignore the darkness, I focus on what's hidden deep inside me. What I haven't touched in eons, since I landed on this realm. My divine energy.

*You can have so much more,* darkness whispers cajolingly.

In the corners of my mind, the shadows inch closer, attracted by the energy within me, wanting it…

*NO!* I yell mentally, and focus on the well of power within me. It answers like a rubber band that's been stretched too much. Surges to the surface, releasing into my hands, and the blade.

A burst of light escapes me, hitting Thor full-force. He flies backward into the nearest tree, crumpling it to dust.

"Lucky shot." Thor rises, shaking himself. His eyes flash. "You won't get another."

The remaining four Valkyries from the sky descend, encasing me in a square. I'm surrounded at all corners, Thor marching toward me.

And then the screeches come. First one, followed by another.

*Didn't take them long.*

My gaze meets Artemis' across the distance. As the Valkyries stare, eyes narrowed, at the skies, I run to her.

"What did you do?" she asks, searching my features.

I shake my head. "What needed to be done."

I'd hoped to use the creatures as a diversion for us to escape. Sadly, what follows next is full-on pandemonium. They descend upon the Valkyries with their dark riders, and both sides engage. Thor glances at me, at the creatures, then back at me. I don't know if he realizes the link between my burst of power and them, or if he's simply picking up on the fact that the riders seem determined to get to me.

Whatever it is, he roars to the closest Valkyrie, "Secure Fenrir! Then we leave."

"Like hell," I mutter.

Two of the Valkyries come at me and Artemis, and we engage them one on one. Another separates from the group with the creatures, while yet another is sporting a wound. The smell of blood and something else, something nauseating, fills the air.

But I have bigger problems than that. Namely, the dark rider who escaped the group and is headed for me.

Thor steps in front of him. "Who are you?"

The man—thing—swipes at him with a blade. Thor delivers a punch that sends him flying. Then he turns to me.

"What is the meaning of this? Did you call these things forth?"

I know it's futile, but I still try. "What you've come here to get me for, I never did it."

Thor's bushy eyebrows connect, then release. "We can talk about this back home. In Asgard."

"No!"

I take a step backward, then another. Realize Artemis isn't with me.

I smell her blood first. Then hear her scream. Fearing the worst—that a creature got to her—I turn. Artemis stumbles, but it's not from a creature's attack. Rather, a Valkyrie's blade nicked her shoulder—or so I think. Then Artemis moves, swaying, and I see the glint of steel out of her back.

A moment of silence lengthens and we stare at each other. Then a roar unlike anything I've ever produced erupts out of me.

Thor takes a step toward me, stops. Sees what has my attention. His eyes flash a warning. "Fenrir, hold on—"

"*NO.*" My voice is throaty, guttural, monstruous. I take a deep breath, but not even that is enough to calm me.

In a flash, I'm by Artemis' side. She stumbles into me, eyes fluttering shut. The smell of her blood surrounds me, permeating every molecule of air.

With slow movements, I pull the blade out of her shoulder, wincing at the blood. Leave it to a Valkyrie's blade to deliver maximum damage on a god of another pantheon. Loki did always warn me away from other gods' weapons.

The fight goes on around us, Valkyries against creatures. Thor's yelling something—all I can hear are muted sounds. All I can focus on is how Artemis doesn't stir.

Ice fills my veins, soon turning to fire. An anguish builds in the pit of my stomach, roaring through me, then flaring out to uncontrollable heights.

Hands shaking, I set Artemis by a tree and face my brethren. Crack my neck. My muscles. The Valkyries close to me sense the change in the air, and Thor takes another step forward. Says something else. I'm beyond listening.

This time, I'm the one who calls forth the wolf. *I will release you, but I maintain control. I need to feel what happens.*

There's a long silence, and for the first time in eons, he speaks to me. *I protect you. I am your darker self, your beast—your protector. Blame me, hate me, but do not ignore me anymore. We are one.*

*I wish to ignore you no longer.*

He says nothing else. Instead, within moments, I've shed my human skin, and become the wolf, grown in size. My rage seems to have fueled me. And when we attack, we hold nothing back.

Snaps of our jaws rip a Valkyrie apart. Another's blade tries to swipe at us, but we keep going. One more dead. And another. A dark rider next. The creatures back away, then fly up in the air, hesitating. Without a rider, they're unsure what to do. I roar, once, and they disappear.

Thor throws his hammer at us. It hits our head, and reverberates. But it's not enough to stop us.

The last remaining Valkyries have already rallied around Thor, their mounts casting nervous glances at us. Our breathing is out of control.

"Fenrir, this has to stop," Thor says. "Come home with us. Answer for what you've done, take the stain away from our reputation, and perhaps we can find a solution."

Our voice is a roar. "What I've done?"

"Hades wants your head for attacking him."

"*I didn't do it.*"

"Much as I'd like to believe that, your record speaks against you."

I scowl at him. "And if I return? Loki will only shut me up again."

Thor frowns. "Your father—"

"Is a trickster god. And he's enjoying this shit a little too much. Aren't you, Father?"

Sure enough, he pops out. Thor takes him in, his expression a thunderstorm. I guess Loki wasn't supposed to have followed him to this realm. But when has the master of trickery and mischief ever listened to anyone besides himself?

Loki smirks. "Very well, son. Here I am, unmasked. So. Does this mean you'll come, like a good little puppy?"

"No."

"Too bad."

He takes a step to the side, making way for Thor

and the remaining Valkyries. They attack. And though they come at me, I sense the quiet descending on me. An almost haze.

*Let me help*, my wolf pleads.

I look at Artemis, at the advancing mini-army… If I want us to survive this, do I really have a choice? Divine energy can get me partway there, but every second I use it is a risk that *he* will take over me. Or…I can allow my beast, the one who got me through eons of solitude, out. Stop muzzling him.

I close my eyes, inhaling, then open them. *Do not harm them. And Artemis—do not touch her.*

*As you wish.*

Then the presence in my mind—the *good* one, the beast—pushes forth, taking over our body, over our power. No longer leashed, no longer held back, he straightens. And, as promised, I'm surprised to find out he hasn't shoved me to the back of our consciousness. Instead, I'm right there, next to him, with every movement.

A *whoosh* fills the air—a Valkyrie's blade, headed for me. I stop it with my paws. She gasps in shock. I use the butt of the weapon to hit her. And do the same with others, each strike fluid, fast, but not overtly damaging. Until Thor and I come face to face. Father disappeared—unsurprisingly.

In one hand, Thor holds his hammer. In the other, his sword. "Do not test me, Fenrir. You will not win this."

"Perhaps I may surprise you yet."

Then I launch myself at him. The blade breaks into my flank, as I'd expected. But my momentum helps me. Thor loses his balance, and I'm able to roll, dislodging the blade onto a branch.

I face him again. Behind me, the air shimmers. Loki's blast of power catches me, but not unaware. I snarl at him, releasing a gust of wind through my jaws.

Loki's pushed back. It won't hold him off—nothing will—but it's enough.

*Let me in*, an insidious voice whispers in my mind.

My massive body shudders with the force it takes to push him—the thing controlling me—back. To draw up my mental barriers and refuse to allow him access.

The effort leaves me panting. Then the air reverberates again, drawing my focus. Thor's swinging his hammer. Only this time, when he tosses it, I catch it in my jaws.

They stare at me—Valkyries, my father and my uncle—and the weight of their surprise is heavy on me. I laugh, low and unlike myself. And then I swing my jaw up and down, up and down, gaining momentum… On the fourth swing, I let the hammer go, and it hits the ground.

A cloud of dust rises, hiding me. Before it has time to dissipate, I run to Artemis, take her in my jaws gently, and run, run, run.

# CHAPTER 14

**Artemis**

I wake up in a cave, my shoulder—hell, my entire body—throbbing. It's dark, though the faint light of the sun tells we're nearing sunrise. Confusion sets in more, my mind like a fog. I'm not used to this. Gods can be weakened, yes, usually by other pantheons' weapons, but I've never been put in such a situation directly.

We'd been in the woods. The wings…

*The Valkyries!* I'd been fighting them. How did I get here? Did they—

"Fenrir?"

I jerk up even more, a hiss escaping me at the

throbbing in my shoulder. All thoughts of pain disappear when chains rattle somewhere behind me, in the gloomy darkness.

"Here." The deadpan voice is hard to miss.

I push up a little more, wincing, then give up. Grit my teeth and crawl around, adopting a seated position once more.

It takes a moment for my eyes to get used to the darkness. All I can make out is a shape. And that incessant rattling… "Fenrir?"

When he doesn't answer, I reach for my bow. An arrow flames at my touch, illuminating the cave. And then I remember the creatures and not wanting to attract them. *Shit.* But my attention is soon on something way more important.

A gasp escapes me. Fenrir's covered in cuts and bruises, curled up on the floor, leaning against the cavern's wall. His shirt is ripped in a few spots, and I can see cuts and stab wounds healing. His cheek is equally bloody, though I have a feeling it's more someone else's blood. And the look in his eyes…is so filled with agony, with pain and regret, it tears me up inside.

"What happened? Where are we?"

"The Valkyries are gone, you shouldn't worry."

"That's not what I asked."

He looks down, his jaw clenching, and says nothing. Wincing some more, I push up. The ache in my thighs intensifies, but I manage to use the wall as support, and walk to him. Crouch by his side. "Why are you chained up?"

He says nothing. A muscle ticks in his jaw.

"Tell me, dammit!"

At last, he looks up. His tone—his gaze—even deader than before. "I did what I've tried hard not to do. Gave in to the beast."

It takes me a moment to realize what he means. "You…attacked your own kin? To defend me?"

"I wasn't about to let what they did to you slide."

"But—" I stop myself, finally seeing what he's telling me. Realizing the extent of his sacrifice. Not only did he go against his own pantheon, which is a crime no matter which way you look at it. But he also allowed his wolf out again. The same wolf who'd tried to hurt me before, but ended up protecting me now. *I was right, to trust that the man inside the beast would win.*

I sit back on my heels, stunned as I finally grasp what he was trying to tell me before. "You've carried this alone. All this time, this is why you didn't want to go back home. Not just because of the darkness—that *dick*—pushing you to attack Hades. Not just because of what you carried within you, either. But because you knew the Norse pantheon would not believe you." A knot forms in my throat, thickening my next words. "You shouldered this burden alone, for how long? Without help, without telling—anyone?"

A derisive laugh escapes him. "Who would I have told? Oh, don't get me wrong. Over the centuries, I tried many a witch, until I gave up. Many took my money, my favors, but had little help to actually give me."

I reach for him. For a moment, I'm afraid he'll flinch away from my touch. But instead, he leans into it like a cat who's been starved for attention, deprived of love.

"You shouldn't have to deal with this on your own, Fenrir. That's what your pantheon is there for. They're your family."

"We aren't like you Olympians. Our bond is one of duty, not camaraderie. As evidenced by my very uncle trying to bring me in."

I shake my head.

He pulls away from my touch. "We should go back to Olympus."

"What?"

"It's what you came here for—to capture me and have me face justice, once and for all."

True. But things have changed. And while I might be a little slow on the uptake, I won't go against what my instincts are telling me now. Which is that bringing Fenrir in without some answers will only work against him.

In an effort to buy time, I say, "We can't, we already tried opening the portal."

Fenrir meets my gaze. "It seems whatever blocks you doesn't block me. I was able to heal you a little—I'm sorry if it's not properly done, I'm not very experienced with that—and open a portal to get us here. The beasts haven't followed yet, I don't know why. But I can use the same power and bring you home…to Olympus."

He lowers his gaze again, then leans his head against the wall with a sigh. For long moments, he says nothing, and only our breathing fills the air. His, more laborious.

"Why didn't you heal yourself?" I whisper.

"Not important. And I didn't want to put you in danger again. It's a miracle the creatures haven't yet come here, given I also used a small burst of energy to chain myself up."

I want to remind him that we're in this together, that his well-being is equally important, but the words die on my lips. I stare at him for a long time, eventually saying, "Tell me about this darkness. Not the wolf, taking over. But when *he* tries. How does it work?"

"Why?"

I move closer, resting my hand on his knee. "Because you've never been able to tell anyone, and you need to. Also, knowing the triggers will help me avoid feeding it. I'd rather keep *you* in your body, not that…thing."

A shudder runs through him. And a wave of sadness washes over me at the same time. All this time, I've seen him as another mission, another task, another inconvenience. But if there's any inconvenience with Fenrir, it's that he feels too much. Impossibly so, for a god who's meant to be from a pantheon ruled by duty.

"It comes upon me," Fenrir finally says. "I don't… I'm not even sure what triggers it, other than me using my divine powers." He hesitates, thinking it over, then shrugs. "Anger, I suppose. Deep emotions." He shakes his head. "It drives me to madness. Takes over everything. My will, my powers, my mind."

"What does it seek?"

"Always to use me as a weapon. Against my own kin, or anyone else. The only way to keep it at bay is to starve it. And even then, I hear his voice, calling."

His words bring back to mind that night, in Olga's cabin. And from one moment to the next, I'm intensely aware of how close we are. How if I were to lean just so, I could brush my lips against him. The intensity of that yearning scares me, and I force myself to lean back a little. Then turn my thoughts away from that night, and onto what Fenrir said.

I've been hunting him for so long, I never stopped to consider his side of the story. Or would have, ever. But he saved me. He stood up against his own kin for me. That earns him a measure of trust, of respect. So without overthinking it for once, I lift the arrow keeping us in the light and touch it to his chains. They break free, releasing him.

"What—"

"We're not going to Olympus. We're going on this witch's quest, and once we get more information, we can return to Olympus *with proof*. To do so now would be suicide for you, and I can't allow that." I narrow my eyes on him. "And you don't need to keep yourself chained up around me, you're not a dog."

"I could have hurt you, that night—"

I step right up in his face now, showing him how unafraid I am. My heart pounds in my chest at the proximity, and I'm eerily aware of the coiled tension in his body. But for a completely different reason than fear. "You wouldn't have. I know it, the same way I know we need to do this."

He stares at me for a long moment, a mix of awe and gratitude shining in the depths of his eyes. The fact he's never had this understanding from his own pantheon is…unthinkable. Or perhaps it's simply that I was lucky.

*Though how lucky have I been, really, when my own*

*father sees me as a tool to be used? When my own worth relies in what I can achieve for him?* I shove the thought away.

"You don't owe me anything, you know," Fenrir finally says. And it takes everything in me not to reach up and kiss him.

"I know. But you could've left me, not dug yourself deeper into trouble." I move closer, touching his shoulder. Trying to ignore the butterflies in my stomach when he stares at me in that way. "And I will give you the same measure of trust, of courtesy. Now, let's go find ourselves a shield."

**Fenrir**

I blindly follow Artemis as we descend from the cave I'd found for shelter, and return to the trail indicated by the map. Apparently, even in the throes of a fight, I'd portalled us closer to the aegis we're seeking.

But that's not even what's in my mind. Rather, Artemis' kindness is. It took me experiencing this to realize how little of it—kindness—I've had in my life. And how I have no idea what to do with it, now that it's been given to me.

My father only ever saw me as a tool. My pantheon as something to fear. Every connection I've made since settling down on Midgard was short-lived and superficial. And the connection to the deepest part of me, my beast—my wolf—was buried for the longest time.

Now, I feel him humming under the surface. Not fighting me, or pushing me, just powering me. If I'd let him, I have no doubt he would be completing my aura in much the same way Artemis' weapons complete hers.

But it feels too soon, too raw. *I need time*, I whisper in my mind.

He rumbles, then gives a deep sigh of acceptance. And the warmth in my chest increases. Perhaps Artemis' kindness isn't the only one I'm worthy of.

After two hours of walking, Artemis stops, signaling for me to be careful. I come up behind her, finding a mother doe and her baby calf eating grass peacefully a few meters from us.

"I normally hunt them, taking care to respect their sacrifice. But...I can't bring myself to." Her voice is barely a whisper.

I'm so close to her, her scent drifts to my nose. The wind tugs on her curls, making them fly in my face. And then she turns to me, green eyes sparkling. "They're so innocent, aren't they?"

I nod, my eyes flickering to them as I try—hard—to hold back from kissing her. The light of her soul, of her kindness, surrounds her even as darkness weighs me down. Yet, that same brightness in her suffuses my being, and I could've sworn it also lights me up from within, for a brief moment. It's enough.

After a beat, it seems the doe senses our presence, as she nudges her calf along, and they disappear into some bushes. Artemis relaxes her posture, then looks at the map again. "We're close by." She points in the opposite way they left. "Another bit that way."

I scan the skies, dreading something will appear before we get there. But, there's nothing. And for the first time, I feel like we've actually got a chance of finding this aegis and returning safely from the quest.

So I follow in Artemis' footsteps once more, lost in my thoughts. Only stop when I bump into her. My gaze goes up, and up.

An old willow tree fills the new clearing we entered. The air crackles with its energy, drawing me in.

"The shield is within it," Artemis says.

"How do you know?"

"Because Athena loves willows."

We move closer to the tree. Artemis goes to touch it. My warning dies on my lips, as the moment her fingertips reach the bark, she shimmers and disappears. I hurry and do the same. My body feels electrocuted, then I open my eyes, not believing what I'm seeing.

We're in an underground cavern of sorts. The walls glint of a whiteish light, and at first I think it's with precious stones. But, no. It's salt. We're in a salt mine.

My gaze is drawn to the middle of the cavern, and the shard of light that seems to glint on the shield. It stands upright, a perfect golden circle, supported by nothing. A few steps closer, and I notice it's actually floating a small distance from the ground. A Gorgon's head—hideous features, snakes for hair—decorates it. With the way the light hits it, it almost seems…alive.

"It's exactly as in the picture," Artemis whispers. She takes a step toward it.

"No, wait." I grip her arm, tugging her back. "If there's a trick to this, let it be me who suffers."

She throws me an annoyed glance. "Don't you think you suffered enough?"

I ignore her, and move closer to the shield. Whatever happens, will happen. My pain is a small price to pay as repayment for her kindness.

After all, nothing should have led Artemis to trust me. On the contrary, I'm the last person she should have been embarking on this quest with. And yet, she did. And that does something to my heart—thaws the fortress of ice around it. I've been lying to myself saying that I'm ready to face the consequences of my actions. Because I'm not. Not if it means being parted from her light forever.

Matter of fact, I'm starting to wonder if I'll ever be ready to part from her light.

# CHAPTER 15

**Artemis**

My annoyance at Fenrir trying to protect me dissipates the moment he starts moving toward the shield. The way the light falls on it looks benevolent, but knowing Athena... I wouldn't be surprised if something *was* bound to happen. Which is why I'd wanted to be the one to get it.

Not like I can argue with a stubborn Norse god, though.

So all I can do is watch him, and hope. *Maybe because Odysseus is the one who hid it, Athena didn't get a chance to add some of her magic to it?* Yet, the subtle power filling the cave tells me otherwise. Odysseus might've hidden the aegis, but there's no way Athena didn't have a hand in this.

Fenrir's now within an arm's reach of it. The light from above—where the hell is it coming from, anyway?—seems to shine brighter, shimmering over him like a waterfall. The shield gleams. Is it me, or did the Gorgon's eyes shine?

"Fenrir, watch—"

Too late. His hand reaches the aegis, and for a moment there's only blissful silence. Then the ground vibrates, nearly knocking me off my feet.

"FENRIR!"

The Gorgon from the shield seems to come alive. The snakes—her hair—slither and hiss, coming off the shield. Fenrir only stares, frowning, at them. His features go from consternation to complete horror, as though he alone hears something. And then he backs away. And they strike.

It's so fast, there's nothing I can do. The snakes jump on him, straight for his face. Within seconds, they've got his entire head surrounded, and seem to be tightening around it. He tries to rip at them with his hands, but falls on his knees.

I raise my bow, notching an arrow automatically. But I can't shoot. I *won't* hurt him.

I take a few steps closer, then hesitate. One of the snakes turns to me, its eyes eerily stuck on me. "What fare you here, sister?"

*Athena.*

Relief spreads through me, and I allow myself to kneel. She's always been one for respect, and given she's the older sister... "Forgive me, sister. And do not harm him, please."

The snake slithers in the air, then detaches itself from Fenrir and comes toward me. And still, it speaks with Athena's voice. "This aegis is Odysseus'. Why have you come?"

"I need it."

The snake stares at me. Then, for a moment, the yellow eyes seem to turn gray, and I know I'm being assessed. Before that can be concluded, behind her, Fenrir screams.

"Release him, please," I beg Athena.

She doesn't get a chance to. Dark light escapes Fenrir, obscuring even the light shining on the shield. The snakes move off him, slithering and hissing away, as though afraid.

Only, the one in front of me doesn't move. It glances to Fenrir, then back at me. Its head bobs up and down in the air. "What have you brought here, sister?"

"I don't have time to explain. Trust that this is needed, and your aegis will not be used for nefarious purposes." At least, I hope it won't be.

The snake nods, then slithers away. Freeing the way, with one last comment. "Only you may touch it. Not *his* tainted hands, whoever he is."

I move to the shield, fast, before she can change her mind. Fenrir lifts his head, his eyes following my approach. The snakes have now returned to the shield, back to being ornaments.

Two-handed, I lift the aegis. Feel its power move through me, lighting up my entire being, healing every scrape, bruise and cut it touches. By the time I turn to Fenrir, he seems equally healed…by the light?

*No, it must be because he touched the aegis, even if only briefly.*

Fenrir stands, stumbling toward me. His gaze is still haunted, but also filled with hope. "We actually found it!" He stares in wonder at the shield in my hands, then at me. "You—"

Without another word, he pulls me into his arms. His hands cup my face, angling it. And then his mouth meets mine in the briefest of kisses. A caress, a whisper on the wind. But it's enough.

The flare is lit, and I move the shield out of the way, holding it by my side. Then I push against him, taking the sweet kiss and turning it to an inferno. Need courses through my veins, enhanced when his other hand shifts to my lower back, pressing me even closer.

It's a small touch, gentle but firm, yet it ignites my senses. The feel of his rough fingertips on my bare back is the sweetest of tortures. One I can't ignore any longer. I'd fooled myself into thinking it was just that old hag's tea, before.

It wasn't.

There's so much more between us, more than even that damned tea could have instigated. His tortured soul pulls at mine, ensnaring it, intertwining us together until I don't know where he ends and I begin.

Our tongues battle for dominance, neither letting up. Fire keeps coursing through my veins, demanding to be put out. But every touch, every sound, only inflames me further.

We emerge for air, staring at each other.

"We should—"

"I—"

We both stop. My eyes drop to Fenrir's mouth again, and he seems ready to say something. Then his body tenses, and he shoves me behind him.

I stumble, the shield nearly falling from my grip. I whirl on him, about to yell at him for once more playing the hot/cold game. But all protest dies on my lips when I see why he'd done what he did—a man steps from the shadows.

**Fenrir**

My fists clench, watching the intruder. He's dressed

all in black, almost as tall as me, but leaner. On his hip is a sword, its silver pommel glinting in the light.

My brain's still addled by my kiss with Artemis, still demanding I go back to finish what I started. My skin tingles with the anticipation, with the need to feel her pressed up against me. Nothing has felt so good, in all my eons of existence. So *mine.*

The beast inside me hums in agreement, but keeps quiet otherwise. At least until my gaze narrows on the newcomer. Then, the beast growls, low and deep in my chest. A sound only I must hear, but which is ever more potent.

"Who are you?" I bark at the intruder.

He says nothing, only advancing. His dark helm prevents me from seeing his features. But the way he turns toward Artemis tells me he's not here for me—he's here for the aegis.

"Are you with them?" I ask. "The creatures."

He still says nothing, advancing.

I clench my fists, stepping away from Artemis, and directly in his path. "You're not crossing any further."

Without turning to me, he unsheathes the sword. The *whoosh* of it fills the air, echoing throughout the cavern. I'd give anything to have my own weapon, but I'll have to make do without one.

"Fenrir…"

I glance at Artemis. She's holding out one of her

knives. It's not much, but it's better than nothing. I take it, holding it by the leather handle so the blade is parallel with my forearm. Tucking it away, as it were, so he won't see it coming. Surprise is my best weapon right now.

I face the man again. "I'll say it once more. Leave."

He finally deigns to turn his head toward me. "Give me what I seek, and I shall leave, Fenrir of the Norse pantheon."

So he knows who I am, and presumably, Artemis, too. Great.

The beast within me rumbles some more, growing ever more agitated.

Behind me, I feel Artemis freeze. Glance at her, but her expression tells me nothing. Is she afraid because he knows of us? Or is there something more going on?

I return my attention to him. Watch him as he moves closer. And closer. His grip on his sword is tight, the leather glove crinkling with the force he's applying.

When he's a mere foot away, I lunge. One movement, intending to bring the knife straight to his throat. But I miscalculate—or maybe he's better than me—and he sidesteps at the last moment. In slow-motion, I see his gaze behind the helm. Cold, lifeless.

I tuck and roll, avoiding the hit of his sword. It clashes with the ground, sparks flying everywhere.

Then he turns back to Artemis, advancing on her. And she's still frozen. Bow by her side, shield in her other hand, she seems unable to tear her eyes from him.

"Artemis, *move!*"

My shout seems to do the trick, as she blinks and backs away. But still, she doesn't bring up her bow. Nor notch an arrow.

The beast within gives me a nudge. It's enough. I push off the ground and, growling, run at the intruder from behind. I tackle him, though it feels like smacking straight into a solid boulder of ice. We both fall to the ground, rolling over. I knee him in the shin, ending up on top. Knife to his throat.

For a moment, everything stills. Then he *presses into* the knife, as though not afraid to die. The tip of it sinks into his neck. No blood flows. Nothing does, in fact.

"What the hell…"

Taking advantage of my surprise, he bucks his hips and throws me off, then jumps to his feet. Before I can move, he kicks me, in quick succession—once, twice, a couple more. The blows land against my abs, but still rattle my entire body. I hug my knees to my chest, coughing. Then crawl onto all fours, trying to regain control of myself.

The beast inside me is agitated, angry. *No. This is my fight,* I tell it. The last thing I need is to morph…again.

Out of the corner of my eye, I see the newcomer advancing on Artemis. And can do nothing to stop it.

## Artemis

The dark knight advances, and I'm unable to move. Immobilized. *Give me what I seek, and I shall.* That voice… *It can't be!*

But still he inches closer, closing the gap between us. And when he's a mere half foot away from me, he reaches for me. Leans in closer. I close my eyes, shivering, because it feels exactly like it used to. Even as he pries my fingers, one by one, off the aegis. There's no violence, no pain. Just determination. And then…he takes it.

I open my eyes. He's already walking away.

Fenrir gasps, looking up from the floor. "Dammit all to the hell!"

With a growl, he pushes off the ground, and then runs after the man.

"Fenrir, no!" But he's already gone.

I stare at my hand, still feeling that cool touch upon my fingers. Still shivering, I try to shake myself out my stupor. We need that damned shield, and we need it now. I just don't know if it's worth us getting into more trouble, especially when the rider looks like one who's attacked us before on those beasts.

*And that voice...*

Nonetheless, I take off after them. "Fenrir, wait!"

The cavernous corridor I enter is semi-lighted, and my bow and quiver bounce on my back as I run. I can't see either of them anymore. Will I emerge out of here in the same woods, or...?

I soon get my answer. Pass a shimmering curtain of something, and the moment after, I'm in the woods again. I turn in a circle, taking everything in—and see someone disappear behind a copse of trees.

I take off after them. The woods seem to close in on me as I give chase, and even my breathing becomes erratic.

*It can't be, it can't be, it can't be.*

Memories of a time long past run in my mind, clashing with others. My heart aches, physically, but still I run. And run. And run.

...and emerge into a clearing. Fenrir's panting, facing off against the dark knight. The latter's holding onto the shield with one hand, his sword with the other. My knife still glints out of Fenrir's hand.

And then he moves, rushing at the knight. He tosses the shield aside, engaging Fenrir's knife attack with the sword. They become intertwined. This time, I pull my arrow and bow, aiming. They're moving too fast though, and I can't find a proper aim.

*Dammit, Fenrir!* "Move out of my way, Fenrir!"

He ignores my shout, instead violently shoving the man apart from him. And then he jumps him again, diving low to the ground at the last moment and swiping his leg at the knight's knee.

The opening's too good to ignore. I take my shot, then. The arrow *whooshes* through the air, and embeds itself into the man's shoulder. He stops mid-strike—his sword frozen in the air—and looks up. The helm still hides his features, but I feel that gaze to the pit of my stomach.

And a dread unlike any other builds up my spine, more and more.

*I should've told Fenrir I saw him in the woods. I shouldn't have held back that part.*

Still, the knight has no other reaction. With his free hand, he reaches up and yanks the arrow out. No scream. No hiss. No groan of pain.

No blood on the arrow, either.

My arm lowers, and lowers some more. Mouth open, I stare at them.

Fenrir takes advantage of the knight's distraction and swipes at his feet again. This time, he's fully successful. The knight falls to the ground, and his helm bounces off his head, and away, away… I follow it with my eyes.

Then, slowly, force them back to him.

My gasp echoes in the meadow. I can feel Fenrir's eyes on me, but I can't tear my gaze away from the dark knight.

He finally speaks, his voice devoid of emotion. "You'd strike at me, Artemis? *Me*? After all we've been to each other?"

My bow drops to the ground, my shaking hand unable to hold on to it. "P-Pegasus…"

And the god I'd loved, the one whose death I'd mourned, smirks back at me. "Hello, love."

# CHAPTER 16

**Artemis**

Pegasus looks different. Completely, utterly different. His previously bronzed skin is now ashen. His cheeks, full of life, are sunken. The blue eyes I'd loved are dulled, lifeless. But worse of all, is the lack of smile.

His smirk widens, the coldness in his eyes enough to make me shiver once more. "No words, love?"

"I'm not—" I stop, clear my throat. Take a few steps closer. Fenrir's watching us, eyes narrowed, gaze uncomprehending. *Can't focus on that right now. There'll be time for his anger later.* And I do feel it simmering in the air. But I shove it away, focusing on the ghost of a man in front of me. "What are you?"

"Pegasus, my dear. Clearly."

I shake my head, taking another step closer. "You're not Pegasus. He's dead."

He lifts his arms. "Clearly very much alive."

"Is that what you call it, then?"

His look turns nasty. Then he glances to his right—the aegis. It's mere meters away from us. And unlike before, though I'm stunned, I'm not about to let him take off with it again.

"Let it go, Pegasus."

His eyes are glued to it. "I can't."

Another step. "Why not?"

"Because he needs it."

"Who does?"

Instead of answering, Pegasus lunges for the shield. But I'm prepared, and in two strides and a jump, I beat him to it. Clutch the shield with both hands and roll away with it. An *oomph* resounds to my right, and I look up—Fenrir has tackled Pegasus again. They fall to the ground, Fenrir's knife digging into Pegasus' chest.

"NO!" The scream escapes me, raw and primal. It's like déjà-vu, but worse. Because I'm witnessing it this time.

And even worse, both men turn to me. Fenrir, uncomprehending and hurt. Pegasus, victorious and…sad? I can't understand his look. But he grabs

Fenrir's knife—my knife—with his hand, and twists it out of his grip. Then knees Fenrir, and climbs out from under him.

He's about to bend over, knife in hand, when I run between them. "Please. Just…stop."

The shield is in my hand. I push it behind me, forcing myself to stand tall. This isn't the man I loved. With my free hand, I pull out my other knife, levelling it at him.

Pegasus looks at it, then me. An odd little smile twitches his lips. Then his blue eyes meet mine—and for a second, an infinite second, they're the shade I was used to. Warm. Lighted with amusement.

I'm so distracted by them, I'm not prepared for what he does next. Which is wrap an arm around my waist and yank me close to him, within a hair's breadth. Lips so close to mine. Lips that delivered so much pleasure…

They meet mine in a butterfly's caress. Cold, un-feeling. And then they move to my ear. "He will not let go of the shield, and I will not be able to refuse him. Run, Artemis. Run back to Olympus while you can."

The second after, he jerks himself away from me, shoving me away in the same movement. I fall to the ground, the aegis still in a death-grip. And Pegasus…disappears into the woods, as though he's taking a stroll.

I stare at him for too long, shaken by what he'd said.

Fenrir helps me up and I dust myself off, still trying to understand what just happened. "I don't—"

"Who was that?"

I meet his gaze then, and the fury simmering beneath. "Someone we long thought lost. Pegasus. Hades' best friend."

His eyes narrow. "And is that all he is?" When I say nothing, he adds, "Only, I imagine not all of your uncle's friends call you *love*. Unless they do?"

His words have the intended effect. I jerk my chin up, scowling. "Let's just get this over with and return the shield to the old hag."

The walk back to Olga's cabin is quiet. Not the comfortable kind of quiet, but the type filled with so much tension, all it would take is one word, one misstep, and everything would implode.

I suppose it's a testament to our self-control that we both choose to keep quiet, and not bring up anything. Not that it helps me, since all I can do is go back over and over the scene.

Pegasus. Alive, but not quite. His words... *He will not let go of the shield.* Why? And who? Is it the same deity who controls Fenrir? Not that big of an assumption to make, given Pegasus is wearing the same attire as the riders hunting Fenrir.

I glance over my shoulder—Fenrir's walking with his gaze glued to the ground, as though not even truly present. Perhaps I should pause, tell him everything. But… How can I? When I don't even know what's happened?

So I turn around, and focus back on the path. The woods seem to rearrange themselves, and we get to the old crone's cabin much faster than it took us to find the shield. Perhaps it's a blessing.

We find Olga inside, singing over a bubbling cauldron. I toss the shield on the table filled with papers. She stops what she's doing, turns, and lets out a gleeful chuckle. Then she moves so fast, I almost don't believe she's the age she says she is.

Her hands move over the shield, as though it's a prized possession. And I suppose it is, to her, otherwise she wouldn't have sent us to get it.

"Care to explain what you needed the aegis for, old crone?" I ask her.

She smiles at the shield. "For protection, of course."

I wonder if any of that has to do with the two visitors we'd seen here, when we first arrived. Or if it's more tied in with the many enemies she must've had, what with all the blood she's taken in these woods.

Before I can ask for more information, Fenrir

speaks. "You got what you wanted. Now tell me. Who hunts me? And why?"

Olga looks between us, a bushy eyebrow arched. "Trouble in paradise?"

Great. Even she feels the tension.

"Don't test me, old woman," Fenrir growls. "Not even my blood or that shield will save you from my wrath if you keep pushing."

"Tsk, such manners." She ignores him for the longest time. Just when I'm about to snap, she says, "Zalmoxis is the god you seek. Have you heard of him?"

We both shake our heads.

"Always a pity when so much history is lost. Sit, please, and I will explain." Fenrir scowls and I lean my hip against the counter. Olga seems to get the hint. "You are aware of the ways your pantheons split the world, correct?"

I grit my teeth. "Yes."

"Do not get testy with me, huntress. I am merely trying to find where to begin." She clears her throat, pours herself a cup, drinks, and nods. "Very well. This story is older, much older than before either of you were born."

"Then how do *you* know it, old hag?" Fenrir asks.

"Do you want to get your answers, or not?" When he nods, she takes another sip of wine. "Every pantheon has their old gods. Older than the enneads or trinities or councils that currently rule each pantheon. Such as the Titans, for the Greeks. Nun and Apophis, for the Egyptians. Indra, for the Hindu pantheon. Fu Xi, in the Asian pantheon…"

I nod, if only to encourage her to get the fuck on with it.

"Zalmoxis is one such old god. And he happens to have mingled a bit too much in human history."

"How so?"

"He had a daughter with a mortal."

I roll my eyes at her dramatic tone. "So did my father, Zeus. *Many* such daughters and sons."

"Tsk, but back then, huntress, the rules were different. And Zalmoxis lost his love, because he tried to imbue her with his divine power."

That bit rings closer to home. Mortals, and how they survive our divine essence, has always been a point of contention among pantheons. My own mother died because she kept insisting on seeing Zeus in all his splendor. And that killed her, because her mortal shell was unable to take it.

"Yes, you would know all about that," Olga says with a meaningful look at me. "So, with Zalmoxis' consort dead, his daughter became his sole focus. He brought her to his divine lair, and he was able to imbue *her* with his divine energy. Being half divine, it did not kill her. But his energy changed her, making her nearly immortal. Nearly, but not quite. Her Achilles' heel was that if she ever was to see life not worth living, she could *choose* to take it away from herself. Only she could do so, no one else."

I glance at Fenrir, but he refuses to acknowledge it.

"That daughter went on to marry a well-known king of these parts… Vlad Dracul the Third, otherwise known as Vlad Țepeș."

I remember our introduction to her other two visitors. Fenrir beats me to it, saying, "He's an urban legend."

"He is most definitely a *legend* in these parts, wolf god. And the visitors you met, before? One of them is his daughter."

That shuts Fenrir up. Olga continues, "Zalmoxis' daughter was named Isadora, and she became queen of her own realm. Zalmoxis found Țepeș to be a hero, perfect to defend his daughter. He took a chance on him and it paid off… Zalmoxis gave him everything—strength, supporters, luck to escape multiple assassination attempts. A shape-shifting ability, and even, by some accounts, magic. All Țepeș had to do was use those skills to protect Isadora. But, alas, he failed. In one of his many wars, Isadora thought him dead, and she took her own life, unable to live without him. The ultimate sin."

"What does all this have to do with me, old

crone?" Fenrir asks. There's such exhaustion in his tone, all I want to do is go to him. But I know he wouldn't welcome it.

"Zalmoxis, as vengeance for what happened to his daughter, later manipulated Țepeș into becoming a vampire, the first of his kind in these parts. And built within that gift was a curse—meant to wipe out his lineage in the worst way possible." She smiles above her mug. "That curse is wreaking havoc with the heirs of the House of Dracul right now, which is why they're coming to my door."

I glare at her. "Will you get to the point already?"

"You are hearing the point right now, but you aren't listening. The vampires are linked to him, and their quest parallels yours."

"This is a godly matter," I mutter, "not a human one."

Olga cackles then, so loud and so hard, she nearly chokes. When the last of her cough is over, she says, "How blind you choose to be. The vampire's curse keeps Zalmoxis involved. It gives him a window of escape, from wherever he is. It *feeds him*, because the closer he gets to the curse obliterating the Dracul line, the stronger he gets. And then there are those praying to him, happily giving him their blood in exchange for a little of his magic…of his darkness. Don't you see?" She looks between us, then rolls her eyes.

Fenrir lets out a long exhale, as though he's trying to keep himself in check. I don't blame him. "So some bloodsuckers are having an issue with a god. Big fucking deal. I'd bet *their* issue isn't as big as mine."

Olga stares at him for a moment, then speaks slowly, as if to a child. "Zalmoxis still has power, despite being an old god. What happened to all the rest of them, gods as old as him?"

I think back. "Imprisoned, most of them. Most of the Titans are, at least. Or else they've had their access limited, and they are under guard constantly."

"Mm."

It hits me then. The vampire link. Zalmoxis getting stronger. "You're saying Zalmoxis still roams free, because of these vampires and the curse that feeds him?"

"Not quite. But he roams, indeed. Somewhere." Her eyes become glazed. "He still maintains power, through the Dacians—witches he created—who worship him. They are the ones who pray to him, who feed him their blood, in exchange for his magic. Through their constant devotion, he has survived, instead of becoming forgotten. It is how he was able to possess the sister of one such Dacian, who dabbled in the wrong enchantment."

"Possess?" Fenrir whispers.

"I see I finally got your attention. Yes, *possess*.

Same as you have been. He has a direct link in her mind, and it is that which the vampires are trying to break."

"We don't care about their struggles," I remind her. "You can help them, or not, after this."

Olga chuckles. "Yes, huntress, and I shall. But if Zalmoxis is doing this—possessing others—it has to be because he's not truly free. Therefore, *somewhere*, yes, he roams. But I know not where."

I shake my head. "I don't understand. If he's imprisoned, how's he able to tap into Fenrir? And why?"

"Because of his worshippers still giving him power. And the curse." Fenrir shakes his head. "Those things don't just feed him and maintain his existence. They help him *break the barriers* of wherever the hell he is. Don't they?"

"Points to the wolf god." Olga smirks. "Yes, the worshippers play a huge role. And the other side of the equation is, that you are a conduit for him. His weapon, so to speak. Zalmoxis is an old god, and he cannot be denied. The curse on the vampires, it saps their strength until they need blood filled with darkness to return it. His hold on you…I assume it gets worse when dark emotions are involved?"

Fenrir says nothing, but the truth is written all over his shocked features.

"Yes, I expected as much." Olga takes another sip of her drink. "Unfortunate."

I think back to what she said. "But *why* would he be mad, imprisoned somewhere? You're saying he's trying to break free through others, like vessels? Same as we chose oracles, in the past?"

Olga nods. "Yes. As for why he is imprisoned… The stories do not say. Only that he did something that broke every rule there was."

"So how do we break his hold on Fenrir?"

She cackles. "I can tell you, but there will be a price."

My restraint snaps and I push her against the wall, arrow notched and ready to fire. "You will tell us, old crone. I'm done with your games."

"Artemis." Fenrir touches my shoulder. "Let it go."

"Why?"

"Because the answers I seek won't lie here. I am cursed, there's nothing more to it."

"You *are* cursed, wolf god. However, it does not have to be the end."

But Fenrir's done with her, it seems. Without another word, he walks out. Again.

I scowl at her, and turn to follow. "Fenrir, wait!"

"No. All of this is a waste. Thank you for humoring me. Allow me one night of getting drunk, forgetting it all, and then we can go to Olympus. At least now we have something to tell them, even if we haven't gotten rid of the creatures chasing me."

I nod, knowing there's not much I can do to change his mind. Not when he feels like there are no other options. Because for the first time, I feel like that, too.

Behind me, I sense Olga watching. I face her once more. "The creatures, the ones Heka priests used to use. Zalmoxis is behind them too, then?"

She nods. "I would assume as much."

"Which means someone of the Egyptian pantheon must have told him how to get them…or create new ones."

A smile plays on her lips. "You are getting closer, huntress."

I take a gamble on my next question. "Why would Zalmoxis want the aegis, old hag?"

"Perhaps for the same reason Athena wished it hidden. To protect himself…from an incoming war."

She reaches for the door handle, tugging it closed. I guess that's as much as I'll ever get out of her.

**Fenrir**

An old god, older than even Odin. Imprisoned somewhere, trying to break free by taking control of others. Me, a god. Another, a witch. And who knows how many more?

I have my answers now, and they give me none

of the joy I'd expected. In fact, they've only worsened everything.

But even worse than that is a darker thought—of Artemis, and Pegasus, and the way she'd seemed when she'd seen him. She loved him once, I'm sure of it. And now that he's back? I can only wonder for how long I'll still have her support...her light. Perhaps she'll soon turn her efforts to saving him. After all, he's a hell of a lot worthier of it than me.

# CHAPTER 17

**Fenrir**

The trek through the woods is as quiet as the one from retrieving the aegis was. Everything we'd built—the companionship, the camaraderie, the chemistry—has gone poof.

"Fenrir."

I ignore her. She's been trying to talk to me since I walked out on Olga, but I don't need this shit. Not now. No amount of placating will fix the fact that I'm screwed, fighting against a god way more powerful than me. A god who's only quiet right now because I don't use my divine energy. But the moment I do, he's there. Always. Like a leech, trying to draw away my control. How am I supposed to ever win?

*We* are *fighting him*, my beast reminds me.

*Sure, because a crippled wolf is enough to take on an old god. What deluded potion were you fed when we were pups, beast?*

Only a whine answers me, and he retreats within me. The warmth I'd felt in my chest seems to dim with it.

"Fenrir, would you wait?"

Artemis runs up to me, and steps in front of me, blocking my way. I keep my gaze resolutely above her head, refusing to give in. To let her see my hurt.

When she reaches for me, I jerk out of her reach.

"I get it that you're mad at me—"

"What's there to be mad about?" My voice is cool, devoid of emotion. She flinches. Good. I want her to feel pain right now. Maybe it won't be at the level I'm feeling it, but I want her to feel it.

"I owe you an apology," she whispers, still trying to catch my gaze.

"You owe me nothing."

I try to move past her, but she simply steps with me.

"But I do, Fenrir. You were right. Pegasus was more than just my uncle's best friend. He was also my lover."

I flinch at the pain in her tone. I'd wanted to cause it, but now that it's there, it doesn't make me feel any better.

"We were very close, for centuries—in human lifespans. No one in Olympus knew, aside from my brother. And Hades guessed, as he does most things, I assume. But he never outright said anything to me." She frowns. "It's not that our being together was forbidden, but it would have been frowned upon by my father. And at the time, that mattered to me…a lot."

Something I can relate to. Instead of admitting as much, I let her keep talking.

"Pegasus died during that second attack upon Hades. At the time, we didn't know what was causing it—but from Hades' descriptions, I'm assuming it was the same creatures that have been after you. I…realized after our first attack the link. Perhaps I should have told you."

"You owe me nothing," I repeat. "I'm your bounty, that's all."

She takes a step closer. This time, I can't avoid her gaze. "You're more than that now, and you know it. I wouldn't have put my reputation on line for a bounty, Fenrir."

We stare at each other for a moment. She seems ready to add more, but I clear my throat. "How is he here, then? If he was killed?"

"I don't know. Hades said he couldn't get to his body. His immortals were focused on taking him away, not recovering a fallen god. When Olympians went back later, Pegasus had vanished, as had any trace of an attack. We'd assumed him dead."

"Great. So now that he's not, you can go find him and have your little happily ever after." I push past her, ignoring her stricken expression. "Like I said. Give me one night, then we'll go back to Olympus, creatures or no creatures, and you can be released of this little *duty*."

After a beat, and another, her footsteps follow behind me. The woods widen, and I know we're near the outskirts. I pull out the taxi driver's business card—the one who'd dropped us here—and my cellphone, and dial the number. Anything to get the hell out of here faster.

**Artemis**

By the time the driver drops us back at the hotel, Fenrir still hasn't said anything to me. We enter inside, and head to our room in complete silence. I drop my bow and quiver to the side of the chair, and take a seat on it.

Fenrir goes to his suitcase and pulls out a different shirt, swapping it out for his torn one. The black looks good with his skin tone, but also makes him seem more…unapproachable, somehow.

When he heads for the door, I call out. "Are you really not going to speak to me?"

He stops, hand on the doorknob. His back muscles tense. "What else is there to say, Artemis? You were so stunned by Pegasus' reappearance, clearly you still have feelings for him. You let him get away with the aegis, for fuck's sake." He turns to face me. "Tell me, what more is there?"

"I—well, there's something else, actually. I thought I saw Pegasus once before. When we were in the woods, and we each got our respective hallucinations… He showed up at the end of mine. I didn't know it was him, his outfit hid it. But he did something that made me think of him. I didn't tell you because I thought he was part of the illusion."

He clenches his jaw. "Right. Thanks for clearing up yet another lie by omission. And what about what Pegasus whispered to you before he left?"

"I…" My throat clenches, the words stuck in my throat. It's not that I don't want to tell him. It's that it physically *hurts* to think of him.

"Right. That's what I thought." He whirls back to the door and leaves.

For a few long hours, I merely sit in the room. Take a shower. Watch the sun set. Somewhere, Fenrir is out drinking himself into oblivion. And part of me yearns to do the same. To let go, to forget everything and simply feel.

I close my eyes, recalling the feel of his hands on me. His mouth kissing me. And then the image is overrun with Pegasus' kiss—from now, not back then.

Fenrir isn't wrong. I do still have feelings for Pegasus, and those will never leave. It's because of the history between us. But they're not as strong as they were. Something else has taken their place…

I toss back on the bed, groaning in frustration.

The air shimmers around me, and then a melodious voice says, "Men. So frustrating, are they not?"

I jerk upright and my eyes land on none other than Ileana. "What are you doing here?" Hope flares in my chest. "Are you here to help us get back into Olympus, as you promised?"

"That depends. What did the oracle say to you?"

I hesitate only for a beat. Then, figuring that I have nothing to lose, I tell her everything. Including about Pegasus.

When I'm done, Ileana has taken a seat on the bed, a stunned expression on her features. "Pegasus? Alive? And…Zalmoxis?"

I shake my head. "I wouldn't call Pegasus alive, Ileana. He's… I'm not sure *what* he is. But his skin is ashen, his lips were cold. And he seemed to be flickering between a zombie state and…the old him. Barely."

A shudder works its way through Ileana, and then she meets my gaze. "You…have stumbled onto a large part of the puzzle, Artemis. Hades should hear of this. All of it. Come, let us return to Olympus."

"And Fenrir?"

"If he comes with us now, he will still be persecuted."

"What would help his case, more than we've already gotten?"

She thinks it over, tapping her chin. "Someone on his side from his pantheon, perhaps. His father, Loki?"

I make a face. "I don't think they're on the same page."

"Perhaps for a reason."

"What do you mean?"

Ileana leans forward. "It seems a bit odd how Fenrir was…taken over. Why him, out of all the Norse gods? Pegasus was a convenient pawn, someone left behind. And we are all paying the price for that. But Fenrir? I can think of a few other gods more suited for Zalmoxis' needs."

"You're saying… He was *chosen*?"

"Or *given*. Perhaps as payment for something. And out of all the gods in the Norse pantheon, none are fickler than Loki himself."

The thought that Fenrir's father could have been the cause of what's happening to him… I look up at Ileana. "I can't leave him, if that's the case. We have to seek more answers."

Ileana nods, a little sadly. "As you wish, huntress. I will inform Hades of what you told me, but he will want to hear it from you. When you are ready, return home to us. With or without the wolf god."

She disappears in a shimmer of flowers, and I'm left thinking. And thinking.

Finally, I stand, discard the hotel robe for my bustier and the jeans I'd worn earlier. Then, on second thought, I do the trick I'd done before and transform the jeans back into the skirt they'd been. Satisfied, I head out.

**Fenrir**

"Another." The bartender does as I ask, giving me a side-glance. He's probably wondering how I'm still standing after half the bottle of whiskey I consumed. "Leave the bottle."

"You sure? I—"

"Leave it."

At the growl in my tone, he leaves the bottle, pockets the money I slide to him, and goes back to his other—more amicable—customers.

I look at the whiskey. Down the one he'd poured, and refill the glass. Like with every bad decision in my life, Loki was the one who taught me to use alcohol to numb the pain. Especially once he figured out it was easier to get me to morph into my wolf form that way. After all this time, I should've learned better. But, some habits…they just leech onto you when you're down.

Just as I bring the drink to my lips, her voice rises behind me.

"Do you think maybe you've had enough?"

I ignore Artemis. If this is to be my last night of freedom, I'll be damned if I don't enjoy it.

"Fenrir."

When I resolutely keep my back to her, she pulls a stool next to me at the bar. Then steals my drink, downing it. "I saw Ileana."

"Perfect. Just in time for the return trip."

She hesitates, then says, "You're too drunk for this."

"Drunk for what? The truth?"

She rolls her eyes.

"Or more the version of truth you want to tell me?"

She leans toward me, lowering her tone. "You're making a scene. And what does it matter to you, if I hide things? Hmm?"

I pull the top off the bottle and pour another shot. "Nothing at fucking all."

Artemis is relentless, though, I'll give her that.

She leans even closer, her thigh brushing mine, her breast pressing against my forearm. Her lips at my ear. A jolt of desire so painful goes through me, I choke on my drink.

"Nothing, and yet here you are, getting drunk into oblivion because of those very things. How mature of you."

I ignore her, taking another gulp of whiskey to wash down the fire in my throat. Unfortunately, it only ignites the rest of my body even further.

"You're jealous, Fenrir. Admit it." When I say nothing, she pulls back, dropping the act. Her voice fills with sadness. "And you have nothing to be jealous of. Pegasus and I, yes, we have a history. And that history muddled my thoughts when I saw him—because of the way he was taken from me. Now I understand, though. Now, I have the answers I'd sought. And painful as they are, they're enough. That chapter is closed."

"Bullshit."

"You want me to tell you what he whispered to me? He said, 'He will not let go of the shield, and I will not be able to refuse him. Run, Artemis. Run back to Olympus while you can.'"

That's not what I'd expected. The surprise is enough to jolt some sense into my jealousy-addled brain. Some, not much. "What…that makes no sense." I meet her gaze. "Why are you still here, then?"

"Why do you think?" She stands, adding, "As for it not making sense… It does. I'll tell you exactly how, if you leave that drink and come back to the hotel with me."

I look at the whiskey, then down the remainder in the glass and stand. "Lead the way."

"Fuck." I fumble with the key to the hotel room, having the hardest time swiping it in the damn slot.

Artemis reaches for it, for the second time.

"I don't need help."

"Stop being a child."

I turn on her, trapping her body between me and the wall. "Would a child do this?"

Without waiting, I cup her cheeks and drop my mouth to hers. It's messy, and not my best kiss. But Artemis doesn't shove me away. All she does is gasp, and clutch at my shirt. Instead of stopping me, the sound spurs me on. I press against her lips until she opens, giving me access. The first touch of her tongue against mine sends me down a darker abyss, one where I only feel her. Not my darkness. Not my curse. Not my helplessness.

*This* is something I can control.

So I take that last step, pressing our bodies closer,

until she's completely glued to me and the wall. Her hands yank on my shirt, as though she's equally desperate to get me closer. There's no more space between us, nothing but the heat of her body seeping into mine, and mine into hers.

When I suck on her bottom lip, she moans against my mouth, and her hips undulate against mine.

I pull away, meeting her glazed gaze. "If you don't want this, now's the time to say so."

Never tearing my gaze from hers, I insert the key in the lock, turn it over, and open the door. Artemis lifts her chin, walks past me inside, and faces me. Then her hands are on my shirt again, dragging me inside. I kick the door shut behind me.

This time, she's the one who initiates the kiss. We come together like two forces of nature colliding, all clashes of teeth and tongues and roaming hands, questing fingers. My hand roams down her back, seeking bare skin, then moving to the front and palming her breast. Artemis' moan makes my erection even harder, and a steady pulse thrums in my head. A drumbeat that drives me insane.

*I can't…let the darkness…*

And then there's no more thinking. She pulls my shirt off. Undoes my belt buckle. Reaches inside my jeans, touching me.

I groan, dropping my head against the wall. She

falls to her knees, and before I know it, takes me in her mouth. The heat of her mouth nearly undoes me, as does her tongue. I grab a fistful of her copper locks, and she moans around my length. I only last a few more thrusts, a few more seconds, before I feel myself ready to come. And I refuse to do so down her throat the first time.

With a groan of my own, I tug her off me, and lift her up. Her legs wrap around me. I flip us over, pressing us both against the wall. I reach for her skirt, pushing it past her thighs, until it's bunched at her waist. Then one hand moves under her ass, lifting her higher, aligning her with my cock. The other goes between her thighs, seeking to remove her panties—

"Fuck." She's not wearing any.

I groan, dropping my head on her shoulder. "You're going to fucking kill me."

In answer, Artemis only spreads her thighs further, and somehow moves against my fingers. Her heat, her wetness, is my undoing. At least until she grips my hair and brings my head up, until we're eye-level once more.

"And you're going to kill me if you don't fuck me. Right. Damn. Now."

I clench my jaw, and align myself with her entrance. Kiss her again, this time biting her bottom lip. Artemis moans, and that's when I thrust inside her.

*Fuck. Fuck. Fuck. I'm about to lose my shit like a damned teenager.*

And I am. She's so tight around my length, so hot and wet, yet I can barely move. I push a bit deeper, and a low groan escapes her.

I stop kissing her, freezing. "Am I—"

She smashes her mouth against mine again, and somehow uses her legs, still wrapped around me, to pull me deeper inside her. Then her lips move down my jaw, peppering it with kisses, until she reaches my ear. "I'm fine. Don't you dare stop."

So, I don't. I push deeper, and deeper still, until I'm all the way inside her. Then I take another pause—not for her sake, but for mine. Because she feels so damned good, I might just die from this experience.

But Artemis is one impatient little minx. She doesn't give me a chance to pull myself together. Instead, she does that thing where she wriggles a bit, then pulls me to her. A growl escapes me, something so near beastly, I'm even more afraid of losing it.

She's not, though. She only drops her head against the wall, moaning loudly. Her hands reach my waist, digging into the skin there as she tugs on me. "Harder."

I do as she asks, no holding back this time. With each thrust, I feel her walls clenching on me. Her entrance grows tighter and tighter, and my dick is near bursting. But I need her, first, to hit that pinnacle with me.

Sliding my hand between us, I touch her clit, feel her tightening around me even more…and she comes undone. I grip her hips then, and finally lose the last of my control as I thrust over and over, losing myself within her.

Artemis' red locks are spread over my chest, tickling some rather sensitive areas. Her breath is slow and easy, as she falls deeper and deeper into sleep. A shot of male pride and satisfaction runs through me—I'd given her this. Me, the screw-up of the Norse pantheon.

The warmth in my chest reminds me of something else. Another someone.

*Beast?*

He doesn't answer, not at first. Then, slowly, a low whine.

*I'm sorry. You didn't deserve it, and I was no better than Loki was to us when we were young.*

Another whine.

*I will be better, I promise. I didn't lie when I said I need time, but I also realize we need to work together toward making this union work. Will you work on it, with me?*

A silence, then, *Yes. I will always be here, to protect and defend you.*

## Artemis

Sunlight pours in the window. I must have been up for an hour, but instead of moving, I keep tracing patterns on Fenrir's chest, thinking. He catches my hand in his, kissing each finger in turn. He watches me, a satisfied expression on his features. Almost…content.

And I hate myself for breaking it, but there's no other way around it. "There's something I need to tell you."

My tone must clue him in. "About Ileana's visit?"

I nod. Then, painful bit by painful bit, relate everything to him—including the bit about her theory on Loki. Fenrir's quiet for a long time after, then he moves away from me, and pulls up to a half-seated position, his back to me.

I stare at him for a moment, then rise up on my knees behind him and hug him, pressing my heat against him in the hopes it lets him know he's supported, and no longer alone. Our closeness lets me feel his anger, the way his muscles are shaking.

When he finally speaks, his tone is eerily calm. "I have no doubt there's some truth to Ileana's theory. But where does that leave us?" He half-turns to me, cupping my cheek. "You have a plan, my huntress?"

"Maybe… Before I bring you to Olympus, I think you should speak to your pantheon. Explain what happened. Demand their protection."

"What will that do?"

I look at him. "It will ensure Zeus doesn't go on a power trip."

He sighs. "I can refuse you nothing. But I don't think any amount of talking to them will get them in my corner, Artemis. And I definitely can't just show up in Asgard after that fight. I'll be imprisoned on sight."

I rest my chin on his shoulder. "What if you give them someone else to imprison?"

"Like…?"

"Loki." I didn't realize it was where my mind was going, but now that it's out there, I can't really take it back. "What if you meet with him, trick him into talking about Zalmoxis? I'll act as your witness. Then, once he's gone, I'll go with you to Asgard and testify on your behalf."

Fenrir inhales sharply, then turns his head toward me. "You would do that?"

"Of course." I bite my lip, trying to figure out the next step. "Is there a meeting spot you could go to, somewhere you and Loki know, where he'd show up?"

He thinks, then nods slowly. "There is a place.

My father brought me there once. Trolltunga, in Norway." Something flashes in his eyes. "And it would be the perfect place to figure out if Ileana's theory is right. Remember those powerful spots you mentioned, that make travelling easier? Trolltunga is one. And if we can portal out of there, Heimdall will ensure no creatures enter Asgard."

I smile, and give him a kiss. "I think we have a plan." Then another realization hits me, and I groan. "Does that mean I have to get into another one of those metal birds?"

# CHAPTER 18

**Fenrir**

We land at the Oslo airport from yet another flight, Artemis muttering throughout. I leave her inside the terminal to do the same as before—hoping it works as it did in Romania, and keeps the creatures off our trail—and then head over to get a rental.

Thankfully, the process is smooth and by the time she exits, I'm waiting by a car. I watch her scan the crowds, her expression guarded. Then her gaze lands on me, and something crackles in the air between us, even across the distance. The guarded look is gone, replaced by a wide smile.

She walks over to me, rising on tiptoes to give

me a kiss. As if drawn to her, my hand moves to her waist, holding her against me a little bit longer. Then I break the kiss, bury my head in her neck, and inhale deeply.

Artemis stills, but lets me have my fill. When I'm ready, I let her go and step back.

"You okay?"

I nod. "I will be."

*Are you sure?* the beast asks.

I give him the same answer. *I will be.*

Then open the door for her, wait until she gets in, and head to the driver's side. I set up the phone to bring us to the Trolltunga cliffs, and we're off. GPS tells me it's a nearly seven-hour drive with traffic, but I'm hoping to cut it down to five.

Curved highways pass by, with the scenery ever-changing. From industrial and cold, to mountainous and imposing, to once-again well-taken care of roads, and finally, back roads.

During the drive, Artemis is quiet, soaking in the snow-covered tips of mountains, and jaw-dropping views. When we finally park, I take a moment to stretch, my back stiff.

"We'll have to walk the rest of the way."

Artemis nods, and pulls one of the jackets I'd bought at the airport from the backseat. The air is biting, its chill digging bone-deep. Hand in hand, we walk the rest of the way, until we're up a cliff that overlooks a beautiful gorge. Water sprinkles with the sky's light, mountains draw up tall and regal.

It's meant to be one of the most amazing, worshipping-inspiring cliffs in Norway. About one thousand and one hundred meters above sea level, with a perfect view of Lake Ringedalsvatnet. The seven hundred meters below feel like a life-extinguishing drop, even when I'm meant to be immortal. And still, I soak it all in. Close my eyes, feeling the wind tugging at my clothes, the sense of freefall from being so high-up.

"It's of another world," Artemis whispers.

I open my eyes, taking in the horizon with the sun setting. It's bathed in indigo and red and orange, like an artist has tossed an entire palette of colors at a wall, to see what would stick.

"You could say that."

Even now, I feel the power in the cliffs. Long ago, this was a special spot for us. It was also an area where Loki loved to bring me as a newly born deity. His own way of bonding...even if it resulted in many scrapes and bruises I couldn't explain to the rest of the Asgardians. My father liked to push my boundaries, all for his own designs. And after he'd been expressly told to stop toying with me and force me to morph, he'd found more creative ways to get me to toughen up. Fighting it out with Mother Nature was one such way.

An odd memory comes forth to my mind. Of the first blackout I'd ever had, here on these very cliffs. I'd woken later in Asgard, back in my wolf form, with Tyr watching over me and my father nowhere in sight. Back then, he'd ignored my worries. Said it was to be expected, because I wasn't normal.

*How many lies did he tell me? Did he really have a hand in all that's happened to me, in this curse?*

I soak in the beauty surrounding me for another moment, then close my eyes and kneel on the stone. Let my hands rest upon it. I'm not reaching into my divine power, not really. More like tugging on a connection with the earth that's existed here since time immemorial.

I can sense Artemis' gaze upon me. Moments go by, followed by more moments.

Eventually, I stand. "It was a waste of time. Loki won't show unless there's something in it for him."

My beast growls, then. It's a sound that raises the hair at the back of my neck. Then, behind me, the air *whooshes* and a chuckle echoes onto the wind.

"How right you are, son."

I whirl, putting myself between him and Artemis. "You came."

"You *called*. What kind of father would I be if I ignored my own son's call?"

I narrow my eyes. "You've got some nerve. After you took Thor's side, and didn't even hear me out?"

Loki looks at me, arching an eyebrow. "Thor is mighty pissed with you."

"He can be as pissed as he wishes."

"You aren't meant to go against your kin."

"Then he shouldn't have pushed me into doing so."

Loki stares at Artemis. "So this is what it's come to? Allying yourself with an Olympian?"

*He has no right*, my beast growls.

*I know. He won't get close to her. We'll protect her, both of us. Together.*

A rumble of agreement answers me.

"At least she's not trying to stab me in the back."

"No?"

I grit my teeth. "You cannot play your game on me, Father." Already, he's succeeded at distracting me. *You came here with a purpose. Stick to it.*

"You always did think highly of yourself." Loki chuckles. His gaze shifts to Artemis again. "Do you not get tired of his arrogance?"

I snort. "You're one to talk."

"Watch your tongue. Questioning me—"

"—is what I should've done ages ago. When darkness first inched toward me and you told me it's normal. That we all have good and bad in us. That it would go away. That our family can withstand anything."

His eyes narrow on me. "What is it you wish?

An apology? I am not some soft-hearted mortal."

"No, you're not. And we're way beyond an apology, *Father*." As I say the words, I realize they're true. Regardless of what Olympus has planned for me, I'm in it alone. No help will come from them, and I would expect nothing less. "What I want to know is why Zalmoxis is after me."

Loki scoffs. "Zalmoxis? What demented bard have you been speaking with? He is a myth."

"Not so much, given his minions have chased me across this realm, and many others." I take another step closer. "Tell me. What do you know of him?"

"What makes you think I know anything?"

Artemis clears her throat, deliberately drawing his attention. I don't know how, but I can sense she's doing this to give me some breathing room to compose myself. "You may not be an old god, like the Titans, but you come from giants whose mischief-grubby paws were all over intrigue and political coups. Surely, you, of all the gods, would know something."

Loki stares at her a beat, then laughs—a surprised, full of mirth laugh. He wipes tears from his eyes, then points at me, wagging his finger. "I like her. For an Olympian, she's got spunk."

"Answer the question, then," Artemis adds.

Loki glances between us, then shrugs. "Tales. They are but tales." He must see something in my features as he rolls his eyes. "Very well. I will humor you, since you're clearly bent out of shape over this."

"Please do," I mutter.

"Zalmoxis was once god of the dead, in some remote corner of this realm." He waves his hand inconsequentially. "The people there were filled with superstitions, but also had desperation for more. It was the perfect place for a god such as him to grow in power."

"And what kind of power was it?"

Loki walks to the edge of the cliff and sits on it, feet dangling in the empty air. He stares at the lake for a long moment, then tosses his long, dark locks over his shoulders and winks at me. "The best type, son. *Dark* power." He looks away again. "It wasn't always so. Or so the tales say, at any rate. When he was in love, his power was pure. It grew things, created life. But when he lost the love of his life"—here, Loki rolls his eyes—"Zalmoxis' power took a darker turn, fueled by his anger. And the angrier he became, the more powerful he was. He was able to unlock things that not even old gods could."

"Such as?" Artemis asks.

"Turning someone from mortal to divine-level. Resurrecting the dead…"

I frown. "Other gods can do that. Osiris, for example."

Behind me, Artemis adds, "Kali, of the Hindu pantheon. Ah Puch, from the Mayans. And let's not forget the Shinigami, from the Asian pantheon. To name a few."

Loki throws back his head and laughs. He gets up from the cliff's edge, dusts himself off, and faces us once more. "I meant he could resurrect dead *gods*, not mortals."

Shock renders me mute for a moment. I share a look with Artemis, who's equally stunned.

I'm afraid to ask the next question, but my beast nudges me. The warmth in my chest is the last bit of encouragement needed. "What… He was imprisoned, or so the tales say. Correct?"

"Mm."

"Why?"

Loki grins. "The story goes, he tried to use those powers to bring a dead goddess back to life." The grin falters. "Now, is that all? Asgard awaits, and this conversation bores me."

Artemis takes a step closer. "There's one more—"

I tug her back behind me, and meet Loki's gaze. "Nothing. You may leave."

A flash of anger crosses his features, then he disappears. The moment he's gone, I turn from the cliffs and stalk away, hands clenched into fists.

*You're mad,* my beast says.

*Damn fucking right I'm mad! How can he stand there, lying to my face that he doesn't know Zalmoxis in person? That he didn't use me, once again?*

*He will never change.*

*No, he won't.*

By the time I reach the car, I've pressed the nails so hard into my skin, they've broken it. Little rivulets of blood fill my palms. I wipe them on my jeans, then get behind the wheel, waiting for Artemis to join me. After a beat, she does, and shuts the door.

"Why are you so angry?"

*Calm*, the beast inside me urges.

I take a deep breath, force it back out slowly... Still, the tension inside me doesn't let up. "Because how else would he know all this, if Ileana wasn't right? The fucker *did* make a deal with Zalmoxis."

"And used you as bait." The disgust in her tone doesn't surprise me. She's finally been confronted with how far my pantheon will go.

"More like payment. Do you really think Asgard is a safe place for me, after this? He's a trickster god, Artemis. He'll twist our words, have us both imprisoned before we can even speak!" I shake my head, slamming my fists against the wheel. Then again. And again.

"Fenrir, stop!"

Her touch is the only thing that stops me. Barely.

**Artemis**

I can sense the darkness rising in him, crackling in

the car. I rest my hand on one of his fists, caressing it slowly. Humming a tune, enough to calm him down. And then unclench each of his fingers until they're intertwined with mine.

After another beat, he drives down the cliffs, and back into the closest town. We stop at the first hotel we can find, and get lodgings. Fenrir makes to head to the bar, but I tug him by the hand to the stairs, and up to our room. "I have a better idea."

He follows me, almost in a daze. Of anger or lust, I can't quite tell.

I open the door to the room—using the card, as I'd seen him do in Romania—and then walk inside. Whirl on my heels, facing him. "You can go to the bar, if you so wish. Or…you can come here. And lose that anger in me."

He takes a deep breath. "I don't want to hurt you."

"You won't."

Another beat passes. And another.

Finally, he steps inside.

I tug the shirt off me, then my bustier, and my pants. Everything, until I'm fully naked. He kicks the door closed behind him, his face in shadows now.

"This won't fix anything."

"Maybe not. But it'll quiet this inferno inside me," I say, and move backward, toward the bed. "And maybe, just maybe, it'll do the same to you."

Face still shadowed, he watches me. I can feel his

gaze on me as I sit on the bed, spread my legs. Arch my back. My breath speeds up, even as my core clenches in need. One hand moves to my breast, lingering around the skin, finding the nipple. Tugging on it.

A hiss comes from Fenrir. But still, he holds himself away at a distance.

I let my eyes drop to half-mast, and allow my other hand to roam free between my thighs. Slowly. Questing. Seeking. My lips part when a finger pushes past my folds—

There's a groan, and then Fenrir's there. Kneeling between my legs, tugging my wrist away. He brings the finger slick with my essence to his lips, and licks it clean. A whimper escapes me. Now, there's a faint light and I can see his burning gaze.

He lets go of my wrist, hoists my legs over his shoulders and then dives between my thighs. I throw my head back, letting every sensation wash over me. His tongue, probing my folds. Finding my clit. Circling it. His teeth, nibbling, then sucking it.

I shoot off the bed, hand dug into his hair, unable to hold back a scream.

Stars. I see stars, constellations, galaxies and universes. My mind shatters, and when it finally comes back down, it's to find Fenrir watching me. One of his hands moves between my thighs, a finger probing my insides. I clench around it, and another whimper escapes me.

He pushes off his knees, rising until he's nearly eye-level with me. His lips clash with mine, and I can taste my essence on his lips. It only makes me kiss him harder, digging my fingers into his hair even more, pulling him closer.

And all throughout, my hips move of their own accord. Riding his finger. Then fingers, as he slides another one inside me.

"Scream for me again, huntress," he whispers in my ear. "Scream for me…tame this beast inside me."

And I do. Like my body was waiting for his command, I come undone once more, my mind shattering yet again.

When I return to the room, I'm aware of my breathing—out of control; my body—poised for more; my legs—trembling from my latest explosion. And perhaps, more to the point, Fenrir. Holding himself up over me, waiting for me to acknowledge him. His hardness—when did he get naked?— throbbing against my thigh.

I arch toward him, moaning. "Fenrir…"

"Yes, huntress?"

"Please."

"Please, what?"

I lift my legs, preparing to wrap them around his waist, and pull him inside me. But he grips my thighs, watching me. His jaw is taut, his eyes are dark pools of lust.

"Say it."

"Fuck me," I whimper. "Is that what you want to hear?"

In a whirl, he's got me on my stomach, and pulls me up so I'm on all fours. Lips at my ear, he whispers, "Precisely." Then he thrusts inside me. He's so hard, so big, I scream at the intrusion—the moan, long and hard.

Each thrust is almost painfully deep, but followed by a wave of pleasure that seems to peak, and peak, and peak…

I push back against him. Begging. Pleading.

Fenrir grabs a handful of my hair, arching my head back. He bites the skin of my neck, hard, then nibbles on it after I gasp. The soothing touch of his tongue reminds me how he'd lashed my clit, and I feel my core clenching more, and more.

As though reading my mind, his other hand moves between my thighs, to my clit. And circles. And circles. And circles.

"I—"

"Fuck, you're tight." He groans, dropping his head against my back. His thrusts don't slow down. If anything, they become deeper, and deeper still.

But I know he needs more. *I* need more. I need to forget everything and everyone, and remember him alone.

Only one word can deliver that, for both of us.

So I whisper it. "More."

Fenrir stills inside me. "What was that?"

"I said, *more*."

His cock throbs, as though in full agreement. But I can feel Fenrir fighting it. Logic seeping in.

I reach behind for his thigh, digging my nails into him, near-growling with yearning. "*More!*"

This time, he moves. Once. Deeper. Twice. Deeper. When I don't stop him, his thrusts increase in speed. And depth. And speed. A raw, primal cry builds in my throat. I bury my head in a pillow, biting it and trying to stifle my pleasure into it.

Fenrir's hand on my clit moves with more accuracy. His thrusts inside me build up even more.

And then—he shatters, with a roar that makes the walls shake.

And my scream? Well. It might've been heard all the way in Olympus.

# CHAPTER 19

**Artemis**

Fenrir falls asleep shortly after. Exhausted though I am, I stay awake, watching him sleep. In dreams, his features soften, as though he doesn't carry the burden he normally has on his shoulders.

And what a burden. I want nothing more than to take away his pain. Erase the loneliness that's plagued his entire existence. But even I, daughter of Zeus, can't do that. Only he can, through his own strength of character.

I hadn't expected to feel this way. If anyone had told me this is how my mission would end—by falling for my bounty—I would have said they're deluded. But the joke's on me. Or maybe it's just what destiny always had in store for me.

Either way, I wouldn't change a thing. Because the love that's blossomed between us does have the power of healing. We're two broken halves, made whole. Forever intertwined.

I rise from bed then, already knowing what I need to do. I shower quickly—my fumbles with the human shower nearly forgotten—and get dressed in silence. No human clothes for me this time, only my regular garb. Bow in hand, quiver loaded with arrows over my shoulder.

I tiptoe to the bed, watching him for another moment. A sliver of moonlight seeps in the room, highlighting his features. My heart does a weird stutter, as though it's pained at the thought of being away from him. Even for a moment. If we're to have a chance, I need to do this.

What does Hera always say? *Love alone can't fix everything. But perseverance, now there's an idea that can break even the thickest of cycles.*

Maybe my perseverance won't be enough to make a difference to our fate. But I sure as hell can try.

I bend over Fenrir, resting my lips to his forehead. "If it takes me a century or more, I *will* return to you. No pantheon, Fates, or power-tripping god will stop me."

I leave the hotel, using the cover of night to make my way out into the woods, then uphill. My feet move fast, faster than mortals. And the entire time, I keep thinking of Fenrir, and how he'll hate me when he wakes and finds me gone. How hurt he'll be, thinking I've abandoned him.

But the idea of him facing my pantheon—my father—without backup is insane. Not so insane if I go through with my suggestion, and try to seek out someone from Asgard myself. They may be ready to cast Fenrir aside, but once I tell them about Loki and Zalmoxis, they'll see there are more important issues at hand.

*You shouldn't have left him.*

The refrain goes on and on in my head. Much like the feel of Fenrir's hands on me, which I'm having a hard time shaking off. But shake I must. Gaining entrance to Asgard won't be easy, least of all when they dislike Olympians.

I stop in my walk. Look back at the town. Hopefully, by the time this is achieved and I return, I'll still find him here. And maybe he'll even forgive me.

I recall his rage at Pegasus, his insecurity, and pray I'm right.

Then I clasp my bow tighter, face forward—and

run straight into Loki. "You!"

He smirks, watching me. I stumble back a few steps, putting distance between us. Unnerved at the way he's watching me, like a cat waiting on its prey.

"What are you doing here, Loki?"

"My son seems quite entranced with you, huntress. Why is that?"

"I think your son is old enough to answer for himself." I try to push past him, and he grabs my arm.

"In a rush?"

"What's it to you?" Even as I retort it, this feels too…convenient. Too rehearsed. Is he here to stop me? Because if he is, that means he's been watching us, knowing we would eventually split.

"Anything concerning my son, concerns me," Loki says.

I scoff. "Don't make me laugh, trickster god." Then meet his gaze full-on. "You know very well where I'm heading. And since you saw fit to follow me here, you can help me enter Asgard, and gain me an audience with Odin."

Loki's eyes narrow, but there's no surprise in them at my words. *He knows.*

In a flash, I raise my bow, notch an arrow, and point it straight at him. This earns me a smirk.

"I don't think that's going to go the way you wish it to, Olympian."

"Let's test it out, anyway."

Loki pretends to mull this over, then tuts. "No. I think not."

My grip on my bow tightens. "It's true, then. You're working with Zalmoxis." Ileana was right. As was Fenrir.

Loki rolls his eyes at my statement. "You Olympians, always with the narrow view of the world. No, I am not *working with* Zalmoxis. I only did him a favor some eons ago, and I would much rather it does not come to surface."

"No, I would imagine Asgard wouldn't take too kindly to it, would they?" He merely watches me, saying nothing. I decide to push my luck. "Tell me, were you ever assigned immortals as guards?"

His amusement drops as quickly as if I'd slapped him. "Watch yourself, huntress. Levelling unfounded allegations against another god could easily cause an incident."

I grin, feeling oddly satisfied. *There's the answer we needed. Another piece of the puzzle.* "Thank you for that. I just hate it when a riddle plagues me for days on end, you know? Anyway, I'm afraid I can't accommodate your request, Loki. You'll have to face the consequences of your actions."

"Very well. Then Fenrir will pay, I suppose."

"What do you—"

"Come now, you didn't think I came without a bargaining chip?" He points behind me.

In the distance, I can see smoke, right about where the hotel is. "Damn you, Loki!"

Ignoring his cackle, I run off in the direction of the fire.

**Fenrir**

I wake to the smell of smoke clogging my nostrils. In the distance, a high-pitched alarm rings. Warning the mortals. *A fire alarm.*

Coughing, I stand in bed. My first thought is for Artemis. I reach for her—only to find the bed empty.

"Artemis?"

I get up, pull on some clothes, and check the bathroom. No sign of her.

I look around—no bow, either. Where the hell did she go?

The smoke rises some more. The sound of people exiting the building gets louder. I massage my temples, stumbling to the exit door. Maybe she's outside.

Even as I follow in the mortals' wake, down the stairs, dread piles in my gut. *She didn't leave me. She didn't.* Everywhere I look, there's no sign of her. And when I get to the outside of the building, there's still no sign. What's left of my hope plummets, facing the inevitable conclusion—Artemis is gone, and I'm alone.

*You're not alone*, my beast says. *Never alone.*

But he doesn't deny that she's gone.

I don't get a chance to dwell on the fact. A screech sounds from above, followed by panicked screams. I look up—the cloudy skies open, and four of the dark creatures come out, a rider atop each. They waste no time descending on innocent bystanders, their razor-sharp claws digging into them.

Watching them, two thoughts hit me. I have no idea how they found me, since I didn't use my divine powers. But I also have no intention of letting them hurt more people.

I close my eyes, reach deep within for my divine power, and stop cowering in fear. *Let the darkness come. Let these creatures try to get me. Are you with me, beast?*

*Always.*

*I'll need you to keep him away…. Don't let Zalmoxis take over us.*

*We will fight him. Together.*

On a roar, I open my eyes. Fire flashes in my hands, and two blades materialize. One of the creatures closest looks at me.

"That's right," I mutter. "Come fucking get me."

**Artemis**

I see the creatures from afar, and panic rises within me with an intensity that cuts my breath. "Fenrir!"

Damn Loki and his trickster ways! To use his own son as bait….

I look up at the sky. It's too late to plead for help now, but I try anyway. "If any of you Asgardians care for him, show the hell up! We're about to be massacred."

Two seconds of a wait is all I allow myself. And then I move, diving back into the city under siege.

And it is. The cloudy skies blot out the light, turning everything into shades of gray and crimson from either fire or blood. Mortals are running this way and that, seeking shelter.

I pay them no attention, focused on one person only.

Amid all the smoke and chaos, I find him. His left arm is bloody, but he's holding a sword in each hand. And unlike before, when even his divine energy was muted, now it's not. He rises from the ground, eyes flashing, and uses one blade to block a rider's attack.

The other, he slashes at the creature's front leg. It screeches. The noise, this close by, is deafening.

He moves in for a second attack, not seeing the duo coming at him from behind.

*How the hell could Loki do this to his own son?* I still can't wrap my head around Loki's callousness and duplicity. Fenrir had told me as much, and it's not that I didn't believe him. But it was hard understanding it, given the environment I'd grown up in Olympus. This type of betrayal would've gotten anyone ostracized if they'd tried it. Since the Titans, Zeus is very much against family squabbles. He demands full loyalty, and we've all given it—and received it in turn.

But this is only more proof of how different our pantheons are. And, like it or not, I need to let it go. I can't change history nor a god as fickle as Loki, and not all families are made equal. I'll let Fenrir know about what happened in the woods and his father's role, once we're safe from this. And I'll make him understand that he *does* have someone to stand up for him. In me.

I raise my bow and notch an arrow, preparing to shoot. And then I aim, and let it go. One rider goes down behind Fenrir in a screech. The other follows after. Fenrir ducks an attack, glances around and sees me.

His expression registers shock, then confusion, and finally frustration. "What the hell are you doing back here?"

He's too far off for me to hear him, but I can read the words on his lips as surely as if I was by his side. So I run to him, shooting arrows everywhere, clearing a path until we're face to face. "Helping you."

He searches my gaze, his tone accusing. "You left."

Before I can answer him, another creature descends from the skies. Out of pure reflex, I push into him, tackling us both to the ground. The creature lands a bit farther.

On wobbly knees, I get back up, raising my bow once more. "Fenrir, we don't have much time—"

"You shouldn't be here. Not in the middle of this. Go, open a portal and head back to Olympus."

I toss him a look over my shoulder. "I was going to come back—"

"Now's not the time." I can feel his hurt, the way he's trying to hold himself together. Only I'm not about to let him. I shoot a few arrows, buying us a millisecond of time.

Then I whirl on him and kiss him, lingering as much as I can in the midst of a near-battle. "I came back," I say when I pull back, meeting his gaze. "And I wasn't leaving you for Olympus but to try and get an Asgardian to help you. Let that sink in."

He stares at me for a long moment. Then shrieks around us draw our attention. We're surrounded, and not in a good way. Fenrir curses under his breath and turns, his back to mine. Swords drawn, he looks every inch the Norse warrior he's meant to be.

The creatures charge, and I lose track of him. Arrow after arrow leaves my bow, but my aim isn't always true. Not this time. Which is why within mere moments of engaging in a fight, I get separated from

Fenrir and find myself face-to-face with two of the creatures and their riders. More would've swarmed me, but with their wings they take up so much space, two alone are enough to cut off all exits, creating a dome around me.

Smoke escapes their nostrils, emitting a noxious fume in the air. My eyes water and I cough. When I reach up to wipe my face, I inadvertently give them the opening they wanted. The riders jump off their beasts, swords at the ready, and advance upon me.

*My bow and arrow won't cut it this time.* I pull out my remaining knife, and prepare to engage. *Here's hoping all that mock-fighting with Apollo from when we were kids pays off.*

The first rider runs at me. He doesn't scream, doesn't speak, nothing. Just runs at me like a brainless soldier. Except, his attack is very much real. The sword misses me by inches as I duck, and evade him. A cut of my knife barely scrapes him. And then I recall Pegasus, and how no amount of wounds was enough to keep him down.

*If these guys are the same…*

I straighten, and tuck away my knife. A measly weapon won't do. So I bring up my hand instead, pulling at my godly energy. Manifesting a ball of fire, and tossing that at the rider. It would've worked, too, had his friend not come at me from behind.

His sword slashes into my shoulder and I yell,

moving away. My scream only spurs him on. He stabs again, this time hitting my side. I shoot a blast of energy, this time striking him full-frontal. He goes flying into his creature, both of them rolling away.

I slap my hand on the wound in my side, imbuing it with healing energy. Normally, I'd need to do this with more focus, but a few seconds is all I can spare. I then move on to my shoulder, while facing the other rider to make sure he doesn't catch me by surprise.

And then…another creature and its rider comes up behind me. Despite the impeding danger, and the fact I'm already hurt and this battle has barely started, all I can think of is Fenrir.

*Fenrir… How are you holding up?*

## Fenrir

*"I wasn't leaving you for Olympus but to try and get an Asgardian to help you. Let that sink in."*

The taste of Artemis' kiss is still on my lips. And it's with her words in my head that I move to attack the first riders before they get the drop on us. I need us both to survive this attack, so we can continue our story. Because for the first time in a long time, I think I have something worth fighting for. Someone who'll stand in my corner, and fight for me as much as I'll fight for her.

With a roar, I launch myself at another rider, hoping my swords are strong enough to cut through their bodies. And though it doesn't seem to stop them—much like no amount of wounds stopped Pegasus—it does buy me time to figure out their strategy.

Long ago, when Loki was toying with me and trying to use me, he was all about strategy and tactics. That's one of his more useful teachings that I still carry with me.

So when the riders seem to be dancing around with me, but not truly hurting me, I realize there's more to this attack.

*They don't want to kill me. They want, to…what, exactly?*

My beast provides the missing piece. *Take you. Take us. To him.*

A shudder runs through me. *Over my dead body.*

The revelation gives me the extra burst of energy I needed to keep on attacking. And attacking. Soon enough, I discover that decapitating the riders seems to *actually* keep them down. I don't know if it kills them—can they be killed?—or just puts them on pause mode until the head is reassembled with the body… nor am I willing to stick around to find out.

After the fourth decapitation, I glance around. Artemis is nowhere to be seen. Between the smoke and the creatures and their massive wings taking up space, I have no way of figuring out where she's gone.

And then something slams into me from behind. A creature and its rider, pushed by a burst of divine energy. By the time I get back my senses and stand, it's to find Artemis a good soccer field distance away from me. And surrounded by one too many creatures.

A second realization hits me, way worse than the first. *These things may have an issue killing me, but they have no such qualms with her.*

Groaning, I push to my feet. Grab the sword I'd lost, and a second one I find lying around. And then I run toward her, pulling deep inside for my own well of divine energy.

The moment I reach deep, though, darkness rises to meet me. *Finally…* The gleeful voice—Zalmoxis'—sounds loud, almost as if he's close by. I clench my fists, refusing to back off, refusing to give in.

*Help me,* I beg my beast. *I need you to fight him, and help Artemis.*

I keep pushing for the well of energy within me. And darkness continues to inch closer to my heart, demanding control. But then the warmth in my chest increases, as does the light in my palm. My beast, joining efforts with me as one once more. Our union doesn't obliterate the darkness—nothing will, short of killing Zalmoxis, I'm sure—but it keeps it at bay. And that's enough for now.

I open my eyes and lunge forward, running

faster, covering the distance between us with the speed of a wolf instead of human legs.

## Artemis

I jump out of the way of a rider's sword, and bend over. Panting, I materialize my bow once more and reach for an arrow. For the first time in forever, my fingers ache, and my muscles protest. I've never wanted to fall to my knees and surrender as bad as I do in this moment.

But I won't.

I grit my teeth and raise the bow, aiming the arrow at a rider. At the last possible moment, I move it just a bit higher, and let it loose—straight into a creature's eye. Blood splatters everywhere as it shrieks, shaking its head and stomping everywhere. One big paw lifts and falls on a rider, crushing it to the ground.

Then the maimed creature moves, stumbling into another. Their roars as they attack each other fill the air, and I cringe at the cacophony in my ears.

A light draws my attention in the distance. I blink once, then again. At first, all I see is blond hair. And then, Fenrir's form takes more shape. He's running like the wind toward me, holding not one, but two swords.

And then he's by my side. Without pausing, he

goes straight for one of the riders, neatly decapitating him. Then he turns to another. And the third.

He turns to me, panting, and walks the final steps toward me. It's only when he pulls me into his chest that I feel him trembling. He's as exhausted as I am from the effort. And the creatures keep on coming. They won't stop, that's for damn sure.

"We can't keep going like this," I say. "Are you ready to portal out of here?"

"They'll just follow us, and I don't want more innocents to suffer."

I pull back, blinking away my tears. "Your sense of duty and honor is going to get us killed one of these days."

Fenrir gives me a wry grin, then kisses my forehead. "You could go."

"I'm not leaving you, so don't even bother."

Above us, screeches resound again, close by. Two more creatures descend from the skies. One of the riders hops off, and straightens with sure movements. Something in his bearing immediately puts me on high alert. When he removes the helm, revealing Pegasus, I'm not even surprised.

I turn to Fenrir. His expression is even more guarded than before. "Can I borrow a sword?"

He frowns.

When he doesn't immediately answer, I reach for one of them. Swap him my knife. "Thank you."

Then rise on my tiptoes and press my lips to his, lingering a moment longer than I should. "Watch your back. Your father's in the area."

I turn to leave, but he moves out of his immobile pose. Reaches for my waist, pulling me close. "Artemis—"

"I'll be fine." My smile is wobbly, I know, but it's the best I can manage.

Without another moment's hesitation, I turn to Pegasus. At my approach, he unsheathes his sword.

Movement from above draws my attention. A portal opens in the sky, looking like the beginning of a tornado. And then…Valkyries emerge, on their white horses.

I glance at Fenrir. He's watching them approach, frowning. And it takes me a moment to realize why. It's not his uncle Thor leading them, this time. But a woman. Dark hair, braided. Harsh features, drawn taut in concentration. And eyes as dark as Fenrir's—though I only see them for a moment.

Whoever she is, she seems to have something in mind. Because instead of attacking us, the Valkyries start going after the creatures.

I turn my attention back to Pegasus. The battle rages around us—creatures with Valkyries, Fenrir with more riders. Pegasus and I, we're stuck in an almost frozen bubble.

"Why haven't you returned to Olympus?" he

asks. "You had plenty of time."

"I couldn't leave Fenrir. And if it's him you're here for, you're not getting him. Not unless you go through me first."

Pegasus shakes his head. "You don't understand what you've landed yourself into."

"Then tell me."

A pained expression crosses his features. "I wish I could." He raises his sword, and I know the time for talking is over.

He strikes at me first. I block the blow, kick at him, giving myself space to move. Then we circle each other.

Time and time again, we clash. I run on automation, blocking his attacks, but not truly committing myself to anything besides defense. And all throughout, I'm fighting the past. Memories of us, assailing me at every turn.

A laugh here, when I'd played a false tune on the lyre. A kiss there, just because. A soft touch, showing me love. A compliment, because he'd seen through my need for love—for being loved just for me.

I force them away, telling myself this isn't the god I knew. And somehow, I eventually gain the upper hand. It happens in an instant. He strikes at me, jaw tense, eyes on Fenrir behind me. I deflect the blow, then duck under his arm and come up close.

Sword at his neck, I still hesitate. "Tell me, Pegasus."

"Just get it over with."

"I know this sword can't harm you." Tears fill my eyes. "What did he do to you?"

Pegasus laughs darkly. "Zalmoxis brought me back to life. I was dead and he…" He shakes his head, as though unable to keep up the pretense. "He ruins everything he touches. Darkens it. He's ruined your boy, too."

"He hasn't. Fenrir can fight him off."

"Not for long."

"Tell me what he plans."

He meets my gaze for a brief moment. Then looks away, speaking in a dead tone. "To exit his prison, and remake the world. Give everyone an opportunity to bring back their loved ones."

"But—that means the dead would never have peace."

This seems to hit him, as he slouches over. His sword scrapes the ground. "Exactly."

I drop mine, too, unable to pretend for a moment longer that I could kill him. "Is there no way to escape his bond?"

Pegasus shakes his head. "Only Zalmoxis can break his hold on me. And he won't. He uses us all to…do his bidding."

"Why does he want the aegis shield?"

"He wanted to have it as a weapon. Melted into

a blade, mixed with Gorgon blood and venom from a particular beast of an older kingdom, it would harm any god or goddess." His gaze shifts to Fenrir. "You know his father contributed to the hold Zalmoxis has."

Now's my chance to get the details Loki avoided. "I do. Do you know how?"

He meets my gaze. "Loki made a deal with Zalmoxis. In exchange for help to bring about Ragnarök, he promised Zalmoxis his first born."

No wonder Loki didn't want me telling this to anyone in Asgard. It's why he loathes Hades, too, as I'd witnessed in previous Council meetings. Hades' inability to let things go, led to the gods being more wary of other pantheons. This entire time, Loki was afraid to be found out.

A cry in the distance draws my attention. I step around Pegasus, and a raw scream of pain escapes me. "No!"

Fenrir's gasping, holding onto the rider's shoulders—the rider whose sword is now impaled in his gut.

I move to run toward him, but Pegasus grabs my arm, whirling me around to face him.

"Let me *go!*" I beat at his chest, but he only shakes his head, his eyes dulled.

"I can't fight you, Artemis. Not now. Not ever."

"Pegasus, please—"

"I did love you. But you must forget me, now. Move on. Be happy. And be safe. Only Olympus can give you the protection you need."

I don't realize what he does, at first. He cuts his palm and dark liquid oozes. A portal forms, shimmering behind him. I stare, in shock. Then I see glimpses of marble floors past the shimmer, and realize it's the portal to Olympus.

It hits me then, what he means to do.

With all the effort I can master, I shove him away. Then I turn on my heels and run to Fenrir. The wind, the magnetism of the portal—the call of home—tugs at me, wrenching me backward. But I force my legs to move faster, and hold out my hands for Fenrir.

Whether my powers feel my desire, or the wind tugs on Fenrir with the same force as it does me, I don't know. But the rider pulls the sword out of him, and Fenrir falls to his knees. He should be on the ground, but instead he's being pulled to me.

When he's close enough, I launch myself on him, and grab handfuls of his shirt. Then I hold on tight, closing my eyes, even as the portal's wind pulls me inside.

We go through, smacking onto golden marble floors.

# CHAPTER 20

**Artemis**

Any relief I feel at being back home is immediately shattered when I hear a screech. A creature got through, with us! Was that Pegasus' plan, all along?

I force my thoughts away from that. He'd meant to protect me, nothing more.

Fenrir groans, and I push off him, straddling him. There's so much blood coating his shirt, and escaping him in more and more quantities. I know, on some level, that a god can't die of blood loss. But I'm also unsure what the hell those swords are made from, and whether they can be used to truly wound us.

*And I'm not about to take any chances.*

I push the shirt away from the wound, then draw within me for the last remnants of power I can muster. Healing energy fills my palms, escaping in pink rivulets all over Fenrir's chest and stomach.

His eyes burst open, and their agony-filled glimmer focuses on me.

"Stay with me," I whisper. "Stay with me!"

The screech behind me grows louder. Is the creature trying to attack us?

I try to look over my shoulder, but then I'm on the ground, thrown off Fenrir. He pushes to his feet, pulling one of the swords he'd still had in his grasp with him. And then he tackles the creature before it can get to me.

*He's crazy—even with divine powers, there's no telling what it'll do!*

Exhausted as I am, I crawl across the floor for my bow, which landed a few meters away. Fenrir's groan echoes behind me, but I resist the urge to look. Once my fingers touch the bow, I push to my back, yank an arrow out of the quiver, and notch it. Aim. And shoot.

The *whoosh* of my arrow echoes for a longer moment. It's only then I allow myself to look past it— see the creature's massive jaws open toward Fenrir, about to bite him. It seems to hear the arrow, turning toward it, and catches it right in the eye. Fenrir's sword then embeds itself into the creature's chest. A louder screech resounds, then…the creature falls.

A few feet away, Fenrir falls to his knees and lets his head drop onto the marble floor, muttering, "Some welcoming."

I crouch up, then slip again and fall. There's no trace of the portal. But I remember Pegasus' last look. Of acceptance. Of resignation.

I shake my head, and am about to head to Fenrir. Is his wound properly healed? I don't see more blood dropping onto the marble, but I need to know for sure.

Footsteps, however, stop me from moving, echoing down the corridors heading here. And from two different sides, gods emerge. As well as some immortals I'm not familiar with—no sign of Ileana or her consort, Frumos.

It seems the Greeks and their immortals are the only ones in attendance. Perhaps it's just as well, as I don't think any variation of a Council is prepared for the tale I'm about to tell them.

I focus my gaze on the gods. Ares and Hermes step out of a corridor. From another one, Athena, Apollo, and Persephone herself.

When he sees me, my brother lets out a pained cry. Then runs to me, kneeling by my side and gathering me in his arms. "ARTEMIS! What…" His eyes go past my shoulder, taking in Fenrir and the creature next to him. He pales. "What's the meaning of this? Who are you, and what in the Underworld is that monster?"

Fenrir gets up, or at least tries to. Some of the immortals surround him—us, really—and raise their hands. Magic lights their beings, reverberating in the rotunda.

Fenrir looks at me, arching an eyebrow. *How do we handle this?* He seems to say.

I touch Apollo's hand. "Fenrir is with me. The creature attacked us. It's a long story."

He glances at me, then at Fenrir again. "Fen... The Norse god who attacked Hades? You found him?"

I squeeze his bicep, a silent message between us. "He is *with me*." *And I, with him.*

Apollo does a double-take. Frowns. Stupefaction replaces the confusion. Finally, he drops his voice. "How can I help?"

"Go get Hades."

His gaze shifts to Fenrir, then he stands. Walks away. Luckily, no one tries to stop him, though I see him disappearing with Persephone down a corridor.

The rest of the gods toss questions our way. Athena is first. "What did you do with my aegis?"

I roll my eyes. "Used it as payment to an oracle."

A flush creeps up her cheeks. Ares, by her side, lets his jaw drop. "You allowed a mortal to take one of our weapons?"

"Oh, don't give me your sanctimonious bullshit, Ares. Athena was first to do so with Odysseus. Or did we all forget how deeply enmeshed she became in the war of Troy?"

A stunned silence descends. I take advantage to stand, and walk toward Fenrir, helping him to his feet.

"It seems to me, huntress," Ares says, "that you forget you played equal parts in the Trojan war."

Fenrir's eyes are filled with questions, but I give a small shake of my head. Then face my brethren. "Squabbles for later."

Ares' eyes flash. "Indeed. How about you explain what this creature is doing here? And why you have with you a god of another pantheon? One guilty of a crime?"

"He's not." To Fenrir, I say, "I will fix this. You shouldn't pay for a crime you didn't commit."

"And what proof do you have of that?"

*No. Shit. Not now.* I whirl, putting myself between Fenrir and the new arrival. "Father!"

Lightning-filled eyes meet mine. Today, he's wearing a royal blue toga held by a brooch on his shoulder. Everyone gives him a wide berth, probably sensing his annoyance.

Behind Zeus, Hermes smirks. That damned messenger god! Meddling fool. I hadn't even noticed his disappearance, else I would've realized who he'd gone to seek.

I meet Zeus' gaze. "There's more going on here than you understand."

"Is there? Because it seems simple to me. You were tasked with something. You achieved it." His gaze rests on the dead creature. "And I see you achieved it just in time. Guards, get him."

I widen my stance. "No! The creature has nothing to do with Fenrir!"

"Doesn't it?" Zeus turns to Hermes, whose smirk widens. "Were you not warned that you should not bring Fenrir back because of the creatures hunting him?"

"I—I—"

Mutters from the other gods rise.

Shit. This isn't how it's supposed to go.

"That's not—"

"You are correct," Fenrir says. "Those creatures hunted me. But not because I was in league with them."

Zeus barely spares him a glance. I feel his dismissal like a waft of cold air, and shiver. "Immortals, get him."

It's as if Fenrir didn't even speak. My worst nightmare, realized. And there's still no sign of Apollo or Hades!

Three more immortals step away from their gods, joining the three already circling us. I place myself squarely in front of Fenrir. "He's innocent. And he deserves a chance to be heard."

Zeus clenches his jaw. His tone is fully condescending, as though I'm a child in need of being reined in. "Of course he will be heard. And tried. If what you say is true, the truth will come to light. Now, come. I'm sure you're tired of your journey."

The immortals advance again. I glance at Zeus's outstretched hand, and shake my head. He frowns.

There's only one way this can go. I'd told Fenrir all about how my pantheon will stick behind me, that we're a family. Well, no better time to test it than now.

I raise my bow, aiming an arrow at my father. "Call the immortals back."

Lighting flashes in his eyes. "What do you think you're doing?"

"Spare me your righteousness. I won't let you take an innocent man. You'll make sure his truth never sees the light of day."

A long silence extends.

Then Zeus speaks. "You dare go against your own kin? Have you completely lost your mind?"

Fenrir moves behind me, touching my hand holding the bow. "You shouldn't have to pay for something I did." He steps around me, holding out his hands. "Take me."

Zeus looks at him. "I will. And her." He jerks his

chin toward me, and the guards advance on both of us.

At first, stupefaction roots me to the ground. What a fool I was. It seems my pantheon isn't that much better than the Norse, at least when things go truly bad. Smokes and mirrors. I'd counted on being the golden bounty hunter, immune to any punishment. Clearly, I was wrong.

But I can't let a small miscalculation screw us both over. Many things run through my mind. The creatures. Pegasus. Loki's betrayal. Zalmoxis.

Only one matters enough to be voiced—the only truth that will make them listen. "Pegasus is alive."

Zeus freezes. Gasps from the other gods resound again.

Athena takes a step forward. "That's not possible. I led the recovery effort, and we found no trace of him! His essence was gone. Completely."

Tears prick the corners of my eyes. "I'm telling you, he's back. I don't…. I don't understand it. But he's under someone's control."

Athena frowns. Ares shakes his head. "You're more level-headed than this, Artemis. What happened to you?"

"I'm not losing my mind!" I look at them each in turn. Weeks ago, I would've trusted them to have my back. Now? "There's so much happening—"

"Enough!" Zeus thunders. "Gods, leave us. Immortals, you stay."

No one moves.

The air crackles then, a sure sign he's getting impatient. I plead with Athena, but she simply shakes her head. Turns her back on me. As does Ares. Hermes shoots me one more victorious glare, then also leaves. One by one, they disappear. All except Zeus and three of the immortals.

I take a step toward my father. "You have to believe me. The one behind Pegasus' death and the attack on Hades—it's not Fenrir. But Zalmoxis."

Something crosses Zeus' expression. Something I've never seen—fear. But it's gone quickly, hidden behind a façade.

"How do you know that name?"

"He's the one behind this. Controlling Fenrir to attack Hades, weaken the Underworld, and escape."

"That's not possible."

"Zeus, please!"

He gestures to the immortals. "Take them both away. No soldier of mine gets to turn their back on this pantheon and not suffer any consequences."

Tears fill my eyes, but I blink them away furiously. I have no choice but to follow the guards with Fenrir.

**Fenrir**

The guards—immortals? They have the same energy about them as Ileana—take us down a long winded corridor. I soak it all in. The golden walls. Lush carpets. Perfumed air. Torches lighting it all.

My gut still aches, but Artemis' healing energy healed it enough so it won't give me trouble.

*What a fucking mess…* The guilt at having gotten Artemis so messed up in this rises in me like a tidal wave. I'm meant to protect her, not get her entrenched in everything else. And having her punished alongside me is pretty much the worst it could've come to be.

She should've left while she had the chance. And I should've listened to her and portalled us out of that hell while I could've. But would more innocents' death have made me feel less guilty, in the end?

*Anything is worth not seeing her in pain.*

The immortals stop in their tracks. The head one says, "Who goes there?"

"Hel, of the Norse pantheon."

"And Anubis, of the Egyptian."

It's only then I lift my gaze from the ground. I hadn't dreamt her, then. My sister, riding a Valkyrie's horse, coming to my rescue in the earthly realm. I soak her in—the long, black hair, braided. Her equally dark habit—she seems to be favoring leather now, though I recall her from eons ago having loved her flowery dresses.

And next to her, Anubis. He wears a thick golden necklace, and nothing else, showcasing a full chest of bronzed skin. On his hips is a beige loincloth, stopping right above the knees. A simple attire, by most accounts. But there's nothing simple in the energy I feel emanating from him.

I turn my attention to Hel. "What are you doing here, sister?"

"Silence," one immortal says.

But the goddess' words are for me only. "Odin sent me in advance of his arrival. He had to take care of some things back home. Work some memory spells on mortals…undo the damage of the attack." Her expression softens. "Why did you not come to us, if you were in danger?"

"I… there was no point. How did you even know?"

Her gaze goes behind me, and I know without looking that it's Artemis she's focusing on. "I heard her plea."

She'd said as much, but I didn't believe her. I'd thought it was a flimsy excuse. Because why would she have gone to get me help from Asgard, when I'd told her how little my pantheon cares for me?

Now, I realize how foolish I was.

"Thank you for coming," I mutter.

Hel nods.

The man by her side speaks for the first time.

"Where are they being taken?"

"In solitude, until Zeus calls the Council," says the other immortal.

"Of pantheons, or of his pantheon?" Anubis asks.

"We do not know."

"Then find out," Anubis growls.

The immortal he's staring at stares back, but loses the battle and takes off to do as much.

I meet Anubis' gaze. "Why are you involved?"

"Because those creatures you fought? And the one who, rumor has it, entered here? They were created by Heka priests. And I trained them."

The pieces mash together in my head, forming a fuller picture. The crazy old hag was right.

Anubis nods at Hel, then glances at Artemis. For a moment, the jackal head disappears, leaving behind his human form. Dark eyes, a hard jaw, a glint of granite in his gaze. "You and I, huntress, we have unfinished business. But today is not the day for it." He then disappears down the hall.

"This is not over," Hel says, distracting me from his warning. "We will make sure you receive a just trial." She looks at Artemis. "Do you know anything that could help with that?"

A beat of silence, then, "No."

Hel nods and disappears down the hall. The remaining two immortals lead us to some pale golden doors. They open, revealing a small apartment. One bed, a dinette area, a bathroom I can see gleaming in the distance. For a prison, it's more than decent.

But when those doors close behind them, I'm under no illusion. Gilded though this is, it's still a cage.

And I've dragged Artemis with me into said cage.

The problem is, another nagging thought has hold of me and won't let go. I think back to Hel's last question. Artemis' silence. The air shifting before she'd taken a breath, as if to steel herself.

I trust her. I have ever since she tried to protect me the first time, and the realization is not as mind-blowing as I thought it would be.

But it doesn't help my confusion. She's been all about helping me. And now that one of my pantheon finally showed up to do as much….

I turn to her, frowning. Take on her dejected expression, the pain in her gaze, the slouched way she's holding herself. Watch as she drops to the floor by the door, head in her hands.

But despite it all, I can't stop the words from tumbling past my lips. "Why did you lie to Hel?"

# CHAPTER 21

**Artemis**

I look up at Fenrir's question. Do my best to shake off the exhaustion tugging at me, the pain in my chest.

I should be used to Zeus's ways by now. But I'd never in a million years thought he'd be so dismissive of his own daughter. Goes to show how little I know my own father.

I clear my throat, meeting Fenrir's gaze. "Sorry, what?"

"Hel's question," he repeats. "About whether you know anything else that could help her support me. Why did you lie?"

I rub a hand over my face, then push to my feet.

"Give me a second, and I'll tell you." I stand, go to the bathroom and run the water, washing my face. Only when I reach for a towel and find none do I realize I could've just as easily used my divine powers. Because now I can… we're safe. Away from the creatures' clutches.

"Artemis."

I tear my gaze from the mirror and step back in the room. Drop onto a small chair by the window. "It wasn't out of malice. But I need to tell you something, and then you can let me know whether I was wrong."

He frowns, but leans against the wall opposite me and nods to continue.

"I left because I wanted to seek out entrance to Asgard. Convince them—or at least one of them—to come support you before we came here. On my way to the cliffs—"

"How did you plan to get to Asgard?"

"I didn't." Rolling my eyes, I add, "Not the best time for me to stop planning, I'll admit that much. But I'd hoped someone was listening." I make a face. "Someone was, but not the one we wanted."

"Loki?"

I nod. "He intercepted me in the woods, by the city. Said he wasn't working with Zalmoxis, but had an understanding. He also confirmed the immortals—the ones you're accused of killing—were his. I called him out on him not wanting the rest of Asgard to find out. In retaliation or distraction, he pointed out the fire at the hotel. I realized he wasn't above harming you….and came back."

Fenrir shakes his head. "You should have left. You—I—"

I want to stand, touch him, but there are no words that can convince him of why I came back. Not until he truly gets it. And to get it, he'd have to see himself worthy of the love.

"There's more," I whisper.

Fenrir stills, warned by my tone.

"Pegasus. When we fought… He looked at you, and said your father contributed to the hold Zalmoxis has on you."

His fists clench rhythmically. "He knew? You told him?"

His question wounds deeper than any dagger. Does he truly think I'd share something so personal with anyone, least of all someone who's an enemy to his eyes?

"No," I say softly. "He guessed. How, I don't know. I can only guess as much, but I believe it's because Zalmoxis has a hold on him, too. And has had since eons ago." I bite my lip. "I think he used you to get an Olympian, that's what the attack on Hades was all about."

"Why?"

"I don't know. Any who might, will refuse to talk to us." I wait a beat, then add, "Now do you understand why I didn't tell Hel? I don't know who of your pantheon can be trusted. I didn't want to believe they would all use you as a scapegoat but… There's no way Loki would've been able to pin the immortals' deaths on you without Odin's approval. And it was Odin who spoke at the Council to tell us about them in the first place. As for Hel… I'm grateful she came to help out with the Valkyries. But until I see more—like some actual loyalty from them to you—I just don't know."

Fenrir stares at me for a long moment, his expression unreadable. His eyes are so dark, I can't tell if they're filled with anger, pain, or something entirely different.

He eventually takes a step away, paces. Sees the golden decanter in the shape of a swan. "Is that water?"

"No."

He nods, almost to himself. "Yeah, you're probably right. No point in giving information to people who'd use it against me. Some family, huh?" Without waiting for an answer, he pours himself a glass. Sniffs. Drinks it all. Pours another. After the third, he turns back to me. "Go on, then. What else did precious golden boy Pegasus say?"

I almost don't want to tell him. But if it were me, I'd want to know. "He said that Loki made a deal with Zalmoxis. In exchange for help to bring about

Ragnarök, Loki promised him his first born. You."

Fenrir nods again. We'd theorized as much, but knowing he was nothing more than a currency to his father… An odd look fills his eyes, but he turns back to the decanter. Refills his glass. Shakes his head. Drops it on the table—loudly—and steps away. Paces.

Then turns back to it, and hurls it against the wall. It crashes to the floor, its golden glint reflecting the outside.

I stand. This is my time to intervene. "Fenrir—"

"No." He holds up a hand. "It's fine. I'm under control." A dark laugh bubbles from him. "Don't worry, I'm not about to go on a rampage."

"I didn't think you would."

The door opens as we're staring at each other, and my brother walks in. I hesitate. Then, when Fenrir heads back to the wall, I figure I might as well.

I walk to Apollo, then hurl myself into his arms. "I missed you," I whisper in his chest.

His arms come around me, hugging me tight to him. "And I, you." He pushes me away, tucking a stray lock of hair behind my ears. Then wrinkles his nose. "You smell like you've been through the swamps."

"And I have."

He shakes his head. "I don't have much time, but I have time for his."

He claps his hands, then rubs them together. Blows on me. Little flecks of gold fall on me in sprinkles, like a golden rain shower. I can feel the grime disappear off my body, the ugliness of the battle. My muscles relax, and my hair goes from grazing my back to falling in soft waves. When I open my eyes, Apollo grins at me.

He glances at Fenrir, seems to decide now's not the time to poke the wolf, and then focuses back on me. "I'm sorry I couldn't bring Hades in time. But he is coming. He's having it out with Zeus right now"—he makes a face—"and it's not going in our favor. You know how Father is."

"Don't I just."

"He won't keep at this, believe me. He can't. You're one of us."

I shake my head. "It's not just me anymore, Apollo. I won't have Fenrir pay for something he's not guilty of."

"Have you considered that he might be?"

My answer is categorical. "He's not."

Apollo sighs. "I'd feared as much. And I know how you get when you're stubborn, sister dear." He glances between us, then says, "I'll go see what's going on. Just…good luck." He hugs me again then heads to the door. Right before leaving, he turns again and claps his hands. His golden dust flies to Fenrir. "Don't say I didn't help."

Sneezes follow his statement as Fenrir accidentally inhales some of the flecks. Followed by some of the most creative swearing I've ever heard. But a moment later, his hair also falls in clean waves. And his clothes have been changed from the mortal ripped ones to something more befitting of his station.

It's weird, seeing him in breeches and armour, as well as a flowing dark cloak. It only brings out the dark blue in his eyes, and I find myself staring at him in stunned admiration. My core clenches with need as memories of many pleasures with him flicker through my mind.

The doors close, Apollo disappears. Fenrir retreats to the other side. Then paces agitatedly.

"Something on your mind?" I say sarcastically.

He mutters, keeps pacing. Until I move in front of him.

"You shouldn't have done that. Why did you do that?"

It takes me a moment to realize what he means. "Taking your side against my kin? It's nothing more than you've done for me. As for why? Because I'm not about to let them demonize you."

"You should've! Now we're stuck here and I have no way of protecting you, of getting you out." He tugs at his clothes, moving away from me. To the doors. Tries to open them, kicks them when it doesn't work. Goes to the windows, punching them—to no avail—until his knuckles hurt.

It's movement after movement filled with rage

and fear and frustration at our situation.

"Fenrir, stop! Everything here is reinforced, there's nothing to do but wait." I soften my voice as I approach him. "Don't forget any divine powers you might try to use here will take a lot out of you. We're on Olympian grounds…"

"Don't I know it," he mutters.

I take his fists in my hands, touching my thumbs over his sore knuckles. "Enough. We are where we are. Together. And I'd have it no other way."

He looks in my eyes, seems ready to say something, then stops.

Before he can, the door opens again and a familiar voice rings. "Well. When I asked you to hunt him down, this isn't quite how I thought things would turn out."

"Hades!"

I rush to the doors, ready to word vomit our entire journey. But stop dead in my tracks, because he's not alone in entering the room. Zeus accompanies him, followed by none other than Odin.

The old man with the eye patch doesn't seem imposing from a distance. But up close? There's a light in his good eye that tells me he sees a hell of a lot more than people give him credit for.

"Let me see my grandson," Odin says. "I don't trust you Olympians to take care of him."

He walks to Fenrir, cups his cheeks. Looks him this

way and that, like a mare. Then turns to Zeus and grunts. "Decent, I suppose. Now what's this about him being imprisoned? Hel was damning in her report."

"And where is she now?" Fenrir asks.

Odin waves dismissively. "Around. I wanted to be here."

Hades watches me. I try hard to ignore my father's scowl.

But when he doesn't answer Odin, I clear my throat. "As you are aware, Hades was attacked some eons ago. He implicated Fenrir. When Hades' Underworld was attacked, some twenty years ago, I was tasked to track down Fenrir and bring him here to answer some questions. The working idea was the two were related."

"Is," Zeus corrects. "The working idea *is*."

I ignore him. "I found Fenrir. But what should have been a find and grab mission became much more complicated when it turned out he was being hunted by some creatures. And that he wasn't master of his own…fate."

I glance at Hades. His mask is impassable but I need to know how much to say. When he doesn't give me a sign one way or another, I shut up, listening to my instincts.

Fenrir bows his head, opening his mouth. Something about his posture tells me he's about to admit to everything.

But before he can, an odd glow like the sun fills the room. It shines brightly into my eyes and I have to close them. When I open them again, I find Odin and Zeus frozen, as though they've become golden statues.

Hades' gaze meets mine. By my side, Fenrir stirs. Somehow, the immobilization didn't affect us three. The answer to my question comes in the form of a light. From it, Ileana and her consort, Frumos, appear.

"We cannot hold it for long," she says. "Hurry."

Hades wastes no time, though he doesn't budge from his position. "Don't move; we must stay exactly as before. I asked Ileana to freeze time as there is no way my brother will let me see you two alone. And until I can force some gods to back me up, this will be our only chance to speak."

I stare at the tiny woman, but Hades snaps his fingers. "Focus. Tell me now, we don't have much time."

And so, the story spills. I try to be as concise as possible but without omitting important details. Everything from Pegasus to Zalmoxis to the old hag to Loki makes it out.

When I'm done, Hades glances at Ileana. "Almost done." He turns his gaze to Fenrir for the first time. "You wished me no harm, back then?"

"No."

"And Pegasus?"

"Neither."

"How entrenched is Zalmoxis' control over you?"

Fenrir sighs, bowing his head. It's enough of an answer.

"Do you feel his voice now? Here?"

Fenrir seems to debate it. As he does, Hades' expression shifts. And shifts some more. It occurs to me, not for the first time, that he's always seen so much more than people show. How, though? I've had my suspicions, but it remains to be seen if I'm right.

"I'm…not sure," Fenrir finally admits.

Hades nods, as though having expected as much. "Don't mention the bit about Loki to them. If I'm right, Zeus will call a Council of the pantheons to try you. In so doing, he'll open himself to vulnerability. That's when you can bring up all the hidden stuff. Where he—and the Norse—can't deny it. And where others will contest him."

"It won't be enough," I whisper. "You know how he is, good with his words. He'll charm them all if he puts his mind to it."

"I do. And it's why I'm working on another angle, but it's taking a bit longer." Hades glances at Ileana again.

"We're out of time," she says and disappears with her consort in a puff of flowers.

Zeus and Odin resume speaking as if they'd never stopped. Except Odin pauses, turning this way and that. His one good eye is frowning. "Something is different."

Zeus blusters. "You accuse me of something, old man?"

And off they go, arguing as they're prone to do. I share a relieved look with Hades. For once, Father's arrogance serves us.

Finally, Odin says, "I agree with your proposal of calling a meeting of the Council. Let them acquit my grandson of these odious rumors."

If only he meant it. As it is, I'm more worried he wants this "acquittal" only so he can have Fenrir back in his pantheon. And I'll be damned if I let that happen.

Zeus grumbles, then nods. "I will send messengers at once."

They all leave, and I breathe a sigh of relief. Now, we wait.

**Fenrir**

When Odin, Zeus and Hades leave, I let out a huge breath I didn't realize I'd been holding. First Hel. Now Odin. Both wanting to believe me? It seems odd, to say the least.

"Are you all right?" Artemis asks.

I slide to the ground, running a hand through my hair. It feels oddly clean. Olympians are weird. In Asgard, we take great pride in bathing our bodies, in doing the little tasks mortals also take pride in.

Artemis crouches by my side, leaning into my warmth. I let her, knowing she needs it. Knowing I need it. More than I want to admit, for fear of losing it again.

"You trust Hades," I say.

"I do."

"Why?"

"Because he's a lot more than people give him credit for. He's...good. Not everyone here is."

I grunt. "Where I come from, no one speaks good things of him."

"I know. Here, too. But he's...there's more to him."

"I trust you. And so, I trust in him."

I only hope Hades' tricks extend to keeping Zeus in check. The head of the Greek pantheon is less than impressed with either of us right now. And something tells me he'd rather have my head on a silver platter than admit Zalmoxis' existence.

# CHAPTER 22

**Fenrir**

At some point, we must've both fallen asleep. I wake up in the dark of night—or what passes for night here—with Artemis nestled in my body. The softness of her, pressed against me, immediately awakens other parts of my body.

As though guessing as much, Artemis stirs in my arms. Her nose nuzzles my neck, then her lips follow the same trail.

"Artemis…"

She pulls back a little, searching my expression. Then smiles. When her lips touch mine, fire ignites everywhere. In one fell swoop, I hover over her, my body tight. Press against her. She arches against me, moaning.

I reach down for her—

And there's a knock on the door, followed by someone clearing their throat.

I jump off her as if burned. The door opens, and Hades walks in, a faint smile on his lips.

To gather myself, I turn to the decanter and pour a cup. Then, on second thought, a second for Artemis. Bring both over to the bed, and perch myself on the edge.

Artemis has no such qualms. She slides over to me, wrapping an arm around my shoulders and kissing my temple. Then turns her attention to Hades.

"I hope I didn't interrupt—"

"You know full well you did."

He looks more stunned than he should at the statement, and I have a feeling I'm missing something.

"Since when have you known?" he asks.

Artemis' expression softens. "You've just confirmed it."

"What am I missing?" I ask.

Artemis stares at Hades. After a beat, he inclines his head, as though silently giving her permission for something.

She lowers her voice. "Hades can read thoughts. No one else knows—at least, I'm assuming except for Persephone?"

Hades nods. "And the immortals."

I frown. The implications are huge. Every secret, every intrigue—

"Yes, it gets tedious," Hades says in response to my thoughts.

It also occurs to me how he knew Artemis and I had been in a compromising position. *Shite.*

Hades shakes his head at that.

"Can you ever turn it off?"

"Doesn't work that way, unfortunately."

Artemis says, "No one else can know. But this is why I've always trusted him. I knew—felt it, even back then—that there was more to him."

I nod. "You have my word, your secret is safe with me."

"Thank you." He clears his throat. "Now, as for the purpose of my visit. Zeus called the Council. It's the only reason I'm allowed in here alone with you, to come get you. They're ready for you to give your testimony."

I stand, but he shakes his head. "Not you. Artemis."

"But…I only have part of the story. Fenrir would be a much better witness. How will they know the full truth, if he does not speak?"

It dawns on me in a flash. "They won't. Your father never intends them to. Isn't that right?"

Hades answers instead of her. "Indeed. But I have a plan, and if all goes well, this should get us finally focusing on the important things."

They've gone now, leaving me alone. I pace the length of the apartment, my thoughts at odds with each other. Hades' plan might work. Or it might not. And if it doesn't, I'll never see Artemis again.

My gaze lingers on the decanter of ambrosia. Then I talk myself out of it. If worse comes to worst, I'd rather have my full faculties about.

*Good idea,* my beast rumbles.

When even a long-dormant wolf tells me to stay away from the alcohol, I know I'm in deep shit.

*Trust in Artemis,* he says. *She won't let us down.*

*That's a first for you, trusting in anyone.* Loki made sure to break that capacity in both of us.

He's quiet for a long moment, then, *She makes it worth it.*

There's nothing else I can say to that. So, I go back to pacing. And pacing some more.

**Artemis**

Two immortals follow us—luckily, it's Hades' own. I don't know how he managed to swing it, but it gives me a break on the way to the rotunda for the Council.

Hades throws me a look over his shoulder. "I simply didn't ask."

It takes me a moment to realize he's answering my thought. One thing to be thinking it, another to have it confirmed.

"Thank you," I whisper. "For trusting me. With your secret."

He reaches a hand for me. Squeezes mine. A small thank you.

Behind us, the immortals are quiet. We reach the doors, and I pause, gulping. "Somehow, when you told me I'd have to plead his case, I didn't think you meant…this."

Ileana opens the door a little, and a quick peek inside is enough to freeze me. The last Council had some representatives of each pantheon. But this time, there are so many more.

Hades grips my forearm. "I wouldn't have asked if I didn't think you capable of this. The question is, are you ready for the consequences?"

I nod, not even taking the time to weigh them. Because I know them all too well. I've seen them with Hades, and the way he's been ostracized for not meeting the ideal standard of Olympus for so long. I tried so hard to, and look where it got me.

"Let's do this," I say.

Hades steps ahead of me, Ileana and Frumos, behind me. The moment Hades enters, all eyes turn to us. Whispers and mutters ensue.

My gaze scans the various pantheons, hoping for some friendly faces. The Egyptians seem off put—but then again, their feud with us goes a long way. Perhaps it will go in Fenrir's favor. The Norse are angry—real anger or not? More to the side, classy and quiet, are the Asian pantheon. The Mayans have come, too. And the African pantheon. They're the ones seated closest to the main circle of the meeting, but there are many more besides them. So many faces…more than I've ever seen here.

I gulp again. Clearly, we've attracted quite a lot of attention.

Zeus stands, clapping three times. All noise fades. "We are here to decide the fate of the accused, Fenrir of the Norse pantheon. His crimes are—"

"Where is the accused, Zeus?" Cernunnos of the Celts asks. He's seated, but taller than most with his head of antlers.

By his side, Morrigan is dressed in a dress of leaves—or so it seems from afar. Next to her is Lugh, Celtic god of justice, oath keeping, and nobility. He holds his ever-present spear, and his green eyes are narrowed on the scene playing out.

Zeus scowls, then his mask returns to neutral. "Imprisoned, for all our safety. Artemis will testify on his behalf. Shall we get on with it?"

Odin clears his throat. "I can confirm Fenrir is

being well taken care of."

More mutters. More glances my way.

Finally, everyone settles. I step forward. "Eons ago, my uncle Hades was attacked. At the time, all hands pointed to Fenrir. When Hades' Underworld was breached, some twenty years ago, he was lucky to have the last remaining zmei help him out. He was able to reimprison Cronus."

More whispers, and shocked cries at my proclamation.

Someone from the African pantheon stands. I recognize his limber form as Anansi, the spirit of all knowledge and tales. "You mean to say, those godless creatures still exist?"

He must've missed the Council meeting when Hades announced as much. Unsurprising, given fewer gods had attended than now. So, I nod. "Two of them. And they are very much on our side."

"We are digressing," Odin thunders. "Keep on point. The attack you refer to, many said my grandson was responsible for it, too."

"Yes. That attack sparked my mission. I was tasked to find Fenrir and bring him back to face a trial."

"And it took you twenty years?" This, from Sekhmet. Bastet's sister doesn't have her feline grace, and her beauty is harsher, enhanced by a shorter haircut and the lioness form she takes on.

I scowl at her, recalling it was Bastet who'd

made me lose time with her fake lead. "Yes. Fenrir wasn't easy to find. My bounty tracking abilities focus a lot on tracing the divine energy of my target. With Fenrir… this was hard. He wasn't using it."

More mutters.

"Why not?" Anubis asks, pushing away from the pillar he'd been leaning against.

I recall his stake in this—because of the Heka priests, as he'd admitted to Fenrir—and wonder if he'll say anything about that. Given the grudge he still seemed to hold against me, I don't want to put him on the spot. But I will, if I have to.

As it is, I answer him simply with, "Because he was afraid his divine energy would bring some creatures on his tail."

"Creatures? What creatures?"

*Is he playing this?* I glance at Hades. He nods.

At a loss, I say, "Creatures that were responsible for the death of one of our own. Pegasus. And perhaps not just that…"

More whispers. More murmurs.

Athena stands straighter. "What are you getting at, sister? That those creatures have a hand in what has happened?"

Zeus gives me a warning look. I ignore it. Instead, I lift my chin up, survey them all, and say, "That's exactly what I'm saying. And the creatures are not doing so of their own accord. They would not have been able to enter the Underworld and attack, not with Hades' barriers in place. But it clearly seems that someone is using them to distract us on the surface while something else is going on underneath. And the aim, I believe, has to do with Tartarus."

"And did your quest provide answers as to whom might be responsible?" Isis, Osiris' consort, asks. Her tone is soft, curious. Open.

*Let's hope they can all keep as open a mind as her.* I take a deep breath. "Yes. Another god."

Pandemonium breaks out. Not at me, but pantheon upon pantheon. Norse yell at Greek. Egyptian confer with African—Anubis yelling he'd suspected something shady for a while. Ix Chel, on the Mayan side, meets my gaze. I wish I could plead with her, but as though sensing this, she inclines her head. Then turns to one of her own pantheon and whispers.

Only Morrigan remains quiet. Her gaze shifts back and forth between me and Hades. None of her pantheon speaks, they only watch what's unfolding.

After a bit more of the pandemonium, Zeus stands. Yells for attention. Eyes blazing, he turns to me. "And do you have any proof of what you're advancing?"

"I would, if you'd let Fenrir come and testify."

Zeus flushes. Before he can blow up, someone rises from the Egyptian pantheon. A woman, tall and willowy, with an ostrich feather in her hair.

"Continue, Artemis. As the representative of truth, justice, balance, and order of my pantheon, I wish to hear more."

To my surprise, Athena adds. "Ma'at is right. I would, too."

"And I." From behind Ares, Aphrodite waves at me.

But perhaps the most stunning is when a bulky god wearing a blood-red robe stands on the African pantheon side. His face is in shadows, but he says, "And I."

Hades lowers his voice. "That's Takhar, the god of justice and vengeance."

"Is that a good thing for us?"

He shrugs. "To be determined. Continue."

So, I do. I tell them about the attacks—the original ones, with Fenrir's additional information; the new one at Tartarus; and the ones we were subjected to, on Earth. I explain how the creatures were able to trace us. How they were focused on Fenrir and not me. How I'd realized someone was controlling him.

When I'm done, there's a dead silence.

Ares thunders, "Still does not explain why you think those creatures are tied to the original attack. Or to what has happened since."

"Because we lost Pegasus in the original attack. And yet, Pegasus is leading these same creatures now."

Athena gasps. It's the first I've ever seen her lose her cool. Zeus does flush, looking ready to slap me. Hades, by my side, wavers. I can only imagine the amount of pressure on him, with all these thoughts.

"Enough!" Odin yells. "I want to hear more."

I glance at Hades. It takes him a moment, but he shakes his head. Now's not the time.

Instead, I focus on Pegasus. And tell them about how I realized it was him. How he didn't seem himself. What Olga said, about the creatures and the god controlling them.

Anubis raises his voice when I'm done and says, "I can confirm the old hag's theory. The Heka priests had this ability because I taught them." His support has my knees weakening. Thank Thanatos and the old gods…

Not everyone seems to share my relief, as more uproar follows.

I wait until everything quiets again.

Odin speaks then. "There is but one problem with this narrative. The bit about someone controlling Fenrir. No god can possess another. Which has me thinking this is all an elaborate scheme for the Greeks to put us in a bad light!"

Hades catches my gaze. He doesn't have to say it, I feel it in my gut. Now's the time.

"That might be true," I say sweetly, "but perhaps it's within your pantheon you should look. As it's none other than Loki himself who made a deal with the god, giving Fenrir up. All to bring about your dreaded Ragnarök."

Stunned silence. Whispers, as some gods try to catch my meaning.

And then, an uproar. "You allow your son to do this?"

"He breaks the laws!"

"Pantheons are families!"

And more. And more. And more.

"How dare you?" Odin says.

My anger, previously tightly leashed, pokes its head. "I dare because truth has always been my friend. And truth alone is what we all seek." I jab a finger his way. "*You*, on the other hand, lied."

Thor, behind him, launches to his feet. "Watch yourself—"

"No. No more 'watching myself' and being quiet." I level my gaze at my father, at Odin, then back at the pantheons. "Odin came in front of a Council of our peers and said they'd found two dead immortals. *Fenrir's* immortals. He let it be implied that Fenrir himself was guilty of killing them. Not once did he clarify that the immortals were never to guard Fenrir, but instead to guard his father—Odin's son—Loki."

"Zeus, get your daughter in hand, right now!" Odin yells.

But my father, for once, is silent.

Next to me, in a whisper, Hades explains why. "Don't be fooled. He likes this, sees that it weakens Odin in the eyes of the others."

I purse my lips. The last thing I want is to give my father more ammunition. So, I pull back, redirecting the conversation. "What do you have to say about Loki's deal, Odin? I received confirmation from your son's very lips."

His answer, this time, is not as strong. "No god would have been strong enough to offer such a thing."

I meet his good eye firmly. "An old god would. Zalmoxis."

And this is where Zeus loses it. "Take her back to the apartment!"

Immortals come for me. Hades gives one sign to Ileana and Frumos, and they surround us in bright light. My voice becomes amplified, with no one able to bypass their barrier.

"I will not lie nor suppress the truth. Zalmoxis is part of the old gods, and he has been imprisoned, but not in Tartarus. Wherever he is, he's coming for all of us. Zalmoxis is the one who orchestrated the first attack on Hades, using Fenrir as his weapon. He's the one who also breached Tartarus, helping Cronus. And he will not stop until he escapes from wherever he is. I will not let an innocent god pay for his crimes, and neither should you. Fenrir should be freed. And our attention should focus on Zalmoxis, no one else."

I take a deep breath, waiting. Mortals at least have someone to pray to in times of need. I have no such option. I can only hope my words got through.

Hades steps forward. "Though this tale seems crazy, we have more proof to show."

He glances at Osiris, who stands. The god's olive-complexion seems pale to my eyes, though he moves with assurance, handing his crook and flail to Isis. Moments later, he heads to the grand doors and lets in a giant of a man. Atlas. He's the only one not imprisoned from the original Titans, on account of not being seen as a threat.

"Atlas, Titan of the old, speak your piece."

Atlas clears his throat, surveying everyone. Taller by almost two heads than the rest of us, larger in the shoulders, he's still somewhat…subdued. I realize why when his gaze lands on me—filled with so much sadness it makes my throat tighten.

Atlas soon looks away, though, and speaks. "We knew of Zalmoxis. Of his crimes. He roamed free when we—the old gods—did. When there were no rules, no boundaries. Except one. Not to mess with the fabric of life and death. He did. And for that, he was punished. And his name erased from history, though I am told some mortals still worship him. But what many do not understand is the impact Zalmoxis' actions had."

He takes a deep breath, his massive frame shuddering as though the words themselves pain him. Hades, by my side, trembles. Even my father, when I glance at him, looks shaken.

"You see," Atlas continues, "Zalmoxis is the reason darkness has entered our realms, including Earth. Shifters. Vampires. Ghouls. Wraiths. They all pull from it. And that darkness entered when he broke the ultimate law, undoing death's barrier. For his dead daughter, a half-goddess. The same one whom he'd first made immortal. Her one weakness was that she could choose when to end her own life. And she did, after her mortal husband died. But Zalmoxis, he could not accept this. So, he tried to undo it. To not only break the barrier between life and death for the gods, but also to take away a choice. And we have all suffered the price for it, in some form or another."

Everyone listens, riveted. There's no other sound than Atlas' booming voice.

"I am no longer part of these meetings. But I came here at Hades' request, to plead with you all. Take him seriously. Find him, before he causes more havoc. And do not punish those he uses as pawns."

He settles in a corner, by Osiris and Isis. My gaze lingers on him, soon torn away when Isis herself speaks.

"This Fenrir… Why do you take his side, Artemis? He is not of your kin. He is not your responsibility."

"You're correct, he's not. But in the days I've spent with him, I've seen goodness in him. I'd gone after him expecting a beast, a monster, and I found…a flawed god. Like all of us. I know I'd like a second chance, if I screwed up. Does he not deserve the same?"

She nods, offering me a faint smile.

Hades takes advantage of the silence that follows and says, "I propose a vote. For Fenrir."

"I agree," Isis says.

"And I," Osiris adds by her side.

"A vote on what, exactly? Surely you don't expect us to let this god go," Zeus says. "No matter what Artemis says, he still attacked another god. *You.* And by all accounts, he still could."

"Because of an outside influence."

"According to one person."

"Who happens to be your daughter, and my niece."

Dead silence reigns as Hades and Zeus glare at each other.

"Or are you calling her a liar?"

I hold my breath. Hades is imposing when he wants to be.

Zeus snorts. "No. Just a besotted fool."

This is the wrong thing to say. More goddesses

in the audience rise up, including Athena. "Are we then all fools because we love?"

"That's not—" Zeus catches on too late on what he has unleashed.

Hathor, goddess of love for the Egyptians, stands too. "Yes, are we? Because love is not a weakness, oh *mighty* Zeus."

Zeus winces at her glare and sarcasm.

A beautiful woman with sharp teeth and a leopard's tail rises next from among the Asian pantheon, who'd been quiet up to now. "What a foolhardy god you can be, Zeus," she says. "To act as though your own daughter is an enemy?"

"Xiwangmu, hush!" Another woman tugs her down. I try to place the name, and vaguely recall she's the goddess of immortality, also known as the Queen Mother of the West.

One by one, more goddesses rise. Ix Chel of the Mayans, Morrigan of the Celts, Aphrodite herself. They don't all speak, but their disdain is clear.

Realizing as much, Zeus drops in his chair and waves his hand dejectedly. "Let us vote, then."

To my surprise, Morrigan steps forward. "What if instead of voting for freedom or imprisonment, you impose a penance, to be carried here? In Olympus, under a guardian."

Shocked gasps and mutters spread. I glance at Hades, but his expression is full-on granite. A look passes between him and Morrigan that I can't decipher. And then another speaks—one I hadn't expected.

"I see nothing wrong with that proposal," Poseidon says.

"Nor I," my brother adds.

I mouth a *thank you* and get a thumbs up back. More gods and goddesses nod.

Bastet adds, "I would still put a collar on him," but that gets more chuckles rather than anyone taking it seriously.

Zeus puts an end to the pandemonium. "And who would be stupid enough to volunteer for this task, knowing their very existence could be threatened at any point?"

Hades looks at me and nods. I step forward, chin up. "I would."

Zeus stares at me. He shakes his head. "Artemis, just because your uncle—"

"Hades has nothing to do with this. Zalmoxis does. Let's put our focus there. I will take on responsibility for Fenrir. Draft whatever contract, I will sign in blood if need be."

Gasps echo all around. While we may not get along on most things, all pantheons understand blood oaths. There's a reason human witches fear them, and it has to do with us.

"That seems acceptable to me," Morrigan says. "All in favor?"

Heads nod all around.

Morrigan pulls out an old parchment and ink from thin air. Then scribbles on it. It flies to me. Without hesitation, I prick my finger, and sign. A reddish glow imbues the parchment. At the same time, I feel a tug in my chest, like a tiny bit of me was yanked out. *A price paid.*

The parchment flies back to Morrigan. She shows it around, my blood signature visible and glowing softly. "All in favor of Fenrir serving his penance in Olympus—for, shall we say, fifty years?—in Artemis' guardianship, say aye."

No one is more surprised than me to hear the ayes all around. Except, maybe, for my father, whose incensed glare never leaves me.

# CHAPTER 23

**Fenrir**

It failed.

Nothing else can explain the dead silence that's been ringing all around. I've tried asking the immortals for an update—might as well have been speaking with a wall. They only shrugged and told me to return to the chambers.

Which I did. Only to more pacing.

Eventually, my thoughts turned inward. To how the hell I'll be able to say goodbye to Artemis, when my heart feels so intertwined with hers, we might as well be one.

If anyone had told me eons ago, when I was on

the run, that the same person responsible for hunting me down would become my biggest supporter…that she would steal my heart…. I would have told them to take a hike.

But it's the truth. A soon-to-be painful truth, now.

My gaze shifts to the bed. To this morning. To wishing I'd finished what I'd started, so I could at least have that memory to cling to.

*I will be with you,* my beast says.

I let out a sigh. *I know. But I'm not looking forward to more dungeons and caverns.*

*Perhaps that won't be the case.*

*Since when did you become the optimist?*

Murmurs of voices outside draw my attention, interrupting my mental squabble with my beast.

A moment later, one of the immortals opens the door. "You're wanted in the Council."

I'm moving before he's even done speaking. "Do we know why?"

He shrugs, and I follow him and the other immortal down the corridor. Every step feels like it takes forever and a breath, all in one.

Finally, I'm brought in front of large oak doors. An energy pulls them from within, and they open. My jaw drops.

Over a hundred gods and goddesses of each pantheon must be joined in one spot. My eyes linger over various aspects of each pantheon—the togas for the Greeks, the armors for my kin, the leaves for the Celts, the silken robes for the Asians, and so on.

Then, in their midst, my gaze lands on Artemis. She turns to me, tears in her eyes. And that alone tells me everything has gone to shite.

The immortal behind me prods me onward, so I take a step. And another. Soon, I'm by her side. Artemis holds her hand out, and I take it. Gulping, I face the plateau where the head gods and goddesses of each pantheon stare at me.

Osiris speaks first. "We have been told quite a tale, Fenrir of the Norse pantheon. You are lucky to have such a passionate supporter."

I nod, my throat tightening. "Thank you. I am."

"In light of all that has happened, I think it only fair you know where we stand. We will secure a task force led by Athena and Ares to seek out any and all information about Zalmoxis. All of us will reach into our pantheons for whichever gods or beings are elderly, and ask for what they know."

The words become muffled to my ears.

"And as for you, Morrigan had a fantastic idea."

She steps forward, a vision in green. "You will serve penance for your attack on Hades for fifty years…."

I close my eyes. So, I did lose.

"…in Olympus. Under a guardianship."

*Wait, what?*

I open my eyes, forcing my lips to part. "What?"

Morrigan smiles. "Artemis volunteered."

I freeze. For so long, all I do is stare at her. Then I turn to Artemis. Read the hesitation in her features—at my reaction. And then I drop all pretense and kiss the shit out of her.

Vaguely, I'm aware of hoots and calls from the gods closest to us. Mutters from others—not everyone is supportive, what a surprise. But above all, I feel Artemis melting against me. Kissing me back. Sighing happily against me when I pull back and hug her.

*Told you we would be fine, with her,* my beast says.

*I'll learn to never doubt you again, beast.*

And somehow, I know it'll be all right.

Everything else goes by in a blur. Morrigan—as Zeus seems quiet—takes over explaining that I'm free to return with Artemis to her chambers. But that Hades or someone would be by to explain the rules of the guardianship.

Artemis is bouncing with excitement, so the moment we can escape, we do. Running down the corridors, laughing.

I grab her waist at the first opportunity, pulling her against me. She's breathless, emerald eyes latched onto mine. I cup her cheek, caressing her lower lip with my thumb. "You're crazy. Doing this, for me?"

She laughs, then pushes on her tiptoes to kiss me. "I am. And I have no qualms about it!"

When her lips press against mine, they remind me of our unfinished business this morning.

"How far away are your chambers?"

She laughs again. "Not too far…"

And then she's running. And I'm chasing. Within moments, we barge through white oak doors into a room. I don't pay much attention to the surroundings. My attention is solely focused on the goddess in front of me.

Her brilliant eyes. Her heaving chest. Her parted lips.

I take a step closer. She takes a step back. Smiles. And we continue the dance. Until her legs back into the wall. And she knows she has nowhere to go.

It's my turn to grin as I take my sweet time approaching her. Place my hands on either side of her head. Nuzzle her temples, her jaw, her neck.

Listen to her heartbeat quickening.

When I kiss the fluttering pulse at her neck, she moans. Everything else is a flurry of motions. Her arms, around my neck, tugging my mouth to hers. Our lips, fusing together in a battle of wills. Her legs, around my waist. My hands, pushing her dress out of the way. Ripping my own garments.

Until we're both standing naked. And I'm so damn ready for her, I could burst. But I still, my tip right near her heat, ready to thrust inside of her.

Artemis moans in my ear. "Fenrir, please. Why did you stop?"

I shake my head. "I'm not going to be a brute this time."

She arches an eyebrow. "And why not?"

"Because I want to worship you like the goddess you are."

I start dropping my knees, but her legs tighten around me, almost viciously. The hand that had been at my nape, grazing my skin gently, now tugs on a fistful of hair. Until our gazes are locked, and she has my full attention.

"Worship me later, Fenrir. Tonight, just fuck me senseless."

She reaches between us, strokes me once, twice, and then positions me at her entrance. The look she gives me dares me to disagree.

And I may be many things….but a fool, I am not.

So I groan, and thrust inside her tight heat. Drop my head to her shoulder, my gaze to where we're joined. A shudder runs up and down my spine, followed by a trail of pure fire.

Artemis gasps, pulling me even closer. "More."

She'll be my undoing. But I'll die a happy god.

Though Artemis got her way, I got mine, too. Worshipped her for the rest of the night, until we both fell asleep, exhausted.

The next morning finds us still in bed, lingering with some food we'd conjured. She fills me in on what I'd missed—including a Titan's apparition, apparently—and how the gods seem to have been split on how much to believe. Though, it seems her speech had been powerful enough to convince them I'm harmless, in her care.

I shake my head. "I wonder whose door they'll be knocking in the Norse pantheon, to look for answers. Odin is the oldest one I know."

Artemis bites into a grape, shrugging. "I'm sure we'll hear news. They said someone would come by and explain us the rules, remember?"

"Did they? All I remember is needing to get you alone."

She laughs, leans over for a kiss, and smiles. It feels perfect, this moment.

A moment later, the door opens and Apollo strides in. Stares at me, on his sister's bed. Then grins and hops onto the edge of it, within a respectful distance. He leans over his sister's legs with a mischievous smile. "Well. I seem to have interrupted."

"Don't be crass, Apollo." Artemis grins, gently shoving him. "What are you doing here?"

"Come to meet my sister's lover, of course, in the hopes of a better mood than last time. Or should I say, charge, not lover?"

It dawns on me. "You came to explain the rules."

Apollo nods, pops a strawberry in his mouth and then says, "Father isn't pleased. I need to preface this."

"Of course."

Though nothing changes in Artemis' demeanor, I pick up on the faint sadness in her eyes. As, it seems, does Apollo.

I reach for her hand, then tuck a stray lock of hair behind her ear. The gesture makes her smile. When I look back at Apollo, he gives me a seemingly reluctant nod. Apparently, I've met his approval.

He clears his throat and a scroll materializes in the air. He unravels it and reads, "Fenrir is to remain at all times in Olympus blah blah blah for the duration of a full fifty years. Such terms can and will be renegotiated by the Council should he do anything untoward any members of the Council or other pantheons which might add to his sentence."

Artemis rolls her eyes. "He won't."

"Artemis, Goddess of the Hunt, is to serve as his guardian. She will be responsible for every misdemeanor and will answer directly to the Council. As part of the blood oath—"

I spit out a mouthful of ambrosia. "BLOOD OATH?" I turn to Artemis. "Tell me you didn't."

She avoids my gaze, finding the tray of food much more interesting. "There was no other way to show them we were serious."

"Artemis—"

She looks up, then—at Apollo. "Go on."

He gulps, and quickly scans the rest. "Uh, the rest is basic. He's not to be privy of Council meetings. He can't meet with any member of his pantheon unless you or someone appointed by you is present. And going forward, he can only wear Olympus garments and use Olympian weapons."

Artemis nods. "I'd expected as much. Thank you."

Apollo glances at me, then her. Stands and kisses her cheek. "Anytime. You know where to find me."

He's gone the moment after. I wait until the door closes behind him to walk around the bed and kneel in front of Artemis. "Why did you do it?"

"I told you why."

"Artemis, I love you, but that's no reason to—"

"You love me?" A grin splits her features.

I shake my head. "Of course I do! But that's no reason to—"

She kisses me, shutting me up. "I don't care."

"Blood oaths are dangerous. We both gave Olga shit for taking our blood. And now you do this?"

She shrugs. "It'll be worth it."

When she kisses me again, I can deny her nothing.

## Artemis

Everything was too perfect, of course. So when someone knocks on the door of my bedroom two days later, I know it can't be good.

Sure enough, Hades soon walks in. Fenrir takes one look at him, and his expression pales. "Did they—change their mind?"

He shakes his head. "No. Got another problem. Come with me, both of you."

We follow him in silence out of the room, down a few corridors. I can see Fenrir trying to memorize the route. I'll have to explain to him later that it's pointless, since Olympus is a mercurial maze, rearranging itself when the need hits.

Eventually, we stop in front of reddish-dark doors. Hades pushes them open, and I'm surprised at the faces waiting for us.

Osiris, king of the Underworld in the Egyptian pantheon. Hades himself, of course. And...Hel, goddess of the Underworld for the Norse.

Fenrir's expression shows stupefaction. She, on

the other hand, simply nods at him as though this was any other day.

"I don't understand. What are you all doing here?" Fenrir asks.

Hel says, "Odin doesn't know I'm here. We each went deep into our respective realms, seeking a trace of Zalmoxis—somewhere he might have been imprisoned under our noses. Nothing. Which means the human witch was right."

"You…believe me?"

She sighs. "I wasn't going to. Until I heard some tall tales of creatures brought to life by Heka priests. And Anubis himself said it was true. But more to the point…. Loki."

I can sense Fenrir tensing, and reach for his hand. Squeeze it in silent encouragement and support.

"What about Father?" he asks.

"He wouldn't have been able to strike the deal with Zalmoxis unless someone facilitated it. Someone who would also benefit from such a trade."

I frown, racking my brain for who she means. And then it hits me. We're missing the American, Asian and African representatives of the Underworld but also… "Aed?" I ask.

Hel meets my gaze, grudging respect in hers. "Bonus points for Little Red. As the prince of the Daoine Sidhe and a god of the Underworld of the Celts, he might have been involved."

"That makes no sense," Fenrir mutters. "His pantheon has nothing to do with any of this!"

"That's what we thought," Hades says. "Until one of my immortals overheard something." He gives us both a look, and I catch his silent meaning. By "his immortal," he means his ability to hear thoughts. "Odin and Loki were arguing, and Odin pressed him on whether he's sure his Celtic connection knows nothing of this, saying that he's kept quiet all along because he didn't want trouble with the Celts on top of the others. All Loki said was to 'leave Aed out of this.' Either he knows something or it's a false trail. Either way, it needs to be followed. Perhaps the old witch would know more."

"The problem is, we cannot find her either," Osiris says. "She disappeared."

An odd feeling runs up and down my spine. Not quite dread…but not happiness, either, at the news. "What about the aegis?"

"The cabin was empty of divine weapons."

I nod, trying to keep my features cool. "So, what then? What's next?"

"Zeus refuses to launch an investigation aside from Ares and Athena on their little quest," Hades says. "He refuses to talk to the Titans, who would know more. Atlas offered to head to Tartarus and was rudely rebuked and threatened with more sanctions. So…. It's up to us. And if Zeus won't allow

Atlas to go...we must head in the one place he seems determined to keep us away from. Tartarus."

My stomach sinks. "I'll go, if it's what you're asking."

Osiris shakes his head. "No, not you. I have someone better in mind. Anubis."

Hades squeezes my shoulder. "We needed to let you know, is all. Away from prying ears. So you'd understand someone is working on freeing Fenrir from Zalmoxis' influence. I promise."

I nod, kiss his cheek, then drag Fenrir after me. Once outside, we take our time returning to my rooms.

Fenrir runs a hand over his face. "This is insane. So many facets to this plot... When will it end?"

"Whenever it does, we'll face it together."

He meets my gaze. "We're of two different pantheons. With two different points of view, and drastically different ways of handling things. This won't be easy."

"Then we'll just have to bring them together." I step closer, gaze locked onto his. "Whatever happens, I'll be with you. Forever."

Some of the tension seeps out of him, and he leans in for a kiss. I take the moment, the simple joy, and allow it to fill me. Something tells me things will get more and more complicated.

# EPILOGUE

Hades waited until the door closed behind Artemis and Fenrir. Then he turned back to his war room, his expression fierce. "I want to be clear. My brother does not intend to do anything about this. And I will not let my niece suffer. Are we understood?"

Osiris nodded. He'd already been on board, unsurprisingly. His own issues with his brother Set had prepared him for all kinds of coups.

Hel had taken some convincing. "I don't know what bugs me more about this theory. Odin knowing, or Loki and his weird connection to the Celts. Why? He's a trickster."

Hades shrugged. "Perhaps he found a better trickster than him…who knows?"

*It is odd, though. I wonder…* Out loud, Hel said, "Would it be worth it if I approach him? I'm his daughter, after all. Maybe if I call him out?"

It took Hades some concentration to focus solely on the part she said out loud. That was the problem with running intrigues—especially when he could hear the thoughts of everyone involved. "If you do, you will attract his attention upon us. And before we do that, we need more allies." He tapped his chin. "Who could we trust?"

Osiris leaned back in his chair. "From my pantheon, many. Sobek and Thoth each have bones to pick with him—something about past grievances. Bastet, Sekhmet and other goddesses… Let's just say it won't take much to sway them. Many other gods have taken umbrage to Zeus and his way of…handling things." *I need to remember I'm speaking to his brother. If this was to go sideways, everything could be used against me.*

Hades watched the god for a moment, debating on how to address the unspoken side, without tipping his hand. Finally, he said, "Understood. And, for the record—I know how my brother is, make no mistake. I'm under no illusion of what he would do, were he to find out what's going on here." He leaned forward. "We're taking matters into our own hands, and if this was to come to light, I am prepared to take the fall."

"It won't come to that," Hel interjected. "We're all in this. And if we amass enough supporters, we should be fine."

"Which brings us back to my question—who can we trust?"

Osiris stood then, pacing. "First, we should approach the gods who deal with death in every pantheon. Perhaps not Aed of the Celts, but what about Ishtar?"

Hades racked his brain, trying to situate the name. Hel saved him the trouble by asking, "What pantheon is she from?"

"The Middle Eastern. You won't have seen her much at Council meetings, she's rarely in public. She, uh, messed with the goddesses of the Underworld in her pantheon and lost. In order to escape them, she surrendered her husband as payment." Osiris shrugged. "I suppose that's not seen very well with the rest of her kin."

"If she's an outcast, you think she'll be open to this?"

Osiris seemed to think it over. "I'm not sure. She's the goddess of sexual love and fertility, but also of war. 'Lady of battles,' they called her. I could ask Isis to reach out, test the waters."

Hades nodded. "Do so. But, subtly."

"My wife is nothing if not diplomatic."

Hades turned his attention to a smaller door, behind a corner that had been hidden from their visitors. "Atlas, you can come in now."

The big Titan entered and sat afar from them all, as though fearing he would scare them.

"I apologize for needing to keep you away," Hades said. "I figured it's best only a few of us know of your implication."

Atlas nodded. "I understand." *I am used to being kept apart.*

His thought sent an odd wave of sadness into Hades. If there was one thing he was very well acquainted with, it was being the outcast.

"I could not help but overhear," Atlas said. "You seek alliances?"

Hades shared a glance with his companions, then considered Atlas. The Titan had much to gain by being on their side, but he could gain even more by going to Zeus. He had not done so…yet. But could he really be trusted?

"I can see why you hesitate, Hades, but I mean no harm." He ran a hand over his face, and sat. "Truly, I am tired. Of being here, living here. I have much information that I could share with you, but in so doing, I ask for one thing only. And it is fitting you are all three here, as it might require input from you all."

Hel arched an eyebrow. "Already with the demands?"

Atlas meet her gaze, but there was no malice in his. Simply exhaustion. "Would you not do the same, if you were presented with a chance to escape your prison?"

Hel went quiet. They all did, and judging by their thoughts, they were willing to listen.

He was first to say, "Let's hear it, then. What is it you wish?"

"To be killed."

"We cannot kill each other."

Atlas waved a hand in dismissal. "Then reincarnate me. Whatever it is you need to do, I wish to be *gone* from here, to no longer be Atlas."

Already, Hel and Osiris' thoughts were going haywire. Hades tried to tune them out and focused on nodding. "I will not speak for my companions, but I agree with your terms."

After a beat, Hel and Osiris indicated their acquiescence as well.

"Thank you," Atlas said, this time in the Old Tongue.

Hades felt a shiver run up and down his spine. "You are welcome. Now, where would you like to start?"

*What the hell? Why is he speaking the ancient language again?*

Hades froze. Osiris was right. He'd slipped into the Old Tongue, once more. Clearing his throat, he repeated, "What is it you wish to tell us now, then?"

Atlas' tone dropped another octave. "As I said, I did not mean to eavesdrop. But if it is alliances you seek, you would do well to seek out the older gods."

Hades frowned. "If this is a scheme to get the rest of the Titans out of Tartarus…"

*As if they deserve to. I may not like Olympus, but I would not wish it destroyed, either.* "No, it is not," Atlas said aloud. "I mean from other pantheons. Avoid the Norse giants, they are tricksters much like Loki. But there is one, in particular, who might be open to help."

"Don't keep us in suspense," Hel muttered.

"He is called the Thunderbird by those who worship him, in the North American pantheon. You would not have heard of him, as the old mortals— the Lakota tribe—would have most of the stories about him. But he goes by Wakinyan."

"And what, exactly, does he hold dominion over?"

Atlas' grave expression seemed to sober even more. "The sky. Some say he is but an assistant god, others that he is the guardian of the sky." He paused. "I met him, once. Long ago. He is powerful, and he is just." A wry smile appeared on his lips. "Zeus would hate him."

"And yet my brother hasn't ever encountered him?"

"No. As you may have noticed, your brother is focused on the here and now. The past, the future, are irrelevant to his way of living."

"Mm." Hades knew it was true. After all, Zeus' refusal to even take the Zalmoxis issue seriously was what was slowly pushing the gods into other ways of dealing with it. "Why this…Thunderbird, though?"

"Because he is constantly engaged, even now, in battling malevolent spirits or serpents of the Underworld of his realm. And unlike most of you, he *is* able to be in other godly realms, without losing much of his power."

"You think he might help us, then?" Osiris asked. "To fight these creatures, and Zalmoxis—if we ever find him?"

"I do."

Hades nodded. "Very well. Isis can try to approach Ishtar, and Hel—could you see about meeting this Thunderbird, and whether he would be willing to help?"

Hel tapped her chin, then gave a mischievous smile. "I can, indeed. Maybe he could even help me round up some of my wayward Underworld creatures."

Hades turned back to Atlas. "Thank you, again. This will be helpful. And if Wakinyan chooses to help us, we may be one step closer."

Osiris stopped his pacing then. "One step closer

to what, exactly? It is one of the questions I meant to ask. If we do find Zalmoxis, what then? The way he was imprisoned was for a reason, I would assume." His gaze went to Atlas at that. "Do you know where he is?"

"No, none of the Titans were involved in it. We heard about it after the fact, from another pantheon."

"Who?" Hades asked.

"The Celts."

"Again, with the Celts," Hel muttered. "This could explain how my father got linked to Aed."

"I will ask Morrigan to dig deeper into her pantheon, then," Hades said.

Atlas cleared his throat. "I do not know where Zalmoxis was imprisoned, but it was done so because it was the only way to keep his power in check. As god of death, the Underworld would have been his source of power. A prison on any other realm would have meant an opportunity to escape. What we were told was that the place chosen for him meant he would never escape."

*And that worked out so well,* Osiris thought.

"I agree," Hades said. Then realized what he'd done—replied to Osiris' thought—and quickly recovered with, "That the Underworld would have been a useless place to put Zalmoxis in. But Tartarus being linked to every one of our underworlds means, perhaps there is a way to Zalmoxis through there. Unless you think that's a wasted attempt?"

Atlas shook his head. "No, I believe it is the right way forward."

"Which brings me back to my question," Osiris pointed out. "What *is* the way forward? Once we find him."

Hades rubbed his chin, deep in thought. None of them seemed to have the answer.

Atlas concluded as much, as he said, "I may have a suggestion." When he had their undivided attention, he added, "Stripping him of his powers would work."

"And how is that even possible?"

"You will need some alliances with less spotless gods."

"You mean, seek out those who break the rules?" Hel asked.

Atlas nodded. "They would know. And if they do not, one of the older gods will."

Hades sighed. "We'll add it to the ever-growing list of this little mission of ours. First, let's focus on alliances and actually finding Zalmoxis. Speaking of, can you tell us everything you know about him? And Cronus." Hades shared a look with Osiris. "If he's heading into Tartarus, Anubis will need all the help he can get. If Zalmoxis himself isn't there... Someone there knows something."

They all turned to Atlas. He bowed his head and said, "I will tell you everything you wish to know."

Anubis thinks he's got it all figured out. But when he meets tiny Rhea on his way to Tartarus, his resolve will be tested like never before. Will her music draw him out of his emotional slumber? Or will her secrets cost them both their lives...?

Find out in the next *Immortal Rogues* installment, Dead Dilemma.
Available for pre-order today!
*To be continued....*

*And if you enjoyed Artemis' story, please consider leaving a review at your choice of retailer. Even a line or two makes a huge difference to an indie author!*

Rogues Extended Universe – Reading Order
Moonlight Rogues
Flaming Rogues
Immortal Rogues
Lost Royals of Transylvania
*(Curious about Elizabeta and her Dacian companion?*
*companion?*
*Lost Royals of Transylvania has alllll the drama!)*

# ABOUT THE AUTHOR

Alexa Whitewolf is a fiction writer, newspaper columnist of daily issues and author of the critically acclaimed *Moonlight Rogues* shifter series.

Alexa has been a lifelong writer and first began creating other worlds and characters at the ripe age of 12. Growing up in the Transylvania region surrounded by epic mountains and a never-ending stream of legends and stories was bound to create an overactive imagination. This shines through Ms. Whitewolf's writing by creating worlds filled with unique folklore, life wisdom and plenty of furry creatures.

An avid traveler, Alexa writes under a penname and spends her days between an office job and writing in Canada's capital, when she's not flying somewhere with lush landscapes and plenty of hiking trails.

Her series focus on strong heroines, kind yet sexy men, fights of good and evil and the never-ending learning curve of humanity's strong—and weak—points. Romanian folklore is intertwined with her writing, more notably in her shifter romance series, the Moonlight Rogues. Her other series draw on world mythology, such as the Avalon myth and Arthurian legend (*The Avalon Chronicles*) and Ancient Egypt (*The Sage's Legacy*).

You can follow her blog at www.alexawhitewolf.com/blog or on social media. Her column in Observatorul also tackles various issues, including health, technology, and a writer's life.

If you want up to date releases, make sure you sign up for her newsletter. For new releases notifications, you can also follow her on Amazon and BookBub.

# Also by the Author

Rogues Extended Universe

**Moonlight Rogues series**
Moonlight Rogues: Origins
First to Fall
Second to Surrender
Third to Tumble
Last to Love

**Flaming Rogues series**
Fanning the Flames
Igniting the Ice

**Immortal Rogues series**
Secret Shadows
Archer's Arrow
Cat's Charms
Trickster's Trap
Fickle Fate

**Lost Royals of Transylvania series**
Immortal Illusion
Cracked Casualty
Deadly Deceit
Blind Burden
Angry Addiction
Primal Protection

Demoni Sancti Extended Universe

## Standalone
Blazing Ashes

## Demoni Sancti series
Fallen
Broken
Unshackled
Risen
Ascended

## The Avalon Chronicles series
Avalon Dreams
Avalon Wishes
Avalon Nightmares
Atrox

## The Sage's Legacy – YA series
The Dragon Medallion
The Dragon Manuscript
Relics of the Underworld

## Standalone novels
Blood Ties, Love Binds
Unconditional Love